WHEN
IT'S
TIME
FOR
LEAVING

WHEN
IT'S
TIME
FOR
LEAVING

A BLUE PALMETTO DETECTIVE AGENCY NOVEL

ANG POMPANO

LEVEL
BEST BOOKS

Originally published by Encircle Publications.

Author Photo Credit: Sara M. Photography

Second edition

ISBN: 978-1-68512-962-0

Cover art by Level Best Designs

This book was professionally typeset on Reedsy.
Find out more at reedsy.com

To Annette—
you turned one concert into a lifetime duet.

Praise for When It's Time for Leaving

"Solid, spare and completely terrific. And though the talented Ang Pompano may wince at this—it's absolutely charming. With an authentic knowing voice and a confident hand, Pompano honors Robert B. Parker's legacy of wry, laconic PIs—smart and engaging detectives with history, honor, and heart."—Hank Phillippi Ryan, nationally bestselling author of *The Murder List*

"Ang Pompano's debut novel, *When It's Time for Leaving*, is a corker. Thoroughly likeable former cop, Al DeLucia, wants to get out of the crime business but inherits one that, fortunately for readers, won't let him go."— Hallie Ephron, *New York Times* bestselling author *Careful What You Wish For*

"In *When It's Time for Leaving*, debut mystery author Ang Pompano has created the most unusual and appealing duo of detectives since Holmes and Watson."—Lucy Burdette, national bestselling author of *A Deadly Feast*

"Author Ang Pompano serves up *the* PI for the double 20s. Al DeLucia is a classic, damaged gumshoe but with a youthful energy that pulls you through the pages."—Barbara Ross, author of the Maine Clambake Mysteries and winner 2019 Maine Literary Award for Crime Fiction

"Crime fiction has boasted some famous fathers and sons, from Inspector Richard Queen and his son Ellery to Jim Rockford and his dad Rocky. Add to that list the unforgettable duo of Al DeLucia and Big Al—building on that tradition but with some provocative twists. Ang Pompano's first novel proves tough-minded and warm-hearted in equal measure. A fine, multilayered debut."—Art Taylor 2019 Edgar, Anthony, Agatha, Macavity, and Derringer Award winner

Chapter One

Every type of rescue vehicle you could imagine was on the bridge. It was standard procedure, even though there was no one to rescue. I refused medical assistance a dozen times before I began the long walk off the span, leaving the mess of angry traffic and the dead druggie, who called himself Psycho, for the state cops to worry about.

A trooper called after me. "Wait up, DeLucia. I'll get you a ride."

"I'm good," I told him.

Truth was, I wasn't good. The red Mustang I had pulled from the New Haven Police motor pool looked like a Twizzler. I was amazed I got out of that twisted mass of metal alive.

"I gotta walk it off," I called back.

I took a selfie with the wreckage behind me, then continued my hike to police headquarters about a mile away.

* * *

Maybe it was the impact of the airbag, or maybe it was the mistake of looking down at the river below, but the city skyline was all wavy like a mirage. At last, I reached the end of the bridge and climbed over the guard rail, slipping and sliding down the snow-dusted embankment until I reached Water Street. A cruiser stopped along the way. It was Charlie Moss, an older cop and one of the nicer guys on the force.

"Hop in, Al."

I waved off his offer. "I'm on it, okay?"

"Sure. Sure, detective. I didn't mean you couldn't take care of yourself."

He took off, and I continued my march toward the station looking at the picture of me and the mangled car every once in a while. On impulse, I sent it in a text to my ex.

Me: You're going to hear about this anyway.

Kim: *R-U-O-K?*

Me: *Yeah*

Kim: *Then try your bartender for sympathy.*

I missed Kim a real lot. I also missed the house we used to own together. She bought me out, I got ¼ and she got ¾. She lives in it now with another cop, my former best friend, Tom Donahue. He turned out to be a relationship lurker, and when he saw we were having problems he hooked up with her before I could make things right. Goodbye, ten-year relationship, house, and old friend.

A van passed me. It was the soccer mom who Psycho had cut off on the crest of the bridge just after he'd recognized me driving alongside him. He had done a double take, then swerved at me. I pulled the car to the right scraping the side of the brand-new structure. Then his souped-up Honda Civic veered toward her.

"Good for you!" I called out to the mom, even though she couldn't hear me. She had done some serious maneuvering to avoid Psycho. Then she gave him the finger and floored it to get the hell out of there.

Psycho totally lost it after that. He jammed the brakes and laid rubber all over I-95. There was smoke, and screeches, and more horns than in Springsteen's "E Street Shuffle." The druggie spun his car around and headed right for me like a runaway Acela train.

My phone rang. The caller ID said it was Kim. I wasn't going to answer at first.

"Jesus, Al. It's already on the news. Where are you?"

"I'm talking to my bartender. Why?"

"Okay, I may have been a little harsh. But it's always something with you."

"It wasn't on me. All I was trying to do was get back to the station to log out. I still am. I'm ordering tickets for the Florida Georgia Line concert as soon as the website opens at 7:00."

"You're thinking of concert tickets. Are you in shock?"

Could be. When we hit head-on, I ended up on the deck of the bridge.

"No shock. I'm fine."

"They said there were gunshots."

"Not on my part. He blew out every window in the car."

He had been shooting like it was *Grand Theft Auto* right there on the Pearl Harbor Memorial Bridge. And like in a video game, he didn't show the least worry about dying, and even less about killing me. They didn't call him Psycho for nothing.

"Why?" she asked.

"He was pissed that I was driving his brother's Mustang. The dude's in jail. It's not like he needs it. Then it was…" I realized I was spilling more than I wanted to.

"Shit, Al. It was what?"

"A mess. A semi barreling down I-95 took out Psycho before I had a chance."

"You sure you're okay?"

It was the nicest she had talked to me in months. Sometimes it pays to almost get your ass blown off.

"I've never been better. Do you want to go?"

"Where?"

"To the Florida Georgia concert."

"You know that isn't happening."

Sure, I did. But I couldn't resist asking. "I just thought I'd ask."

"Al, I worry about you. You're self-destructive."

"Are you saying I caused the accident?"

"I'm saying you're always trying to prove something and you don't use common sense. Why can't you be more mature like Tom?"

I was almost killed and not only was she blaming me, but she was comparing me to Donahue, the laziest cop on the force.

"I gotta go." I shoved the phone into my pocket.

* * *

Word must have gotten back to headquarters on Union Avenue that I was on the way because everybody in the building was standing in the lobby when I got there. I was so pissed from the conversation with Kim that I couldn't look at them. There was a buzz of voices as they watched me head toward the chief's office where I lifted my fist to knock on the door. I changed my mind and barged in. He happened to be in a conference with the mayor when I threw my shield on his desk.

It bounced off the desktop and landed on the mayor's lap. He picked it up, looked at it for a second, and then tossed it to my boss.

"What's this, DeLucia?" the chief said.

"I'm gone."

I shouldn't have taken it out on the chief. He's a pretty laid-back guy who doesn't bust the chops too much.

"I thought you were waiting until you turned thirty-six to cash out."

After the breakup, I'd invested my share of the house in a condo out in LA. It wasn't under construction yet which gave me a year. Then it was going to be guacamole pizza with a woman on my arm every night.

"I decided what happened today was a sign to speed up my plans before the job kills me first."

"DeLucia, I'm going to consider you're upset right now and give you a chance to think about it before you throw away your career."

"Career? What kind of career makes you drive around waiting for the next loony who wants to bag a cop?"

"As I said, think about it." The chief turned to the mayor and added. "That's what I was saying. We're spread too thin."

The mayor didn't say a word. Those faces on Mount Rushmore show more emotion.

When I walked out of the chief's office it was as quiet as Starbucks at midnight. Then someone clapped. Someone else joined in and before I knew it they were all clapping, and congratulating me.

"Way to go, Al." Bill Collins, a rookie I had taken under my wing, put out his hand.

"For quitting?"

Bill put his hand in his pocket. "For taking out Psycho."

"I had nothing to do with it. Some dude with a semi took care of him. And I'll bet he's trying to wash away the memory at some bar right now."

The poor bastard would be dealing with it the rest of his life even though there was nothing he could have done to stop it. Little did he know he probably saved a lot of people from a fentanyl overdose by eliminating Psycho.

I trudged to my desk. There was paperwork to do. Tons of it before I could go online to buy the concert tickets.

Documenting every detail of what happened on the bridge took that much longer because I kept thinking of how the guys cheered for me as if I were some kind of hero. Why? I didn't need their kudos and I didn't want the burden of phony valor.

Three hours later I was still at it with my two-finger typing when Charlie Moss, the officer who offered me a ride, came up to my desk.

He stood there for a minute smirking and shaking his head. It was his way of saying he was glad I came out of the ordeal alive.

"I got you a going away present. After they hauled the car away I found this on the bridge. Look at it if you ever question if you made the right decision."

He put a pretty well banged-up GPS on my desk. The same gizmo that had been stuck on the window of the Mustang with a suction cup.

I dipped my head in thanks and started pecking at the computer again. I worked for another hour and a half making sure I got everything right.

On the way home over the Pearl Harbor Memorial Bridge, I glanced to the southbound lanes where Psycho and I had our showdown. The traffic was moving freely by then and no one would guess that a few hours before, I came close to checking out there. And Psycho. Nobody, no matter how bad, deserved to be obliterated like that.

My car began to drift. With an abrupt move, I pulled my attention back to my lane and got that same feeling that I'd had when I was walking off the bridge. My vision blurred and I felt cold and sweaty at the same time. I tapped the brakes and rolled down the window for air. As I got off the bridge, the feeling went away as quickly as it came.

By the time I got home to my computer, the Florida Georgia Line concert was sold out. I was tired and I was hungry. Not a good combination for me. I found a couple pieces of pizza in the back of the refrigerator. Only God knew how long they had been there. They weren't moldy so I ate one cold while I heated the other in the microwave. Even old New Haven "apizza" is better than pizza from any place else. I was washing down the second slice with a beer as I watched Steven Colbert when I got a text. It was from Charlie Moss's number. Charlie was also our union president.

Charlie: *By contract, physical required within twenty-four hours of a trauma.*

Me: *That's just to cover the department's ass.*

Charlie: *It covers URs 2. Do it.*

I wouldn't have bothered except that I didn't want to lose my pension. The next day I was on the way to Yale New Haven Hospital to get checked out when I had another spell of light-headedness as I crossed the bridge. I hoped that this wasn't going to become my new norm.

I mentioned the dizzy spell to the doctor. Playing it down, I explained that I was probably over-tired. The doc declared it due to the stress of the incident. I was too proud to tell him that it had happened twice. He gave me a clean bill of health and I didn't take the bridge home.

CHAPTER ONE

*** *

Once back in my apartment, I headed to the backyard to relax. I was streaming music on my tablet when my cell rang. I almost didn't answer because nobody I know makes calls unless it's to break the chops like Kim, but the caller ID came up Blue Palmetto Detective Agency and I was curious. The caller was a Mrs. Greenleaf and before she'd hung up I knew that while the Florida Georgia Line concert was not in my future, a trip to Ava Island off Savannah, Georgia was.

I was still taking in what Mrs. Greenleaf had told me when I got another call. Bill Collins.

"Do you have Florida Georgia Line tickets yet?" he asked.

"Nope."

"Well, you do now. I punched in the web address over and over for four hours before they even opened up the sales and I got in on time! I got four. Two of them are yours."

He sounded like a kid on Christmas morning.

"Thanks, but I'm good."

"You're not hearing me, man! They're yours. Free."

"I won't be around to use them. But I'll give you the money for them. Give them to Donahue. Tell him you won them."

"Donahue? But you hate him."

"Kim likes the group. He'll take her."

"I don't get it."

"Just do it."

I didn't think I had to explain to him that I wanted to leave Connecticut at peace with Kim, even if she didn't realize it.

Chapter Two

A month later, my dream of LA and guacamole pizza on hold, I drove to Savannah with Psycho's GPS stuck to the window of my F-150. I bought the truck because I fell in love with the silver stripe on black package. I realized too late that it didn't have a built-in GPS. Psycho's device was retro, but it did the trick in helping with some creative route planning to avoid monster bridges, just in case whatever was going on in my head happened again.

Even with the added mileage, I made it down to Savannah in less than fifteen hours. There I was able to duck a huge bridge that looked like a sailboat with two giant sails. The alternate route though, put me right in the heart of the city. While I was there, I took a spin through the town to get my bearings as much as to put off the inevitable face-to-face with my old man. My first impression was that there was more to the community than southern Gothic and Spanish moss.

I had read that River Street was paved with ballast from the old sailing ships, but I didn't expect the jazz and southern rock streaming from every bar and restaurant that lined it, any more than I expected to see a paddlewheel riverboat, or an open-topped hearse giving a city tour. The place looked young and upbeat. I was ready for young and upbeat now that I wasn't a cop. I just wondered if Savannah was the right place for it.

I stopped in a place that advertised Savannah's best chicken sandwich. I was wolfing it down along with a craft beer when the waitress stopped by for the obligatory how's-the-food check.

"You're here on business, aren't ya?"

I wiped some juice off of my face with a napkin.

"How can you tell?"

She looked at the sandwich that was already three-quarters gone.

"I don't know. You seem to be eating with a purpose. You know what I'm saying?"

I could feel myself blush.

"You're right. I have to slow down. I'll take another one of these." I picked up the beer bottle.

"That's better. Savannah should be taken in sips, like wine, not in gulps like Coke. Save that for Atlanta."

She made me smile. I wanted to stay longer but it was time to get this over with.

"How do I get to Ava Island?" I asked.

"Well now, I suppose the best way would be to follow RT. 80. In fact, it's the only way. Shouldn't take you but 15 minutes. You'll see the sign for the bridge."

"You mean, The Bridge?" I looked out the window where I could see the monster that I had masterfully avoided, when I came into town, thanks to the GPS.

She laughed. "The Savannah River Bridge? Not unless you want to go to South Carolina. It's a small drawbridge to the island. Careful you don't miss it."

I realized my arms were crossed against my chest. I dropped them in relief.

* * *

"You own a detective agency and a home on Ava Island," Greenleaf had said.

According to my Internet research, Ava is 1.47 square miles of self-governed paradise at the mouth of the Savannah River, between Savannah and Tybee Island.

As I crossed the drawbridge, I could see the humongous Savannah River Bridge upriver.

When I heard the words, "You have arrived at your destination" I was, well… surprised. Maybe I had been a little hasty in judging my old man a loser.

I drove up a cobbled driveway and parked in front of a huge brick Southern Colonial house, complete with a palladium window and a columned portico. As I walked around back, where I could see sailboats racing on the Savannah River, I felt as if I had won the lottery.

The smell of the refreshing sea breeze and the beautiful landscape had me beginning to think that this might be cool after all. Then I remembered why I could never handle living on Ava Island, paradise or not. The house and the agency came from my father. But I'd bet selling the place would get me more than enough money to finally get to LA.

"Can I help you?"

I turned to see a young woman by the pool bent forward on one leg. Her black compression shorts and a white muscle tank showed off a perfect tan. My father's secretary? Correction. I'd won Power Ball.

"Nice imitation of a flamingo," I said.

She dropped the dumbbells she held and stood straight.

"Single-leg deadlift. It strengthens the core. You could use it. What did you say you want?"

The voice may have been soft and sweet but the tone said she could be total badass if she need be.

"I don't want anything. I'm checking things out. I need to take it all in, ya know?

"Listen, what you need to do is leave."

I whipped off my sunglasses. "I'm the new owner."

She whipped off her sunglasses in turn, stood up, and shook her caramel-colored hair.

"Damn it! Not again. I hate to break the news to you dude, but you've been scammed."

I walked toward her. "Scammed?"

"Yes, scammed. I bought this house last year and someone used the pictures from the Multiple Listing Service to put a phony for-sale-by-owner ad on

Craig's List. You're the third one to show up this month. Did they take you for a $1,000 deposit?"

"Nobody took me for anything." I was beginning to wonder if I'd been punk'd. "You called me and said my father gave me his house and a detective agency."

She laughed as if she finally understood what was going on and then moved in to give me a kiss on the cheek. "Ah, so you're the long-lost son. Al Junior, right?"

Long lost son. What had the old man been telling people?

"Al. No junior, okay? You Mrs. Greenleaf?"

"Not exactly. I'm Max Brophy. I call your dad Big Al but I can see Little Al won't do for you." As her eyes lowered and lingered, I shifted on my feet. "You're going to have to be plain old Al until I think of a better name for you." She poked a finger at my chest. "Fine detective you are. You're at the wrong address. Your place is next door."

She pointed to a thick bamboo border above which I could see the second story of a boxy contemporary style house of concrete and glass.

"Okay then. My mistake." The other house was way too modern for my taste but it would put some nice coin in my pocket when I sold it. "It's nice."

She frowned. "Actually, that's the house beyond yours." She led me to a path through the bamboo. "This is yours. Welcome neighbor."

I guess I was punk'd after all. The place was old Georgia all the way. The one-story wood frame cottage, complete with tin roof, sat in the middle of a narrow lot darkened by the spread of a giant live oak tree hung in Spanish moss. Unlike the thick lawn next door, patches of green that resembled crabgrass grew through the soil in the sun-starved yard. A handmade sign with orange lettering on a cobalt background to match the paint on the house hung on a screened-in porch: *Blue Palmetto Detective Agency*. This must have been what all the houses on Ava Island looked like before it was taken over by hipsters who had tons of money to burn. Thanks for nothing Dad.

"If you ever want to sell the place give me first dibs. That guy on the other side of you would love to squeeze another monstrosity like his in here."

I took a minute to pull off some sand spurs that had stuck to my socks. When I straightened up she was gone. As I looked around the yard I noticed a yellow Mercedes sport convertible sitting on the crushed shell parking area between the cottage and the street. Sweet, sweet, sweet. The vanity plate read *Classic 1982*, the same year I was born. I admired its SL badge, long hood, and short rear deck. It must have been the rich man's Mustang back in the day.

I decided that I had better go next door to retrieve my own vehicle. I went through the path into Max's sunny yard. When my eyes finally adjusted to the sunlight she was nowhere in sight. Too bad. I would have liked to get to know her better even if I was only going to be on the island for a short time. I got my truck and drove it to my new, although temporary, home.

When I pulled my truck in next to the convertible I spotted an older woman standing on the cottage porch with her arms folded.

"If you had called, I would have told you how to find the place. And I'm glad to hear the resemblance between Max and me wasn't lost on you." She primped her gray streaked hair.

"News travels fast around here. You must be Mrs. Greenleaf. I didn't call because I have a GPS. Right?"

"A lot of good it did you. Call me Greenleaf. That's what your father does."

Greenleaf brought me through the porch into the cottage. The inside surprised me. It was totally updated with light colored walls and an open beamed cathedral ceiling that made it seem light despite the shade from the huge tree outside.

"This is my office. I'll show you the rest of the place." She led me to the room behind it. It too was modern with a big window that looked out at the mouth of the river. "This is your father's office—yours now. Mine's bigger because I do most of the work around here. I don't see that changing, so we'll keep the offices as is."

"I don't think so." When she wasn't looking, I tapped a button on my phone that set a ten-minute alarm.

She gave me a look with one eye closed and her frown slightly twisted. "You want my office?"

"No. What I'm saying is that I don't want my father's office. Show me the rest of the place."

"Millennials," she said, not caring that I heard.

The rest consisted of a bedroom and small kitchen-living room arrangement with French doors that opened to a patio. "I'll work at that couch so I can put my feet on the coffee table and look at the river."

"Have it your way. I'm semi-retired so I come in at 10:00 and leave at 2:00. That's not going to change either. I have all of your paperwork filed with the state of Georgia, so you're good to go."

"Yeah, good to go."

She gave me the stink eye again. "You have a problem?"

"A month ago, I didn't know my father was still alive. And now I'm supposed to run his detective agency."

I'd help her dispose of his remaining cases and then I was out of Ava Island and Georgia. I whipped out my phone and took some pics so I could bring them to a real estate agent.

Greenleaf spoke like she was talking to a kid who didn't get it. "Your agency. You own it. I explained all of that to you. Did you go to see him on the way in?"

No, I hadn't. How was this her business? "Show me the outside. Okay?"

She took a moment to get a stack of folders that she had left on my father's desk and placed them on the coffee table. Then she took me out back and I saw that I had the same view of the mouth of the Savannah River that my neighbors in the million dollar digs on either side of me had. While the building might be a teardown, the land was certainly worth something. I was only there a half hour and I already knew of two people who were interested in the place. I lost that thought when I noticed a dock with an awesome Grady White tied up to it.

"Whose boat?"

"Yours. It comes with the house and the agency. Your father used it for surveillance work, but he wasn't against doing a little fishing too."

I guess my old man was living his version of the good life all those years. The problem is, my version of the good life was living in LA, with the surf,

13

and traffic, and energy, a place I learned to love on the many visits Kim and I had made out there when we were together. "I'll help you get things in order and then I'm moving on."

My alarm that I had set for 10 minutes went off.

I pointed to the phone. "Hey, I appreciate your showing me around, but I have something I got to do. Okay?"

Greenleaf rolled her eyes to let me know I wasn't fooling her.

"I was leaving anyway." She surprised me by putting a hand on my shoulder. I pulled back and she frowned.

"You didn't ask me for advice, but I'm going to give it to you anyway. Let go of the past. That's the last advice I'm ever going to give you."

I had the feeling that was not the last time she was going to give me advice.

She walked over to an ancient pink and chrome Schwinn with fat white walled tires that was parked in an iron pipe bike rack that was something out of the last century. She slid onto the seat.

"Isn't the yellow Mercedes out front yours?"

"Nope. That's yours too. You can get rid of your truck and the lousy GPS. That car's a classic. Take care of it."

So even my car and boat had been picked out for me.

"I kind of like picking out my own transportation." I thought of how that worked out when I pulled Batshit's car from the motor pool. But still, no thanks.

She pursed her lips and glared at me. "I've never been one to tell people what to do," Greenleaf said. "You get yourself familiar with the place. Tomorrow I'll get you up to speed on a few cases that must be wrapped up. And look, for your own good, go see him. He's at a place over in Savannah called The Palms. That's not advice. It's something you need to do. It's easy to find. Use that GPS of yours."

Chapter Three

Until I got the call from Greenleaf the month before, I hadn't heard from my father since he left when I was an eight-year-old kid. Over the years, I put him out of my mind. I kind of got used to him not being there. I had a friend in school named Davie whose father got killed in a construction accident. Somehow the story of his dead father and my missing father got twisted up in my mind and I convinced myself that my father was dead too. My mother's brothers were cops. My uncles filled in for the father and son stuff like the Pinewood Derby and Little League so I still had a pretty well-rounded childhood. When kids would ask, "Where's your father?" I'd say, "Dead." That would be the end of it. It kind of made me special like Davie. No big deal. My father's dead, yours is alive. Let's play ball.

Of course, when I grew up and became a police detective sometimes I'd wonder what ever became of him, but I never pursued it. He had been a cop like my uncles. Who knew he had become a private investigator? With both of us in the same line of work you wouldn't think that it'd take twenty-eight years for us to find each other. Maybe neither one of us had thought about it, or cared enough to take the initiative.

* * *

That night I stayed up until 2:00 a.m. going over files that Greenleaf had stacked on the coffee table before she left. I was wiped out but the quicker I got the loose ends of Big Al's cases tied up the better. Then I could be on my way to the West Coast.

I must have been more tired than I thought because I slept until almost eight the next morning. Greenleaf had supplied me with a full refrigerator and after putting on a pot of coffee I whipped up some fried eggs and toast.

I brought my breakfast to a herringbone patio out back, chevrons of interlocking blocks; a simple pattern in snapshot but maddening in wide-angle, like life.

"Big Al laid the pavers for this patio himself," Greenleaf had told me when she showed me around.

"Apparently, the old man was good at almost anything he did; except for being a father," I had replied.

As I ate looking out at the million-dollar view of the Savannah River, for a minute I thought that maybe I could get used to this. As I realized I could see the bridge looming upriver at Savannah, the moment soon passed. I didn't ask for the Blue Palmetto Detective Agency and I wasn't going to let my old man push me into something I didn't want. Since the incident on the bridge up in New Haven, I didn't feel like chasing bad guys any more.

While I was on the island already though, I had no problem with getting to know Max better. I was thinking of going over to see her with the excuse of asking her if there was a good place to work out nearby when I noticed splashing down by the dock.

At first, I thought it might be an alligator. I walked down to the seawall and hopped onto the dock to see what the heck was going on in the water.

I'd seen a lot of bad stuff when I was a cop. Still, I almost tossed my breakfast when I got a look at what was happening. Hundreds of frenzied little fish nibbled on the body of a young dude trapped in the lines between the dock's float drums and the Grady.

I pushed the boat away from the dock and tried to move the body. There wasn't enough slack and the boat kept bouncing back against the dock. I loosened the lines from the stern leaving the bow tied so the boat wouldn't float away then laid on my stomach and grabbed the body under the arms. Several of the fish nipped at my flesh before they turned in unison and disappeared. I tried to lift the guy out. No way that was going to happen. I tried again and realized his hands were caught in the lines.

"I need help here!"

An older guy with hair the color of a Q-tip stood on the dock of the contemporary house next door. I called out to him again.

"Yo! I need a hand over here. It's an emergency." He stood there gawking as if he didn't hear me.

The school of fish returned and resumed their meal. There was no time to wait for the next-door neighbor. I kicked off my shoes and jumped into the drink. If it was up to me, I would rather have jumped in with an alligator than those nippy little creatures. As I swam toward the body the crazed fish once more turned tail and disappeared. The tide was too high for me to stand and every time I pushed the boat away it slammed into us. Finally, I freed the man's hands and floated the body to the end of the dock. I was having trouble getting him out of the water when Max charged onto the platform.

"I called 9-1-1." She knelt on the dock and grabbed the body. "Push," she said.

We almost had it on the dock when it slid back in. It landed on me and we both went under. I grabbed the guy and swam to the surface where I maneuvered it close to the dock. Max grabbed his arms again.

"This isn't working. I'm getting out," I told her.

I hopped on the dock and we both pulled until we managed to get the man up on the landing. The guy looked to be maybe twenty-five, about ten years or so younger than I was. He had blond dreadlocks and wore a thin black leather necklace with a silver Hawaiian fishhook ornament hanging from it. A windsurfer I thought, as I checked for life. His lips were blue and I found nothing.

Then Max tried. She checked for respiration and looked for a pulse in his neck. She shook her head.

I started CPR anyway. Within minutes the yard became a madhouse of activity.

So much for a quiet breakfast by the water.

Chapter Four

Giving CPR takes a lot out of you. Although the EMTs were there in minutes, when they finally took over I was ready to dissolve to black.

Max and I went up to the lawn and flopped down to dry out and watch. It didn't look good. My arms were stinging from salt water in scrapes and bites I had gotten on my arms. I wondered if he had been alive when the fish started nibbling him.

The guy next door was watching from his dock.

"I guess the old geezer didn't want to get involved," I said to Max. I'd seen it a thousand times before.

"They're a little different over there." She motioned toward the contemporary house.

"Well I'm glad you heard me and came over."

"Actually, I didn't hear you. I came over to get a file I needed."

"File?"

"Didn't Greenleaf tell you? I'm senior investigator at Blue Palmetto."

I thought it was a one-man agency. "What about Big Al?"

"He's president, of course."

"Senior, huh? There are other agents?"

"Yes, you."

Between the dead guy and now this, I couldn't think straight. I was the owner of the agency, but my father and Max were above me in pecking order. I was about to clarify what she was saying when three officers approached us. I shook off Max's offer to help me to my feet.

"I'm good," I told her as I got up.

One of the cops asked Max to go with him to the table up on the patio. I knew the drill; separate the witnesses, get statements right away because people easily mix up recollections. Even at that, most statements are unreliable. Max went without hesitation.

Another officer with graying hair and a paunch came up. He motioned for me to stay where I was. "I'll handle this," he said to the third cop who went down to the dock.

"I understand you found the body, Mr. ..."

"DeLucia. Al DeLucia." I noticed the gold oak leaf insignia; a major on the police force. I wondered why I deserved such attention.

He broke into a grin.

"Thought so. The other Al DeLucia and I go way back to Granville."

"Is that so?" I don't know if I was supposed to know what Granville was, but I didn't and I didn't ask.

He put out his hand. "Major Gil Johnson, AIPD."

"The island has its own police department?"

"Yep, and you're looking at about half of it; five full-time and four part-time officers including the chief. Ava Island is a special service district of the Savannah Metro Area. Our population swells from 680 to over 3,000 in season so we police ourselves."

Nine officers; a regular NYPD. Roaming dogs were probably the biggest crime on the island, so this must be a huge deal. No wonder why half of the force showed up. The EMTs had the guy Max and I pulled from the water on a stretcher and were running him out toward the front yard.

Johnson shook his head. "They stuff them into an ambulance and rush them to Georgia Regional Hospital over in Savannah even if there's the slightest hope. I don't make the call."

I understood what he was saying, but I knew the man was dead even before the EMTs took over. I thought of Psycho's lifeless body under the truck on the bridge. That hadn't been a pretty sight but the thought of this guy possibly being nibbled to death by the school of fish was even worse.

A white skiff with a gold badge and Savannah–Chatham Metro Police lettered in blue and yellow on the side came up slowly without a wake so as not to disturb the scene.

"Here we go," Johnson said. "We could have handled this ourselves. Technically, I can't stop them from showing up. The river is their jurisdiction."

A diver went over the side. I knew he was checking that there wasn't another body under the dock.

Meanwhile, a photographer had been taking pictures and a couple of other uniforms showed up who didn't seem to have much to contribute other than gawking. Johnson spoke to them privately and they left.

"I was a cop. We used to get that all of the time; our own men compromising the crime scene to be nosy." As soon as I said it I realized it was a mistake.

I didn't mean anything by it but, Johnson didn't take my remark lightly. Still, I knew what I said was true.

Johnson straightened up his sagging old shoulders. "Do you know something I don't about this being a crime scene?"

I decided to ease up.

"Nope. Not my call."

"Good." Johnson relaxed his shoulders a bit.

"Although...I was wondering how a body could get wedged between the dock and the boat."

Johnson glanced toward the dock. "I've seen it before. Boats are tied loose enough to allow for the tides and the current pushes a body in there."

"Are you saying he was dead before he got trapped?"

"You were a cop, so you know I'm not saying anything of the sort. We are investigating a death." Johnson took some gum out of his pocket and plopped a piece into his mouth.

"I had a hard time getting the body out. His hands were wrapped up in the lines. My neighbor had to help me." I motioned toward the patio where Max was being interviewed.

"Why did you move the body from where it was found?"

"The fish were eating him and I had to give him CPR."

He must have known as well as I did that actions to save a life take precedence over preserving the scene. I knew I'd been put in my place.

"Well, were his hands tied or only tangled in the lines?"

"I don't know. I was concentrating on getting him free to see if I could save him. His hands were wrapped in the lines. That's all I'm saying."

Johnson then caught me off guard when he changed the subject. "I heard Big Al was in the hospital. How is he?"

"A nursing facility. The Palms over in Savannah. He has beginning Alzheimer's. I was told he signed himself in."

The major made a face. "Damn hellacious disease. So, you took over the agency?"

Hellacious. Who uses that word? I was surprised that he didn't make a comment about the old man signing himself into the Palms.

"I got here yesterday. It seems to be getting more complicated, but my plan is to tie up a few cases then I'm moving to California."

"Good idea." Johnson's words almost came out as a snicker.

"Tying things up or going to California?"

"Both. My daddy used to say, you should do what you have to do, then do what you want to do."

"Judging from the files I looked at last night, it's mostly small stuff, divorces and insurance cases."

Johnson wasn't all that interested. Kind of like when someone asks how you are but they don't want to know. He lowered his voice and stepped close to me.

"You all set with your license? I know people."

That was nice in a good-old-boy kind of way. I guess any friend of Big Al's is a friend of Johnson's. "Experience and criminal justice credits fast tracked my license. Mrs. Greenleaf got everything in order before I came down."

"Got it."

"Look, can I go change? I'm soaking wet."

"Just hold on a bit. I only have a few questions to establish a time line then we're done."

The few questions lasted forty-five minutes.

Chapter Five

After the cops left and Max went back to her place I called Greenleaf and told her I wasn't opening the office that day. I wasn't going to tell her why, especially since she didn't keep me in the loop as far as telling me that Max worked for the agency, but the old woman pressed me until she had the whole story.

"Your father never closed the office on a normal working day."

Finding a body getting eaten by fish didn't qualify as a normal day, but I did my best to hold my tongue. I certainly wouldn't get into a back and forth with an elderly woman.

"I'll pay you for the day."

"You think it's the money? If I was worried about making money, I'd be working at McDonalds."

"Is there a McDonalds on Ava Island?"

"No. And lucky for you there isn't." The phone went dead.

I wasn't surprised when Greenleaf wheeled her Schwinn around back and parked it in the iron bike rack. I was down on the dock looking at the spot where I'd found the body.

Greenleaf was quiet as she came on to the dock.

"Is that where you found him?"

"Yeah."

She stood next to me looking at the water. "It's too bad. Do they know who he is?"

"I don't think they found any identification on him. He was in swim trunks.

Did you ever see a young guy around here with blond dreadlocks?"

She rubbed her chin as if she were trying to think of something.

"There are a lot of young people on the island but they mostly hang out down in the village or at the beach. Around here the people are older and you hardly ever see them." She looked out at the mouth of the river and the Atlantic beyond. "Maybe he fell off a boat."

I looked upriver. "Or jumped off the bridge."

"Either way, not much of a welcome for you on your first day on the island."

"It might be an omen. You know, I think you're right about opening up today." I might as well get started on cleaning up business. I'd get to LA that much quicker.

Greenleaf sighed. "Whatever you say."

As if she didn't intend to open in the first place. Why else would she be here?

I followed her up the dock. As I stepped off a glint of light caught my eye as Greenleaf's shoe kicked something. I saw it roll under a bush with large red and green leaves. I picked up a small stick and probed under the plant. I found what I was looking for and used the stick to pick up what turned out to be a circular piece of brass.

"What's that?" Greenleaf eyed the ring when I held it up to get a better look.

"Too big for someone's finger." I made it spin on the stick.

"It's nothing. Let's get to work." She started walking up toward the house.

"Everything is something." Whether it was significant or not was another story. I set the ring on the patio table and asked Greenleaf to go in the house for a baggie. I used my phone to take a couple of pictures of where it was when Greenleaf kicked it. When she returned with the bag I dropped it in. "I think I should show this to Johnson."

"I thought we were going to get some work done today."

"I went over the files before I went to bed. I prioritized the cases I wanted to wrap up. There's a list on the coffee table starting with the back-injury guy who likes to jet ski. Check it over and see what you think."

There was an awkward silence and I was about to ask her why she didn't tell me Max worked for the agency. We both started to talk at once. I deferred to her.

"There's something else you should know. Max works for the agency."

I fidgeted. "She's the senior investigator."

"You know then. I was going to tell you, but you were talking about closing the agency and I couldn't get a word in edgewise."

"I still intend to close it after I clean up my father's cases."

Greenleaf scoffed. "Max has cases to close too. Look, I know it's a little awkward. She moved here after she quit her job. She was a TV reporter in Atlanta. Investigative stuff, but the industry has a glass ceiling thicker than a bowl of two-day old oatmeal. Big Al was having trouble keeping up, so he hired her. It was a perfect fit for both of them."

"So now I'm the owner, but she outranks me?"

"You can't handle that?" There was a downward turn of her mouth.

"I didn't say that. I'm going to see Johnson. I should be back soon."

Chapter Six

As sweet as the old Mercedes was I chose to take my own ride because I didn't want anything from my father. The traffic was horrendous and I realized it was because of people going to the beach.

With the help of my finicky GPS I found the Ava Island Police Department a block from the beach in a white building with an impressive rounded portico held up by scroll topped columns.

It was well into afternoon when I stepped into the station and approached a female officer at the front desk. I didn't think the small brass ring was relevant but it was an excuse to ask if I could get a look at the report on the body. I was curious. Once a cop always a cop.

I knew that the public had the right to see police reports but I also knew that the chances of getting the paperwork were a crap shoot.

"I'm here to see Major Johnson."

"He's in a meeting right now. Is there something I can help you with?" The woman hardly looked up from her computer. And there I was giving her my most charming smile. Her loss. I'd have a better chance of getting the report from Johnson since he and my Old Man seemed to have that Good Old Boy thing going.

"I'll wait."

A display of old-time pictures of Ava Island above a row of chairs caught my interest. Photos of bathers on the beach in 1895, a doughboy parade in 1917, and a seaplane at a dock in 1935 told me that the place had quite a history. Eventually I took a seat. After about fifteen minutes the officer directed me to Johnson's office in the Criminal Investigations Section.

Johnson was as convivial as he had been that morning.

"DeLucia, sorry for the delay. I was in a meeting. Everything alright? How's the old man?"

"I never got out there to see him. It's on the to-do list."

Johnson shrugged his shoulders.

"I had a feeling you'd be showing up. Sit down, I'll get you some coffee. It's not your usual police department swill. I make it myself."

I took him up on the coffee.

"I'll take it black," I said.

Johnson walked out of the office and I used the time to look around. It always interests me to see how a person chooses to present themselves to the world by what they display in their office. In a way, we are each our own PR man. Johnson didn't overdo it, having just a few personal pictures around. They were enough to tell me what he wanted the world to know. He was a family man judging by an older picture of what I assumed was him with his wife and two young boys. A more recent picture showed him with the same woman, quite a few years on them both, cutting an anniversary cake. The third picture showed the couple in mouse ears with a little boy and girl on their laps. Grandkids, I guessed. Wholesome. Exactly what the public wants from a major in the local police department. When he came back I was looking at a picture of him by a white truck. He was holding a fish and had a huge smile on his face.

"Striped Bass. I know a spot where they're huge. I can show you sometime."

"I don't do much fishing. Nice truck."

"'89 Ram. I still got it. Solid as the day I bought it. I couldn't kill it if I wanted to."

I took a gulp of coffee. He was right. It was good for station house java. "I came to show you this."

I slid the baggie with the ring in it across his desk. He picked it up and looked at what was in the bag without opening it.

"A brass ring. Have you been on a Merry Go Round?"

"Sometimes it feels like it. I found it near the dock."

Johnson picked up the baggie and took a close look at the ring. "It's cracked.

I suppose it could have fallen off something."

I hadn't noticed it was cracked. He handed me the bag and I examined it. "But what?"

"You think it has some significance?" While he wasn't being overtly dismissive, his seemingly friendly tone struck me as patronizing.

"I don't know."

Johnson frowned. "I'm a bit surprised. You know if you thought it was relevant you should have called us."

He was right of course. "It had already been kicked away from where it was lying. I used a stick to pick it up."

I showed him the pictures I had taken with my cell phone. "Right there on the grass at the beginning of the dock."

"No harm done, I guess. I don't think it has anything to do with the deceased. You found him in the water. The ring was on the lawn. It could have come from anywhere."

"Okay." I picked up the baggie.

Johnson put up his hand. "Leave it."

"You said it wasn't significant."

"You never know. Do you?"

I knew what he was thinking. Me bringing the ring in to him meant more paperwork documenting where it came from, why it wasn't found at the scene, and how it finally got in the possession of the police department. All because I didn't follow procedure.

"I was wondering if I could get a copy of the report."

There was a moment of silence. I don't think it was in honor of the drowned guy. It was more like Johnson was sending me the message that I was butting in to someplace where I didn't belong.

"No can do. It's not typed up."

That told me a lot. In most departments, minor reports waited to be typed up, as the budget would not allow for a lot of overtime. If it was a major crime, such as a murder, you'd ask the super for permission to work overtime, if need be, because the detectives would want a report to follow up.

"Do you believe it was an accidental drowning?"

"People fall in the water all of the time, especially if they've been drinking."

"So, the victim was drunk?"

Johnson was straightening up his desk like he was getting ready to go home. "I didn't say that. We don't have the toxicology reports. Listen, the deceased was a young adult. Ava Island is loaded with bars. Why would you be surprised if he was intoxicated?"

"I take it you're thinking it was an accident."

Was he totally discounting that I said the victim's hands were wrapped in the lines?

"So far there isn't any evidence that it wasn't."

"Have you IDd him yet?"

"Not yet. Still waiting for the dental records. Why are you asking so many questions about an accident?"

"I'm curious."

Johnson laughed.

"So, you're having regrets about taking early retirement, are you? Look I get it. I'm a lot older than you and could have retired long ago but that's exactly why I stuck with it. It's in the blood."

Things were happening fast when I found the body, but I didn't remember telling him I took early retirement.

"You did a background check on me?"

"Curious, as you say." He made an effort to smile, but I wasn't buying that it was a joke. "It's procedure, DeLucia. I shouldn't have to explain that to you." Another long pause.

"You're right. I would have checked everything and everybody too." What an asshat.

"I also don't have to tell you that if I wasn't a friend of your father this conversation would have been terminated long ago."

"Got it. You've got your job to do."

"Right. And look, I know you're going to do your job no matter what I say. Just don't get in our way. Plus, I'm going to ask you to keep me informed if you find anything significant. Here's my number. Keep me informed and we'll have no problems."

I gave him a firm handshake and thought the conversation was finished but instead of showing me to the door Johnson leaned against his desk. "Wasn't there something else you came to see me about?"

"Such as?"

"To ask me about what your father was like during all of those years when you didn't know where he was?"

That caught me off guard. I know I didn't tell him that my father walked out or that we had no idea where he was or even if he was alive.

"No. I'm not interested."

"Maybe you don't think you are. I knew who you were when we responded to the call."

"Yeah, well, I was wondering why someone of your rank was there."

"It wasn't the time or the place to go into details. When you do get around to seeing your father, tell him I send my regards."

Chapter Seven

On the ride back from the police station the conversation with Johnson played over and over in my mind. The guy was friendly enough, but he seemed to be making it clear that neither his friendship with my father nor my professional past was going to gain me any privileges. I understood and respected that. What I didn't get was why he was putting his two cents in when it came to my relationship with my father. He was almost as bad as Greenleaf.

I was halfway back to the office when my cell rang.

"Mr. DeLucia, this is Maryann Fena, the Care Coordinator at The Palms. Your father's carrying on is causing a problem. What you need to do is come in."

"How did you get this number?"

"From Mrs. Greenleaf at The Blue Palmetto Detective Agency, if it makes a difference. Can I expect you in say a half hour?"

I didn't need more stress right then. "I need the address."

She told me, and I punched it into my GPS as she gave it to me. Then I hung up and headed toward Savannah. To my surprise, the voice in the little box was not bringing me on the same road that I had taken to the police station. Instead it brought me east, toward the Atlantic side of the island and a bridge closer to the mouth of the river. It wasn't a nice low drawbridge as the one I had used to come onto the island the day I arrived. This one was high enough to allow a sailboat to pass under it, but certainly nowhere near as high or long as the bridge up by Savannah. I gave it a shot, but the minute I drove onto the span and lost sight of the horizon I began to sweat and tighten my grip on the wheel. It passed as soon as I was over the crest and I could see a park below where the bridge met the mainland.

Twenty minutes later, I pulled up to The Palms Skilled Nursing Facility out by the Hunter Army Airfield. The place looked like a country club, a southern colonial brick building on manicured lawns surrounded by trees. When I was buzzed in I entered a lobby that would do justice to a 5-star hotel. Leave it to my father to set himself up in style for his old age. The charge nurse didn't know who I was so she put me through the third degree. Eventually, she sent me to Maryann Fena's office. Fena was a dour little woman with tiny wrinkles on her face to commemorate every cigarette she had ever smoked, including the one in her hand. The office smelled like she had stock in R. J. Reynolds. She was on the phone when I appeared at her open door. She waved me in to take a seat and ended her call. Then she crushed out the cigarette in an ashtray and hid it away in a desk drawer.

She exhaled heavily, sending out a lungful of smoke. She got right to the point.

"Your father is becoming a problem. He wanders the halls and he refuses to take his meds. He yelled at me today and told me to go to hell because he was going outside whether I liked it or not. He doesn't have to like me, but he does have to follow the rules."

I don't like to make snap judgments, but there was something about her manner that I didn't like either. It's nice to know my father and I agreed on something.

"I'm told he has Alzheimer's. Doesn't all of that go with the territory?"

She pulled back her shoulders and gave a little shake as if she were startled that I should be so impertinent. "I was afraid that he might strike me."

"Did he?"

"No, but the potential is there. I don't trust Italian men."

"Maybe the problem is with you then. Besides, he's an American." Like me.

"But he upsets the other guests."

"He's a guest, as you call them, too. I believe you knew he had dementia when he was admitted here."

31

"Well, then bless your heart Mr. DeLucia, I hope that you will visit often. Visitations from family often help keep a patient under control. It's nice to see a man take an interest in his father's well-being. Usually we deal with daughters."

What did she mean by that?

"Bring me to him."

Reunion time. Twenty-eight freakin' years. Whoop-de-do. Let's get this over with.

She directed me to the solarium where about a dozen "guests" were seated as if waiting for a bus that would never come. A nurse pointed out a guy sitting in a wheelchair by the window. He wore a khaki bush hat with the brim raised on one side.

"That's your Dad over there," she said.

"So that's him. I expected him to look much older."

"He is comparatively younger than most of our guests." She was staring at me. "Is there something wrong?"

It took me a while to realize that she was talking to me.

"No. I'm fine. It's been twenty-eight years. That's all." I had expected to feel a lot more than I did. Should I have been angry? Happy? Something… but what? For years, whenever I needed him I had practiced a hate-filled diatribe for when this day came. "What am I supposed to say?"

"Say what's in your heart," the nurse said.

"That might not be a good idea. He's in a wheelchair. I didn't realize he can't walk."

"He can walk. He's just a little unsteady sometimes. We find it easier if we can keep the guests in wheelchairs."

Skilled nursing facility my ass, it was nothing more than an expensive convalescent home. And keeping the people in wheelchairs sounded like a control thing to me. I was willing to bet that they were all sedated. I was going to question her but before I could Big Al started acting up.

"Go! Go!" He was tapping the window with a fancy walking stick and shouting at a squirrel that was raiding a bird feeder outside. "Damned monkeys!" he yelled.

"He's not what I expected," I said. "At least not with the bush hat and the walking stick."

"He knows what he likes," the nurse said. He always wears the hat. As for the stick, he refused to use a walker or even a cane. Finally, his secretary bought him that stick a few weeks ago. It was a good idea. The alligator handle and brass tip doesn't make it look so orthopedic. It meets regulations, so we allow it. But Ms. Fena's warned us if he falls it's on our heads."

He knows what he likes was her way of saying he always wanted his way. That much I remembered about him. He turned enough so that I could see his profile better and even after all these years I recognized him as the guy who took off without so much as a good-bye when I was eight years old. The years had been good to him and although he was wearing the hat I could see he had hair more pepper than salt. He didn't look as old as the rest of the people in the room. Would he have reached seventy yet? Probably not.

I inched my way through the sunny room trying to formulate what I was going to say. Would I call him Dad? I didn't think so. Would I even tell him who I was? Would I be able to hold it together without telling him what I thought of him?

I caught a break when a lady of no more than ninety pounds, her cheeks smeared with red make-up, waved me to come over.

"That man over there said we're going to get two feet of snow. I have to get home before it starts."

I looked in the direction she was pointing. Al Roker was doing a national weather report on the flat screen that hung on the wall.

"You're fine," I assured her. "No snow for us. He's talking about Rochester, New York. Far from here."

"Are you sure?"

"Positive. Today's all about sunshine for us. See." I pointed to the window where my father was now sitting quietly.

"He's always coming around telling stories," she said.

I think she thought Roker was in the room. She motioned with her crooked fingers for me to move in closer. "I skipped school today," she whispered, letting me in on her secret.

"Good for you. Enjoy the day."

No sense in putting this off. I went over to the window and positioned myself to the side of the old man. I swallowed hard. I didn't know how to address him. Sir? Mr. DeLucia? Not Dad. Definitely, not Dad.

"Al." No response. I walked between the wheelchair and the window so he could see me. "It's me."

His eyes were closed. What the hell? He was yelling at the squirrel a few minutes before. Dead? No, I saw his chest move. Sleeping then. I sat in a chair next to him.

"Long time no see," I said in a low voice. He moved a bit and I wondered if he was pretending to be asleep. "What's it been twenty-seven, twenty-eight years? Where the hell did you go to get that pack of cigarettes, China?"

The corner of his mouth curled up. Was that a smile or was he burping gas like a baby?

"Do you know who I am?"

"Yeah."

"Who?"

"My father. I'm not going home. I like the women here. Except for their madam. Don't get on the wrong side of Miss Fena."

"I'm not your father. I'm your son."

"My son." His face grew serious. "My son. What are you doing here?"

"I came to check on you. Why are you giving the nurses a hard time?"

He sat up and looked at me. There was a mischievous twinkle in his eyes.

"They give me a hard time. You want a sponge bath? They'll do that for you." He chuckled.

"Well, you have to knock it off. Okay?"

He closed his eyes again. "Yeah, yeah."

"Good, then."

"Who did you say you were?"

"Your son. Al. Yeah I know you forgot about me a long time ago."

"My son." He looked like he was searching way back in his mind. Then there was a glimmer of recognition. "What the hell happened to you?"

"What happened to me? You're the one who disappeared."

34

He screwed up his face in a scowl. "I mean what happened to you? You used to be a cute kid. You look like shit."

Two, three, four, five. He's old. He's old and sick. He's paying. Hold it together. "Hey, I met someone you know today. Gil Johnson. He said you two go way back. You know how we met? A body washed up at the dock behind your house."

"What body?" That seemed to catch the old man's attention.

"I don't know. A guy was wedged between the pilings and the Grady White."

"What body?"

He began to squirm in the wheelchair.

"Hey, hey, sit down. You can't get up. You'll fall." He stopped squirming. "Some guy who must have fallen out of a boat or something. Probably drunk. Johnson is investigating."

He began squirming again. "God damned monkey!"

I looked outside. The squirrel was still raiding the bird feeder. "Yeah, well the squirrel's gotta eat too. Maybe it's stealing to feed its family. Ever think of that?"

"Johnson," he said.

"Right. He mentioned Granville. What, was that your one and only big case?"

"At least I had Granville. Did you ever think of that? I had Granville. What do you have?"

How about that. The old bastard was looking for an argument. I wondered if he had been acting up only so I would be called in so he could start a fight with me.

"I have my self-respect for one thing." I took pleasure in the knock.

"Go!" he said.

Ah, so I struck a nerve. "I didn't ask for Blue Palmetto or your house. In fact, if I had a choice I'd be in California right now."

"Go, damn it."

I stood up. "I'm not sure when I'll get a chance to stop by again."

There was anger in his eyes and I felt a tinge of regret that I may have gone a little too far.

"Granville, Granville, Granville!" He yelled as he swung his walking stick. I jumped back in time not to get hit in the face by the brass alligator handle.

He was shouting so loud that two nurses came over to calm him down. One of them motioned for me to sneak away.

Before I did, I put my hand on his shoulder and he fell silent. But now instead of a twinkle in his eyes they looked dead like the eyes of a fish.

"I'll tell Johnson you said hi." Then I left.

Chapter Eight

I should have trusted my instincts and kept the hell away from the old man instead of listening to people like Greenleaf and Johnson. Sure, they meant well, but whoever they knew as "Big" Al DeLucia was not the deadbeat that I knew as my father. Lesson learned. You can't create a family based on a two-bit PI agency that someone threw in your lap.

I could have rehashed my visit with the old man all afternoon but I chose to put it out of my mind the same way he had put me and my mother out of his. I decided to focus instead on what I had to do to close the agency. Still, I kept wondering about the identity of the dead guy.

When I got back to the office I didn't bother going inside. I went directly through the path in the bamboo hedge and knocked at Max's back door. When she answered, she was struggling with a large wooden easel. There was a smudge of blue paint on her cheek. On her it looked good. Her smile told me she was pleased to see me.

"Who's that guy with the white hair that lives on the other side of me?"

Her smile faded and I realized it wasn't my best opening line.

"Are you asking me as a member of your detective agency or as a neighbor?"

"Whichever one has the answer."

"Why do you need to know?"

"He was on the dock when I found the body."

"I know. I was helping you. Remember?"

Of course, she was. We both knew that. Why did I have to watch every word I said with this woman? I let it go.

"Maybe he saw something."

"So why are you here instead of over there talking to him?"

Beats me how someone could go from happy to annoyed in thirty seconds. It seemed like it was my day to piss everyone off. I tried again.

"Do you know his name?"

"You could have asked Greenleaf."

I shrugged my shoulders.

"Maybe I would rather ask you."

That wasn't a lie. I did want to get to know Max better although at that point I was beginning to wonder why. Plus, technically she was my boss in the agency.

"You're right. I should have asked Greenleaf," I said.

I heaved a sigh of defeat. I started to walk back toward the path.

"All right. Come back. Put this easel by the pool for me while I get the rest of my stuff."

By the time I figured out how to open and set up the stupid thing she was back with a half-finished painting of the mouth of the river.

"I like it." I pointed to the painting.

"You don't have to butter me up just because I'm your superior."

She may be my superior, but I hoped she wouldn't forget who owns the agency. "I'll tell you what you want to know. Your neighbor's name is Percy Lynch."

Percy Lynch. Where had I heard that name before?

"What else do you know about him?"

"I thought you wanted his name. I didn't know this would be an interrogation."

"I thought you could give me some background on him before I went over there." I like to know as much as I can about someone before questioning them. It helps me read them and avoid surprises.

She softened a bit. I think she was flattered that I asked her. "He lives in England most of the year but goes back and forth a few times each winter with his wife Jane. He used to be with the circus before he retired."

That was it. Percy Lynch was the ringmaster who fought for better treatment of elephants until the circus finally decided to stop using them.

"See now that wasn't so hard."

"There's something else you should know before you go over there."

She had an amused look on her face.

"What?"

"Nothing, it's not important. You can handle it."

"What?"

"They're... Oh never mind."

"You started it. Tell me."

"You'll find out. I will tell you this, even though they are retired, the circus is still a big part of their lives."

I waved her off. "That's all? I thought you were going to say that they were killer clowns or something."

"Go see for yourself."

I distinctly heard her chuckle as I left her yard.

* * *

The gate across the Lynch's driveway was closed. I pressed the call button but there was no answer. I could hear music coming from their property; someone was over there. There was no convenience of a path between the two properties so I walked through my backyard up to the water. The tide was low and knowing that any land below the high tide line was public I walked to the back of the Lynch's property. I hopped up onto their seawall.

"Hullo, hullo?" I called out.

"This is private property."

The woman's voice came from a hammock by the pool. A head popped up. I don't know which I noticed first, that she was naked or there was a giant snake wrapped around her. I'm pretty sure that the snake came second.

"Mrs. Lynch?" She was in her mid-forties and had the athletic body of a circus performer. She got up and the monster snake slithered around her and down her body. Then it zigzagged across the lawn and plopped into the pool. I tried to keep my eyes on the snake for more than one reason.

I cleared my throat and tried to make my voice sound like nude women playing with colossal snakes were something I saw every day. "Is that a boa constrictor?"

"A Python. Monty loves the water, don't you baby?" She dove into the pool and swam along with the snake.

The guy who had only watched when I found the body, came out of a shed carrying a pool skimmer. Unfortunately, Lynch, who must have been a good twenty-five years older than his wife, didn't even have the courtesy of wearing a snake. Bleah. If I could pull my eyes out, I'd wash them in the pool. Very funny, Max, for not warning me.

"Really Jane, see what the gentleman wants so he can be on his way." Lynch had an upper crust British accent not all that different from what you would hear on Long Island's east end.

"Mr. Lynch. I have a quick question. It's important."

He scooped up a net full of leaves from the pool and dumped them into a plastic barrel.

"Bloody messy tree."

I knew the tiny leaves were from the live-oak tree in my yard.

"My name is DeLucia."

I kept my eye on the snake in the pool. It was swimming in circles around Jane.

"Who did you say you were with, Mr. DeLucia?" Lynch gave a fake yawn.

"I'm an investigator."

"Insurance? Newspaper? TV reporter?"

"Private," I said.

"A private investigator?" he waved me off, "I wish I could help."

"I'm your neighbor," I said. As if that was going to get me anywhere with this jerk.

"Yes, yes. Now I'm putting it together. DeLucia. You must be related to that detective from next door. Disagreeable fellow, I must say."

Yeah, he had my old man's number all right. Disagreeable was putting it mildly.

"I'm living there." For the time being at least.

He actually smiled, but it was the smile of a used car salesman.

"Why didn't you say as much."

There was a stir in the pool.

"Offer our guest a gin and tonic, darling," Jane said. Then she dove under the water followed by the snake.

"I'm good." I waved off the offer. I don't take drinks from naked bartenders.

Lynch wasn't interested in offering hospitality anyway.

"What's the asking price?" He asked.

What the hell was he talking about?

"Excuse me?"

"For your property. You've decided to sell. That's why you're here. Correct?"

"What makes you think that?"

"I presumed."

"When the time comes, I'll let you know."

I did intend to sell but he would be the last to know. I'd give it away before I'd let this wanker get it.

"I guess you know there was an incident next door yesterday. I noticed you watching from your dock when we were taking the body from the water."

He could have tried to help. He seemed to read my mind.

"Yes. Well. You and the lady seemed to have had everything under control. I thought it best to keep myself to myself."

"Did you recognize him? The dead guy."

"I couldn't see him from my dock."

"What about anything unusual out on the water that morning? Did you see anything?"

"I'm afraid I wasn't paying attention. Had I known there would be an incident, I would have done. Jane, did you notice anything unusual?"

Lynch scooped up another bunch of leaves from the pool startling the snake. It wrapped itself around his wife again and she giggled. Then her eyes glazed over and she started to make weird sounds.

"Hoom. Hoom. Hooooom."

I walked toward the pool and bent down by the edge. The snake eyed me.

"Mrs. Lynch, even the slightest thing might be important."

She spit out a mouthful of water. "Hoom, hoom, hoom, hoom."

I looked toward Lynch. "What's she doing?"

"Chanting. The Hum Mantra drives out negative feelings and stimulates a positive flow through the body. Apparently, you are sending pessimistic vibes." Mr. Lynch couldn't have been more condescending.

"Mrs. Lynch, please. If you could answer my questions."

"Hoommmmm."

"There you have it then." The husband started walking toward the seawall indicating I should follow. "When I purchase your property, the first thing that goes is that blasted tree."

I jumped down from the seawall to the beach. Don't be so eager, dude.

* * *

I walked the waterline past my property until I got to Max's place. I was going to tell her she'd pulled a fast one on me by not warning me the Lynches were nudists, but when I didn't see her in her yard, I decided I wasn't going to give her the satisfaction of laughing at me so I walked back home. Besides, I had set a realistic goal of wrapping up the work at Blue Palmetto in a few months and I knew Max would be a big help, so I didn't want to argue with her. I put the drowning incident aside although I still wondered about the identity of the dead guy that I suspected from his necklace to be a windsurfer.

Chapter Nine

I capped off a long day, that started with a lifeless body and ended with the weirdest couple I had ever met, by fixing myself a late-night home-made Mexican dinner. As I streamed a Grateful Dead concert on the Internet, I washed my meal down with lots of Patrón I found in my father's liquor cabinet. I had to say he had good taste in tequila.

I don't know what time I fell asleep on the couch, but I stayed there until a knock on the porch door woke me up. Greenleaf and Max were the only people I knew on Ava Island. Of course, I knew the Lynches but nudists didn't count in my book. It was still dark, so if it was Greenleaf or Max I knew there was a problem. I drew in my breath when I opened the door to find Max on the porch.

"What's wrong?"

"Nothing."

Why would she be bothering me at this hour? She didn't have an office at Blue Palmetto, her house being steps away from the small agency. If she was there to get something from the files she was being a little overzealous. I had noticed a spark between us when we updated each other on our cases, but it wasn't like we were ready for Hulu and commitment. I'd only been in Savannah for two days. Although I wouldn't mind if she was there for something other than business, despite the awkward situation of her outranking me.

"Come on, you're going to miss the sunrise," she said.

"I've seen the sun come up before."

"Not like here on the island. There will be hundreds of people there."

Watching the sun come up with a bunch of tourists, that was the last thing I wanted to do with the buzz going on in my head from the tequila.

"I don't know. It's still dark."

"That's the point. Come on, it will be fun."

On second thought, hanging out with Max wasn't a bad idea.

"Cool," I said.

She had a smirk that fell somewhere between that of the Mona Lisa and Obama. I didn't have to look down to realize I was in my boxers.

"Put on some pants first."

"Yeah well, it's not like I needed a dinner jacket to have tacos. Besides compared to those two weirdos next door this is formal."

Max laughed. "I guess I should have warned you about the Lynches."

"Very funny. I'm more pissed that it was a waste of time. Neither one of them would admit that they saw anything."

"Hurry up, maybe we'll see the green flash."

I was decent and outside in less than a minute. When I headed to my F-150 Max stopped me.

"It's only a five-minute walk."

Before we knew it, we were crossing a boardwalk pass over the grass-covered dunes that separate the beach from the picnic area along the street. On the other side was the widest beach I had ever seen. The shoreline was covered with people taking photos and video with their cell phones like they had never seen the sun come up.

As twilight appeared on the horizon the crowd turned their collective gaze eastward in anticipation.

People argued if they saw the green flash or not as the sun popped above the skyline. Cheers and clapping filled the air as the atmosphere turned a pale peach, and then quickly took on reds, yellows, and blues.

"Selfie time!" We positioned ourselves with our backs to the sun.

We put our heads together and I held out my camera and snapped. The first one caught the brilliant sunrise but our faces were in silhouette.

"Let me try," she said. She repositioned us so that light hit our faces. Perfect. I hoped it would be the first of many happy pictures of us together.

"Send it to me," I said.

As she was texting it to my phone, I spotted two windsurfers about to start their day a distance down the beach.

"I'll be right back." I raced up to them.

"There's a guy who hangs out down here, white dude with dreads. You know him?" I asked.

"You mean Keller?" The taller one said.

The shorter of the two looked at me with suspicion. "Why are you asking?"

"He had an accident. I'm looking for someone who knows him."

"An accident? How bad?"

"He's dead."

"Andy dead. No way." The big one said.

"I'm afraid so. Someone should be notified. What can you tell me about him?"

"We have to go," the suspicious one said.

The taller one was obviously the more concerned of the two. "Don't mind my brother. We only know him from down here. He was a cool dude. Totally radical surfer. I don't know much more, other than he was some kind of blogger."

"We gotta go." The shorter one pulled his brother's arm.

As they walked toward a path over the dunes Max caught up with me. "Why did you disappear like that?"

"The body has a name."

* * *

The name Andy Keller didn't ring a bell with Max. We sat on a bench by the edge of the sand dunes, Max relishing the beautiful colors in the clouds. As much as I wanted to pay attention, I kept trying to sneak a peek at my phone.

"Look at that. You're missing it. What's so important?" She sounded more inquisitive than annoyed.

"Sorry." I put the phone in my pocket. "He had a blog and I'm curious to find out more about him."

"Give that to me. I'll find it."

I put the phone in her outstretched hand. "You wanted to watch the sunrise."

"I've seen the sun come up before. Keller?"

"Right. Andy Keller."

She typed something in. "Here it is, it's called, *Stirring the Savannah Sands*." She showed me the screen.

Along each side of the screen were ads for restaurants, bars, and beach businesses. "He must have a decent number of followers to generate so many ads."

Max tipped her head.

"I know most of these places. Some are here on Ava and some are on Tybee Island. A few of them are good, most are tourist traps."

Max and I read together. In addition to the business links, each edition had a blog article written by Keller, relating to the Savannah area seashore. The current blog was an exposé of landlords who gouged tourists on rental properties. Past articles included a dredging dispute between Ava and Tybee Islands, the question of the possible merger of the Ava Island Police Department with the Savannah-Chatham Metropolitan Police Department, and how not to get ripped off by unscrupulous businesses selling hurricane shutters.

"It looks as if Keller was a rabble rouser," Max said.

"But was that enough for someone to want to kill him?"

"I should hope not. I covered the same kind of stories when I was a reporter." She studied my face. I assumed she was looking for a reaction, which she did not get. "I didn't tell you I was an investigative reporter. Did I?"

I hiked up one shoulder and took the phone from her. "I have to call Johnson." I got the Ava Island PD. The house mouse that answered connected me to Johnson's voicemail. I left a message for him to get hold of me.

Max still wanted to give me her credentials. "So, did you know what I did for a living before your father gave me a job?"

"Yeah."

"You Googled me?"

"I heard it some place."

"Tell me something. Is your passive aggressive behavior because you resent that I outrank you?"

"I don't resent anything."

"Not even your father?"

"Well yeah, I admit that."

"And you don't resent that your father set it up so that I outrank you even though you're the owner of the agency?"

"I'm still going to sell it so it doesn't matter. Right?"

"If you say so."

One thing I learned from my time with Kim was that a guy has to know when to diffuse.

"Look I wasn't trying to be rude and I don't resent anything. I'm just psyched at learning Keller's name. I mean talk about good luck."

"Luck?"

"Yeah, as far as me finding those two surfers." She looked as if she was waiting for more. "And you finding Keller's blog."

"Ah."

Situation diffused. "Want to go down to the village to celebrate our lead with breakfast?"

"No."

Crap. This was me and Kim all over again. Was she still angry that I took off down the beach? Or, could it be this crazy idea that I was jealous that she was senior agent?

"What?"

"Nothing." I have never met a woman who said something was nothing who didn't mean it was something.

"Let's go to your place for breakfast out on the patio," she said.

Chapter Ten

It was warm considering it was still April and a light breeze brought in the lemony-sweet scent of what Max had told me was Magnolia.

As she sprawled out on a double lounge chair by the seawall I poured her a mimosa and climbed in next to her.

"Perfect morning." I held up my glass and we clinked.

She moved in closer. I put my arm around her. My cell phone rang. I declined the call and let it go to voicemail. I took a gulp of my mimosa and spit out a bit of orange pulp.

"Does anyone use voice mail anymore?" she said as she moved her face closer to mine.

"I don't." I put my arm around her again. She cuddled in as the waves lapped at the seawall. Then she pulled back when we heard a loud bump as Lynch hit the dock with his boat. He pulled out into the river and tried again, this time smashing his motor into a piling.

I was laughing at Q-tip Head's lousy boating skills when my cell phone rang again. Caller ID told me it was the same number.

Max moved to the other side of the lounge. "You may as well answer it."

I tried to make my voice show how pissed I was. "DeLucia here."

"Mr. DeLucia, thank goodness you picked up. My name is Estelle Brewer. You found a body at your dock."

I knew that. "What can I do for you?"

"I have to talk to you."

"No problem. Call the office later, Ms. Brewer. We open at nine."

I could detect a hitch in the woman's voice.

"But I called yesterday and Mrs. Greenleaf told me you were out of the office. She gave me this number and assured me that if I mentioned her name you'd see me right away."

There was a loud thump from next door as Lynch crashed the boat into the dock again.

"Go ahead, Ms. Brewer."

"Actually, I'm in your driveway. May I come in?"

If Felicia Greenleaf hadn't been with the agency from day one, I would fire her. Besides, I didn't think I would be able to run the place without her—or I should say close the place without her. Still, a talking to was in order.

Within minutes Estelle was on the patio. She accepted Max's offer of a mimosa, took a deep drink and got to the point.

"I need you to find my daughter. I haven't heard from her in two months."

Judging from the woman's age I took it her daughter wasn't a child.

"Are we talking about a minor?"

"Oh, goodness no. She's married."

"Tracking down estranged family members isn't the type of case we handle." We. The word caught me by surprise the minute I said it. I cringed at my slip of the tongue. I certainly did not identify myself as part of the Blue Palmetto Detective Agency.

"But she and I have a good relationship. She's gone missing."

I heard that line dozens of times when I was on the force. Inevitably the so-called missing person only wanted to be left alone. I had no reason to believe this was not the case with Estelle's daughter.

"People lose contact all of the time for one reason or another. Have you notified the police?"

"They said there is no evidence of a crime and to come back when I have something to go on. That's why I need a private investigator—to get them something to go on. And I understand you are good. After all, your father solved the Granville Kidnapping."

Again, with Granville. This was the first I had heard it was a kidnapping.

"Are you saying your daughter was kidnapped?"

"It's the only explanation I can think of. There isn't a trace of her. And since your father…"

"Listen, Estelle. That was Big Al's case. I'm not my father. I'm sorry."

Max was standing behind Estelle frowning at me. I pretended I didn't notice her.

"But you're my only hope," Estelle said.

"In all honesty, I don't see how I can help you. I'm not taking on any new cases."

"But, this could be your Granville."

I didn't need a damned Granville. "As I said, I'm afraid I'm not interested. Sorry."

Estelle put down her mimosa and stood. She had tears in her eyes and a bit of orange pulp on her front tooth.

"I guess it's not easy following in somebody's footsteps," she said.

That might have hurt except that she had it all wrong. I wasn't following in anyone's footsteps, especially not those of Big Al DeLucia.

She looked so dejected that I felt bad that I had to refuse her. The woman had no way of knowing where I was coming from.

Max shot me a look that asked how I could do that to an old lady.

"May we have a word?" Max inclined her head toward the kitchen and I followed her inside.

"As senior agent, I still have a say, don't I?"

"Yeah."

She had a say and I knew she was going to exercise it.

"I think we should help her."

"I intend to close this agency."

"And I'm sure you will, but as long as we're open we have an obligation to do right by people who need our services. That's all I have to say."

I threw up my hands. "I'll get the details. Maybe we can find someone who can help her."

I went back outside where Estelle was looking out at the river.

"Sit down," I said.

"You'll take the case?" Estelle asked. She had such hope on her face that I was already regretting my decision to hear her out.

"I'll listen and see where I can direct you. Let's start with your daughter's name."

"Jill Hicks. She lives here in Savannah. I'm living up in Aiken at a spread I inherited. It took me 3 1/2 hours to drive here with all of the highway construction around Statesboro."

I knew Aiken, South Carolina—it was just on the other side of the line from Augusta, Georgia. "Horse country. I passed through on the way down to Savannah."

"Yes. That's why I'm worried. Jill has a horse we keep at our place. Its name is Butternut. She would never leave and not check up on him. That's why I have been coming down every chance I get to look for her. I went to her house but it was empty. I don't know where to turn."

"Do you see your daughter often?"

"We communicate often. She calls to check on Butternut every few days and she comes up whenever she can sneak away from her husband. I know that he tries to keep her away so I hardly ever go to her house. Sometimes when your kids get married you have to back away a bit to keep the peace. Isn't that the truth? So, I don't ask too many questions."

I raised my eyebrows at that statement.

"Wise thing to do," I said. "What's her husband's name?"

"Roscoe Hicks. I know that they were having problems and I'm worried for her safety."

"Problems?"

"The last time we spoke she said he was accusing her of cheating on him."

"I'm sorry that I have to ask this. But, could she have run off with another man?"

Estelle looked hurt. "No. She would never do that."

"But you said she was cheating on her husband."

"I never said such a thing. I said her husband accused her of cheating. I didn't say she was for sure."

She was making my head swim and I didn't want to hear any more.

"Mrs. Brewer, you can stop. I'm only here temporarily until I close my father's caseload. Then I'm moving on. If you call Mrs. Greenleaf when the office opens, she will give you a list of other private investigators you might try."

Max edged her way in between us. "Mrs. Brewer, What Mr. DeLucia is trying to say is that when he has to leave, I'll take the case on if it's still not solved."

I was surprised, but Max was pulling rank on me. I wasn't going to argue in front of Estelle, but I'm sure the look on my face spoke volumes. I positioned myself so Estelle could see me.

"Mrs. Brewer, I'm confident this will be a case of your daughter simply looking for some privacy, but if the Blue Palmetto can set your mind at ease…"

"But you're not listening to me, Mr. DeLucia. The man Jill's husband was accusing her of having the affair with was Andy Keller. The man you found dead."

Was she kidding me? I studied her face to see if she was trying to pull off some kind of elaborate con. "How do you know I found a body? And more to the point, how do you know the victim's name?"

Estelle looked at me as if I had two heads.

"I read in the paper that you found Andy Keller's body."

It hadn't been an hour since I'd found out the guy's name was Keller. "In the paper? His name is in the paper?"

Who reads newspapers anymore?

"Yes, it's right here." She pulled a newspaper out of her bag.

"It's on the television too." She handed me the paper. "You are the one who found the body. Correct?"

So, Johnson identified the body and didn't bother to tell me. I suppose it was my fault that he didn't fill me in on the news. I did tell him my only interest was in closing the agency and getting to the West Coast. Although by the same token, he could have kept my name out of the papers so I wouldn't get involved in situations such as this one. For the second time in five minutes I was trying to recover without looking like a fool in front of Estelle.

"I did find him. Right over there." I pointed to the dock.

"That's why you have to help me. I think my son-in-law killed Mr. Keller and either he is holding Jill against her will or..."

I knew she didn't even want to think about the other possibility that Hicks might have already killed her daughter. Max spared her from having to say the unmentionable.

"Don't you worry." She took Estelle's hand.

I had no choice but to go along. "We'll look into it. You'll be hearing from us soon."

The old woman's face brightened. "Bless you," she said.

It had been a long time since anyone blessed me. The way my life had been going an exorcism would have been more in order.

Chapter Eleven

When Estelle left, Max turned to me and said in a meek voice, "I'll bet you didn't see that coming."

"Are you talking about your coup or the part about Andy Keller?"

"You're actually mad that I was in favor of helping her? Listen, if you're not happy with me for following my instinct you can fire me."

"I didn't say I wanted to fire you. And your instinct was spot on. This time."

Max glared at me. "Let's drop it there then. I don't need mansplaining. I have work to do."

* * *

When Greenleaf parked her Schwinn in the backyard later in the morning she found me at the dock on my hands and knees trying to force a noodle float between the boat and the submerged float drum. Max's mansplaining remark still bugged me.

"You'll be happy to know that I saw my father," I said to her when she hopped onto the dock.

Greenleaf made the sign of the cross in the air over my head. Between her and Estelle, all of this blessing was making me feel uncomfortable.

"There may be hope for you yet. I was beginning to give up on you," she said.

I looked up at her. I could swear that I detected on her face what for

Greenleaf would pass for a smile.

"Don't get your hopes up that we're going to become BFFs. He's completely out of it. He was banging on the window with a walking stick trying to scare away a squirrel that he was convinced was a monkey."

Greenleaf seemed to pale a little. Maybe I had upset her. But she did know that my father had Alzheimer's. She's the one who told me he had checked into The Palms. Her moment passed quickly and she seemed composed again.

"So, he's still using the walking stick?"

"I told you, he was banging on the window with it. I find it kind of funny. I wouldn't have thought of him as the type to carry a stick."

She sighed. "He's even less of the type that would use a walker. That's what they wanted him to do and he flatly refused. I think they want him using some type of walking aid to cover themselves legally. I got him the stick a few weeks ago. I'm glad he's using it."

"Oh, he's using it all right. He almost hit me with it."

Greenleaf changed the subject as if it was my fault if I didn't watch out for Big Al's temper. I was beginning to get the impression that as far as she was concerned, Big Al could do no wrong. I wondered if maybe there was a little more to their relationship than I knew about.

"What on earth are you doing?" she said.

"I'm trying to figure out how anything could get caught between the dock and the boat."

"It's obvious. The current pushed the body in there." Greenleaf spoke with the authority of someone who knew what she was talking about. As far as I knew she wasn't an oceanographer, but even if she was I wasn't buying her theory.

"Johnson said the same thing. I still don't see it." I demonstrated by pushing the boat away from the dock and showing her that the lines only opened the space between them eight or nine inches. "The body has a name by the way."

"I know, Andy Keller."

"Am I the only one who didn't know that?"

"It's in the newspaper. You should read one sometime. You can't get all of your news from your phone."

While we were in the telling it like it is mode, I started to tell her that I didn't appreciate her giving out my private phone number, but she cut me off as soon as I said, "You know..."

"Speaking of the phone, a Mrs. Brewer was looking for you yesterday. I shouldn't have given her your cell number but she sounded desperate. I hope that wasn't a problem for you."

Well, what was I supposed to say to that? I knew that was as close to an apology as I was going to get. There was no sense in belaboring the point.

"Did she call you?" Greenleaf's voice was all business.

"Yeah. Mrs. Brewer wants me to find her daughter. She thinks the daughter's husband killed Keller and her daughter might be next. I decided to see what I could do to help her. But it doesn't mean I'm taking the case. Right?"

Greenleaf seemed relieved. "Good."

I was still kneeling on the dock experimenting with the noodle. As hard as I tried I couldn't get it to go between the dock and the boat.

"I see what you mean about the unlikelihood that a body could stick in there. But, I'm sure you'll figure it out," she said.

I didn't know her well, but it seemed a vote of confidence wasn't something that she gave readily. She put her hand on my shoulder to get me to look up at her. "What does this mean?" she asked.

"I'm not sure. I don't know that much about currents."

"I don't mean the case. Are you going to keep the detective agency?"

I didn't answer her.

Chapter Twelve

Estelle had given me her daughter's picture; a pretty girl in a delicate way, with a small nose, big green eyes, and long brown hair. If you saw her on the street you would look twice, but maybe not a third time. She also gave me her last address, on Seiler Avenue in Savannah. My first hunch was that Jill didn't want anything to do with her mother and moved without telling her, but this Andy Keller connection intrigued me. What if Estelle was correct and Hicks did kill him, and Estelle's daughter was in danger? There was too much at stake for me to ignore.

I got off the Harry S. Truman Parkway and made my way to Seiler Ave., a tree-lined street in the heart of Savannah. My hope was to find a neighbor who could give me a lead as to where the Hicks family went. I found the early 20th century bungalow defaced by a modern addition covered in delaminating texture 1-11 plywood.

I parked in front of a huge tree that had lifted the sidewalk and put a crack in the low brick wall that enclosed the lawn. The grassy area, small enough to cut with scissors, was dominated by a huge truck tire filled with sad looking geraniums. The place was empty all right, the only sign of it ever having been occupied was the icicle style Christmas lights that still dangled from the addition's overhang. I spotted an elderly man next door watching me.

In contrast to Hicks' place, his house was a tidy Arts and Crafts home that very well could have come from a Sears catalog. The wall in front of his place was of concrete blocks no more than sixteen inches high and painted bright red to match the foundation of the house. The wall made a perfect backdrop for the small yellow flowers, each precisely spaced, that lined it. As I walked toward his yard he picked up a rake then met me at a line of little shrubs that defined his property line.

I held out my card, something that Greenleaf had taken upon herself to make for me, which he didn't take.

"Al DeLucia. I'm a private investigator. Mr...?"

"Roman. Nate Roman. Are you carrying a gun?"

For several reasons, I hadn't carried a gun since I left the force. Most private investigators that I've known over the years don't, even in Georgia where open carry with a permit is legal, from what I understand. That's mainly because it's rare to get caught in a surprise situation and it usually freaks people out to the point where they won't give you any information if you enter their home packing. That's not to say that there isn't a nice compact Glock 19 locked in the compartment of my truck. I wasn't wearing a jacket but I spread out my arms to show him there were no bulges under my shirt.

"I'm not."

"Humph. What kind of detective are you?"

Wise ass octogenarians. If he and my father were any indication, Georgia must be loaded with them. But, you got to love them for telling it as they think it is.

I gave him a friendly smile instead of telling him what I was thinking.

I have this theory that people will open up to you if you appeal to them for help. Maybe 99% of folks feel good about being able to assist. "I need a little help in finding Roscoe Hicks and his wife Jill. Would you know where they moved to?"

He put his lips together as if he was going to spit, but he didn't. "No idea."

"When did they move?"

The man shrugged his shoulders. "Can't rightly say when I realized no one was living there."

"It's important that I find the Hicks couple. Did they give you their new address or maybe a phone number?"

"What are you writing a book? I don't know nothing." The old guy shook his rake at me in a gesture that seemed to mean go away, and then he walked into the backyard. My luck that I had to run into one of the 1% who doesn't give a crap about helping out.

As I started to leave I heard the front door of Roman's house open. An elderly little lady came out on the stoop. She was wearing an apron which, from the neck down, had a picture of a curvaceous woman's bikini clad body imprinted on it. I stifled a smile as I read the words *Don't Hate Me Because I'm Beautiful!*

"Don't mind Nate. He acts madder than a wet hen since his stroke."

"Are you Mrs. Roman?"

"Miss Roman. I'm his sister. I was listening at the window. So, you're looking for our old neighbors?"

"Do you know where I can locate them?"

"I don't want to start with Nate. Do you know where Forsyth Park is?"

"I can find it." If that damned GPS is cooperative that is.

"I'm taking my constitutional shortly. I'll meet you by the fountain. You had better leave before Nate has a dying duck fit."

With that she scrambled back into the house.

* * *

When I got back to the truck there was a folded piece of notebook paper under the windshield wiper on the driver's side. I checked to see if I was blocking a driveway. Nope. Then I checked the driver's side front to back to see if someone scratched the truck. Nothing that I could see. I flicked open the sheet and read the block letters.

Some detective you are.

It wasn't the first time I'd heard that. In fact, besides Nate saying something similar, my own father had said those words to me. But he certainly was not the one who left the note. He was back at The Palms living in his own little world. But who? I didn't see Nate leave his backyard. Back home any number of friends would come to mind, here I hardly knew anybody.

I looked toward Nate Roman's yard. He was standing on his front lawn watching me. I held up the note. He shook his rake at me and walked into the backyard. Asshat. I had too much to do to play games. I balled the note up and threw it on the passenger side where it took up residence on the floor with a bag from a fast food joint. This gumshoe doesn't litter.

* * *

I parked on Drayton Street and found the beautiful white fountain on the north end of the large park. I took one of the many benches that circled the huge water feature that sat in the middle of a circular pool that was surrounded by flowers and an iron fence. I admired the classical lady at the top of the main fountain and the eight smaller fountains that stood in the pool, four tritons and four swans. A fine mist carried by the breeze, and the sound, like gentle rain on a pond, had a soothing effect on me. I closed my eyes for a second.

"Nate told me you're a detective named DeLucia."

I bolted upright.

"I am."

Miss Roman wasn't wearing her apron. Instead, she was dressed in a colorful spandex running outfit. I liked the old lady's attitude.

Her mouth turned down. "That changes everything. I thought maybe you were a relative of theirs."

"I'm working for a relative. Jill Hicks' mother. She's upset that she hasn't heard from her daughter."

"I see." I could tell she was still trying to decide if I was on the up and up.

"Do you know where they moved to?"

"No. They left in the middle of the night like they were running from something. Then not long after that I read in the paper that Mrs. Hicks was dead. Her mother doesn't know?"

Mrs. Hicks was dead. That explained why Estelle hadn't heard from her daughter. It looked like Estelle's biggest fear had been realized. Maybe Hicks did kill his wife.

"Are you sure that Mrs. Hicks passed away?"

"Of course. I read the obituary in the paper. At my age that's the first section you turn to. There was an accident. The paper had an article about that too. Her car went into a canal. The poor dear drowned." Miss Roman choked up. "I liked her. She seemed kind. And she was quiet. You know what I mean? Him, I didn't care for so much. Too loud and full of himself."

It was too late to find Jill but I still wanted to talk to Hicks.

"So, you have no idea of where Mr. Hicks would be now?"

"Like I said, they moved in a hurry. But, Nate must know. He and Roscoe were thick as thieves. Two of a kind those two."

"But your brother's not talking," I said.

She shook her head. "Why don't you check the plumbing supply house out on Ogeechee Road? He works there. When you find him, tell him I'm sorry about, poor Jill." She pushed a strand of hair back off of her face. "I have to get back. Nate gets worried." She brisk-walked around the circle to the other side of the fountain and then took a path into the square.

I had to smile. Nate's sister was a 99%er.

Chapter Thirteen

Miss Roman said there was an obituary for Jill Hicks. I wanted to read it for myself. I sat in the truck and did a search of the Savannah Morning News website on my phone. I found that indeed a Jill Hicks died in an automobile accident on the Coastal Highway in Burroughs, a town south of Savannah. Another search found me the article on the accident. Jill Hicks died when the car she was driving skidded into a canal and she drowned. According to the article, the police think Hicks may have been texting at the time.

Apparently, Miss Roman didn't care to share the tragic details with me.

* * *

I was bothered by the fact that it was so easy for me to find Jill's obituary. How could it be that Estelle didn't know her daughter was dead?

Estelle was staying at the Riverfront Hotel in Savannah's Historic District not far from the big bridge. I'd notified next of kin many times when I was a cop. It never gets easier and I wasn't looking forward to breaking the news.

The desk clerk called up to the room then told me Estelle would meet me in the lobby. As I waited, the smell of sizzling sausage from the free buffet made my stomach growl. I helped myself to a bowl of grits and threw a couple of slices of bacon on top. As I ate, I listened to the local weather on a TV above the table with the cold cereals and toaster. It was going to be a nice day in Savannah. What else was new?

When Estelle came down her hair was a mess and she looked as if she hadn't slept all night. I think she could see from my face that there was something wrong.

"Is there a problem, Mr. DeLucia?"

"I'm afraid I have some bad news."

Estelle's mouth pulled back and her eyebrows arched as if she were more annoyed than worried.

"Oh, for the love of Mike. You're not going to tell me Jill died in a traffic accident, are you?"

"You know?"

"No. I do not know because it is not true that she's dead. I've been trying to tell the police that they got it wrong."

I couldn't understand what was going on. The woman had me looking for a dead girl. She was obviously in denial. I was glad that I hadn't put too much time into the case. I had Greenleaf and Max to thank for this.

"Why didn't you tell me the police told you she was dead?"

"Would you have taken the case?"

It was bad enough that I looked at my future when I had visited my father, I didn't need to deal with the dementia of strangers as well.

"Of course not."

"I rest my case, as they say. I was told that my daughter died in a car crash. If that is true, then why is she trying to contact me?"

"Who's trying to contact you?"

"My daughter. I'm telling you she is not dead."

"Someone must have identified her body."

"Not someone. Some thing. Roscoe Hicks, that no good husband of hers."

"Didn't you see your daughter," I paused trying to find a kind way to say it. "you know… at the funeral?"

"I was up in Augusta, in the hospital. Jill's husband had her cremated before I even heard of the accident. He sent me the ashes. But I know they're not hers."

Poor Estelle. I wondered what her relationship with her daughter was like that made her fall so deeply into denial.

"Sometimes you have to face what is, no matter how much it hurts," I said to Estelle.

"My daughter is alive. Who else would have sent me money on the first of the month?"

"The Social Security Administration would be my guess."

"Listen, Mr. DeLucia. I'm not crazy and I wish you wouldn't joke. I received a parcel the other day. There's $1,500 and a bag of Hershey's Kisses in it. Only Jill would send that to me. The Kisses have been a joke between us since she was a child."

"Okay, I'm listening. But you said the police confirmed she was dead. Even if you don't believe the husband, that's pretty irrefutable."

"They confirmed the car was hers, maybe she didn't die. Maybe she was sent to a hospital and recovered."

"You said you have the ashes."

"Roscoe sent me the ashes, he said she had told him she wanted to be cremated when she died. But that can't be true. She was afraid of fire. She never would want that. They could be the ashes of a dog for all I know. I wouldn't put anything past him. He's a little younger than her, if you know what I mean."

"How much younger?"

"She's forty-two and he's twenty-seven."

"How was that money delivered to you?"

"A small Priority Delivery box from the post office; as I told you, there was a bag of candy kisses in it. Don't forget the kisses. I know she's trying to send me a message."

"Did you look at the return address?"

"There is none. But the box was stuffed with newspaper. The Ava Island Sands."

"So, you concluded that the package was mailed from Ava Island."

"Wouldn't you?"

"Tell me about Andy Keller's relationship with your daughter."

"My daughter confessed to me that things between she and Roscoe were not going well."

"And she told you she was having an affair with Andy Keller?"

"She didn't have to. The next time I called her, it was the last time I spoke to her, a man answered. I knew it wasn't Roscoe. When I asked who it was he said his name was Andy Keller. He put Jill on the phone and when I asked who he was she was evasive. She said he was some kind of blogger. When it comes to men my daughter doesn't have the sense she was born with. She goes from bad to worse. At least Roscoe had a job. Who can make money as a blogger?"

"I don't know much about blogging, I'm afraid. But you do think Roscoe killed Keller because he thought he was having an affair with you daughter?"

"Exactly. Are you looking for him?"

"I had a lead that led to a dead end."

I left Estelle drinking her coffee surrounded by snowbirds at the other tables. I grabbed a coffee and a cruller on the way out and headed back to the office.

Chapter Fourteen

As the morning edged on, the stifling humidity beat the ambition out of me. I cranked up the air conditioning in my F-150 and fantasized about the dry Los Angeles air. When I returned to the shady Blue Palmetto parking lot I was pleasantly surprised to realize that it must have been fifteen degrees cooler in the shade of the huge tree that darkened the lot. I drove onto a patch of live oak leaves that covered the crushed shell parking area. I was beginning to understand Lynch's complaint. Georgia live oak must be the messiest tree in the world, shedding thousands of small leathery leaves in the spring.

As I walked toward the porch I spread my arms to catch the refreshing breeze coming off the water. Since I had been missing in action I expected to hear an earful from Felicia Greenleaf. As soon as I opened the door on the tiny screened porch she called out from inside. For a little woman, she had a voice that could be heard halfway to Atlanta.

"Well, it's nice of you to decide to come in. I've been fielding calls all morning. The insurance company wants to know if you have the pictures. Mr. Drysdale wants to know if his wife is cheating. Mrs. Halifax wants to know if her late husband had a safe deposit box or not. And I want to know if you brought me coffee."

"Yes. Yes. I'm not sure. And here. I brought you a cruller too."

I put the coffee and pastry that I had picked up from the hotel buffet on her desk. I didn't tell her where I got them.

"You're learning. It's too bad that I have to train you then lose you." She took the lid off of the coffee and smelled it. A broad smile spread over her face and she took a sip followed by a big bite from the long, braided donut.

"I was trying to find Estelle Brewer's daughter if you were wondering."

"Did you take on the case?" Crumbs of cruller exploded from her mouth as she spoke.

"I guess I did." I made a face.

"I'll consider the coffee and cruller a thank you. So, what's your problem?"

"Oh, no problem. I didn't need something else to work on, I've already got a ..." I hesitated.

"I know, you have a shit load of cases to work on and you want to get out of here," she said.

"Yeah. Something like that."

"Did you ever think of asking Big Al for advice?"

It took a minute for me to process what she was saying.

"My father? You want me to ask my fly-by-night father who has Alzheimer's for advice."

"Why not? One: you're a big boy now so it's time you got over what happened more than twenty-five years ago. He's in your life now, like it or not. Two: he's in the early stages of the disease and can have a lot to offer. Think Glen Campbell going on tour after he was diagnosed with Alzheimer's. And don't forget Ronald Regan running the free world with the illness."

I thought about my unpleasant visit to The Palms. "I don't think he comprehended who I was and probably only understood half of what I was saying."

"Maybe you should try listening to your father a little. It doesn't matter what he understands. It's what you understand that matters."

"Understand what? That he's a self-centered bastard?"

"Well even self-centered people get it right once in a while."

"Like?"

"Granville."

"That's the last thing I want to hear about."

"Well I'm going to tell you anyway. Then you can do what you want with the information. What do you know?"

"That Big Al solved the case of the missing Granville girl. I heard it from day one when I got down here."

"Well there's a little more to it than that. Martin Granville was a well-known race-car driver in the '80s. He had it all, a beautiful young wife, a small daughter, a large spread northwest of Savannah not far from Augusta, and a cocaine habit. One night while he was in his car barn working on one of his vehicles his little daughter was kidnapped from her bed while his wife was upstairs reading and the nanny was out of the room. Al Sr. tracked down a man named Georg Gerber who was sent to jail and there he died."

"As you said, everyone gets it right once in a while."

"The thing is he didn't get it totally right. The little girl was never found. That always bothered him."

Was she kidding? I was supposed to feel bad that he couldn't find the little girl after he abandoned his own family. "Spare me, please."

"He's a good man and you can still learn something from him. Take my advice or leave it. I'm trying to help; nothing more."

I was tempted to tell her that she had said she wouldn't give any more advice, but the fact is she was indispensable to Blue Palmetto and if I was going to close the agency in a timely manner I was going to need her help. But I think we were talking about two different kinds of help.

"It would be a bigger help if you could get me all you can on a guy named Roscoe Hicks. I want to wrap this Brewer case up quickly."

I escaped into my office at the back of the cottage where I set my mind on how to find Roscoe Hicks. Miss Roman told me he worked at a plumbing supply house out on Ogeechee Road a little past the Home Depot and Wal-Mart. Maybe someone there could tell me where Hicks was holding up. A quick search came up with Sampson Brothers Plumbing Supply on Ogeechee. It had to be the right place. I called.

"Yeah, hi. I'd like to speak to Roscoe Hicks."

The guy that answered had a voice that sounded like a rusty gravel crusher. "He ain't here. What do you need? I can help you."

"Do I have the right supply house? He does work there, right?"

"Not no more. He quit a week ago."

"I see. I'd like to contact him. He seems to have moved. Would you have his new address?" It was a long shot, but it was worth a try.

"Who the hell is this?"

So much for the long shot. "I'm an old friend and I'd like to reconnect with him. He must have left a forwarding address."

"Maybe he did and maybe he didn't. My brother is off today and I'm trying to run this whole operation myself. I got better things to do than giving you personal information about my employees."

Gravel voice hung up and I decided it was time for a little DIY.

"Greenleaf. Do we have a tool box around here?"

"In the supply closet on the floor between Big Al's fishing rods and the copy paper. Don't forget to put it back when you're finished," she called back from the other room.

Fifteen minutes later after watching a YouTube video on how to take apart a toilet, I was in the front office with the overflow tube and float ball to our ancient commode in hand.

"Did you find out anything about Roscoe Hicks?"

"Where should I start? He's been arrested for everything from assault to extortion. What's that?" She pointed to the toilet parts.

I looked down at the overflow tube. "The uh, lavatory is going to be out of commission for a while. I'm going to the plumbing supply house now."

Greenleaf made a face that told me she thought I was the biggest idiot in the world.

"Thanks for the heads up after I drank that coffee. If I have to go, I'll use your sink."

She went back to work mumbling to herself.

Chapter Fifteen

You won't find tourists on Ogeechee Road. Inland, running parallel to US 17, it's hotter and grittier than the rest of Savannah. The commercial strip of metal Butler Buildings housing construction suppliers and trucking companies runs through a community of gloomy little bungalows that seem plucked out of the 1950s. It's the kind of neighborhood that is hidden away like an ugly stepchild, yet is essential to keeping a city like Savannah running smoothly.

I almost missed Sampson Brothers Plumbing Supply because it has a side entrance facing a parking lot that doesn't look onto Ogeechee Road. When I walked in I noted the position of the security camera by the ceiling at the far end of the store. I lowered my head and put the guts of the Blue Palmetto's toilet on the counter. As I did so I wondered about how Greenleaf was holding out after her coffee.

"Can you match this?"

The counterman tending the place had a grizzled beard and a sour puss. He looked at it almost in awe. "That baby is old. It must be thirty or forty years old at least."

From the sound of his voice, I had no doubt that it was the guy I talked to on the phone.

"You have it?"

"Might." He looked at a computer on the counter next to a security monitor that showed alternating views of inside and outside the warehouse. "It looks like we do. But I'm going to have to go out back and search. My brother isn't here. I'm holding down the fort."

But I knew how overworked the poor martyr was from the phone call.

"I can wait. Thanks."

Behind the counter were rows of metal shelves full of plumbing fixtures. I could see Sampson on the security monitor as he walked down an aisle toward the bowels of the warehouse. He seemed to be having trouble finding the part. Just what I had hoped for. The other three scenes on the monitor showed me at the counter, the front of the building where my truck was parked, and the back of the warehouse where a guy was filling a Sampson Brothers delivery truck from a tanker marked Dirty South Heating Oil.

I spun the computer screen around and brought the computer keyboard to where I could use it. As many small businesses do, Sampson Brothers kept track of its employee records and its business inventory on the same computer network using inexpensive, outdated software. I minimized the inventory record that the owner had been looking at. I found the brothers didn't bother with passwords, so it was easy to find the employee file labeled Hicks. Too bad I didn't get a chance to open it.

"All right. Do you want to tell me what in the hell you're up to?"

I must have jumped a foot when I heard the gravelly voice. While I was looking at the computer I missed Sampson coming back to the service counter. He had the part in one hand and a gun in the other. At times like this I wished I didn't leave my G19 in the glove compartment.

"I'm only checking out the specs on the part. No harm done. You can't blame me for not wanting to get the wrong part." I pointed to a sign stating a $25 restocking fee."

I stole a glance at his hand. It was calm and steady as it held the gun pointed at me. That was a good sign. There's nothing worse than someone nervous aiming a gun at you. On the other hand, the look in his eye told me he meant business.

"You're the one who called looking for Hicks. I recognize your accent," he said.

Accent? People from Connecticut don't have an accent.

"How about putting that thing away?"

"How about you telling me why you're so hell bent on finding Hicks."

"Okay, I'm with the Blue Palmetto Detective Agency; Al DeLucia is the name." Sometimes it's better to be upfront. "I have a client, who is a relative of Hicks, who wants to find him." I had no intention of being so upfront as to tell Sampson that I suspected Hicks was a murderer.

"I told you on the phone, I ain't giving you any information about an employee. Now, get out." He waved his gun toward the door.

"I'll leave when you tell me where Hicks is."

"You think you're slicker'n owl shit, coming around here trying to trick me into giving him up. But I told you it ain't going to happen."

"It will, because I took a picture of your security monitor showing someone putting untaxed heating oil in your delivery truck. That's a pretty big offense."

Sampson began chewing at his lip. I could see from his expression he was trying to figure what his next move should be.

"You see this gun? I could blow you into next week and say you was a robber."

"I already texted the picture to my office manager. She'll send it to the police if you try that. They may begin to question if I really was a robber. Especially since I'm unarmed."

By this time, Sampson was working at that lip so hard that it was bleeding.

"I've had a little problem once. I can't afford any more trouble. Hicks was living over on Tybee Island. Let me find the address on that computer. Then get the hell out of here."

"I'm going to still need that part." I knew that if I didn't fix that toilet Greenleaf would make me wish that Sampson had shot me.

$145 later I was headed out to my truck. Accent my ass.

* * *

I was feeling that I was finally getting someplace now that I had a new address for Hicks, Unit B 84 Village Avenue, Tybee Island. I jumped into the truck and turned on the ignition. Mr. Hicks, prepare yourself for an unwelcome visitor. I was about to pull out of the parking space when I noticed the green flyer under my wiper blade. I put the gear in park and got out leaving the truck running and the door open. If someone came along and hijacked my vehicle I would have been less surprised than when I looked at the flier. No garage sale, no lost cat, or grand opening announcement there. It was simply a handwritten note in block letters that read; **Some detective you are**.

Well, it couldn't have been Nate Roman this time. I must have missed whoever left the note while I was looking at the computer. I wondered if one of the guys from the department was down on vacation and decided to break my balls. If he was, I wished he would show himself and say, "Hey." Or maybe not, if the idiot was following me around. Then once more Hicks came to mind. Did he know that I was looking for him and he was playing a cat and mouse game? Again, I balled the paper up and threw it on the floor with the other note and fast food trash.

Chapter Sixteen

It seemed that Maryann at The Palms had some kind of radar that told her when I was busy. I was headed back to Ava Island to check out Hick's place when my cell phone began playing the dirge that I had designated as the ringtone for the nasty ass "care coordinator."

"This is Maryann Fena from The Palms. Is this Mr. DeLucia?"

I'll be kind and blame the Bluetooth for making her sound like that witch with the flying monkeys.

"Yup, this is me."

Who else would be answering my phone? I waited for her to go next, my patience growing thin, as I was in no mood for games.

"Are you there, Mr. DeLucia?" She sounded quite annoyed that I wasn't talking but I thought it would be best to let her go first.

"I am here," I said.

"It's your father."

Oh Jeez, I hoped she wasn't going to say he was dead. What was I supposed to say if she did? I hardly knew the guy. I opted for a simple, "Yes…"

"I don't think we are going to be able to keep him here at The Palms." There was a hint of satisfaction in her voice that worked its way under my skin.

One side of me wanted to ask her why she was telling me her problems, and the other side wanted me to come to Big Al's defense.

"And why is that?"

"He insists on going outside."

"He signed himself into a nursing facility not a prison. Let him go outside if he wants." It was my turn to sound annoyed.

"I'm sure you realize that we can't allow that. What you need to do is come down here right now."

What I needed to do was find Hicks.

"I'm kind of busy right now. Maybe in a few hours."

"He's being ugly and I'm fixing to send him to the ER for a psych evaluation. I can tell you now they will call you to go in."

Which would waste even more of my time. "I'll be right there."

I turned the truck around and was at The Palms within ten minutes. I marched up to Nurse Fena's office. The door was open and she was hovering over some papers. I knocked at the doorjamb a little harder than was necessary to get her attention.

She looked up and snapped, "We are not an Alzheimer's facility. You're going to have to find another placement for him."

Wasn't that the social worker's job? "You knew his problem when you took him in." I didn't go into the fact that he paid upfront.

"I didn't know he could be as aggravating as a rock. You'll have to do something."

I could see this was going nowhere. Meanwhile, I had to find Hicks.

"Fine, I am going to do something. I'm going to take him with me for a few hours. That should give your staff some respite."

Maryann stared me down in what seemed like a practiced deadpan look meant to show that she was going to be unrelenting on the issue.

"And then."

I had my own determined look. "And then I'm going to bring him back. He paid you. He's your responsibility."

"You can't take him out."

"Because?" Was she kidding me? She said that she couldn't handle him.

"He has to learn to be comfortable in this environment. If he leaves the comfort zone that The Palms provides, then he will be even more unruly when he comes back."

Was there no pleasing this woman? "It's the only solution I have right now."

Believe me, taking my father with me on an investigation was the last thing I wanted to do. I looked at my watch. "Please have someone get him ready."

Ten minutes later my father joined us in the building's foyer decked out with his bush hat and fancy walking stick with the alligator handle. Maryann wasn't happy that I was taking him out of the home but legally she had nothing to say about it. I didn't need to be babysitting my old man but I didn't have much choice. As Maryann punched in the code that slid open the glass door at the entrance my father stuck out his tongue and gave her the raspberries.

"Aren't you precious?" She tried to pinch his cheek but he waved her off and pulled back. Then she huffed and walked back toward her office as we headed to the parking lot.

"She thinks I don't know it." My father had this irritating grin that I took to mean he was trying to impress me with his cleverness. I shouldn't have fed into him but I did.

"Know what?"

"1998," he said.

Here we go. This was going to be a long day.

"No, it's 2019," I said.

Big Al shook his head as if to say get with the program. "I know what year it is. I'm talking about the numbers one, nine, nine, eight. That's how you open the door."

"You know the code to open the door?"

He pointed to the cornerstone of the building. "There. It's written right on the building."

For the first time, I wished that I had known the old man in his prime. I knew that when we got back I'd have to tell Maryann that her passcode wasn't so clever.

When we got to the truck I opened the door for him. He stuck his head in and tried to climb in by putting his knees on the seat. Was this the same guy that had told me the secret pass code to the nursing home?

"Hold up. Hold up." I guided him out and turned him around. "Here get your rear end on the seat." When I tried lifting his left leg into the truck he pushed me away.

"I can do it!"

Fine. So, do it. I must have been crazy for even thinking of taking him out, let alone bringing him on an investigation. Once we were on the road we both sat in silence. I put on the local oldies station for him. It was "his music." It wasn't mine, but at least it broke up the silence. Every once in a while, he would hum along with a familiar song.

"Where are we going?"

"I have to find someone," I said.

"I used to find people. One time a kid went missing."

"You found the kidnapper. I know. I heard."

"You did?"

"Several times. At least once from you."

From what I understood, he didn't find the little girl though. I wanted to ask him about that but I didn't want to start an argument.

As we headed down Route 26 we passed the bridge that led to Ava Island.

"I saw you look toward that bridge. I know that island," Big Al said.

That took me by surprise.

"I live over there," I said.

"No shit? I think I know someone who lives around here too."

He had some flicker of recognition of the area he had lived in for years up until a few weeks before, but he wasn't quite sure what. Yet he remembered other less significant things. Someone told me once that if you've seen one case of Alzheimer's, you've seen one case of Alzheimer's. I didn't get it at the time, but I was beginning to see what they meant.

"You did. You lived there. You gave the place to me. I'm your son. Remember?"

He sat in silence trying to process what I had said.

Chapter Seventeen

The conversation was getting too bizarre. I couldn't get to Hicks' address on Tybee Island fast enough. Tybee Island is next to Ava Island, but is much larger. It is known as Savannah's Beach. The bright pink duplex was only a few blocks from the beach; a prime rental area for tourists. There was a sign on the lawn that read seasonal rentals. Apparently, unit A was available. I told my father to wait for me in the truck and I walked up the steps to unit B. The front door was open and I could see into the sparsely furnished apartment. I knocked on the screen door. No answer.

"Open it," my father said. He had followed me up the stairs. I could see what Maryann meant about him having a mind of his own. He pushed ahead of me, opened the screen door, and walked inside the house.

"You can't do that. Get out here," I said.

"Someone might be hurt in here. Have to check. It's called probable cause." I couldn't believe he said that. What a strange disease. It seemed that when he was in his element he was perfectly coherent. He disappeared into the next room. I had no choice but to follow him in to bring him out. It was hardly breaking and entering to look out for the safety of an old man with Alzheimer's.

My eyes swept the room as I entered. I checked the corners and behind the sofa and chairs in the living room looking not for my father, but Hicks. The living room clear, I headed into the hallway; clear. In the first bedroom, I noticed an unmade bed. The closet door was open, exposing the empty interior. Where the hell did my father go? For all I knew Hicks had him. I went to the side of the bed by the window so no one could come behind me and then made a quick look under the bed. I went to the second bedroom and did the same. Nothing.

I found Big Al in the kitchen hunched over the counter and reading a piece of paper.

"The place seems abandoned," I said to him.

"I know. I checked. I'm faster than you."

"Oh yeah, I forgot I was with an ace detective," I said.

"Somebody was expecting me. Listen to this." Big Al began to read. "I don't know what you want from me DeLucia, but lay off." He handed me the note. "How did he know I was coming?"

"I think that note was meant for me," I said

"You? Is your name DeLucia too?"

"I'm afraid so," I said.

He closed one eye and screwed up his face. Then he looked me up and down. "What's your first name?"

I did not want to get into this. I picked up the note and studied it. The handwriting didn't resemble the writing on the notes I'd been getting on my windshield. "It's Al," I said.

"Ha! I knew you were pulling my leg." His voice seemed to be coming from another room.

I looked up from the note. He was gone.

"Dad?"

No answer. I called again. He came out of the living room carrying a plastic card.

"It was on the floor." He handed it to me.

It was a room key from the Riverfront Hotel in Savannah. The same place that Estelle was staying.

* * *

"What's wrong with you?" Big Al said.

"Estelle told me she didn't have any contact with her son-in-law. Why

79

would there be a key at his house from the same hotel where she's staying? That hotel is a half hour from here."

Big Al gave me a blank look. Of course, he had no idea of who Estelle was. Hell, he had no idea of who I was.

"What are you going to do now?"

"I've got to find Hicks. He's Estelle's son-in-law. But he keeps moving. This is the second address I've had for him."

We heard the distinctive whine of a mail truck coming down the street.

"Leave it to me," Big Al said.

I snickered. I didn't have time to humor the old man. Yet, I marveled at the fact that in spite of having forgotten most of what happened in his life, he remembered that he had been a detective. Before I could stop him, he ran down to Hicks' mailbox and flagged down the mail carrier.

"I want to send something to my old neighbor but I lost his new address. Can you help me out?" he said.

I'll be damned.

The mailman clucked his tongue. "Hold on, I'm new on this route. What's his name?"

That blank look came over my father's face again. "His name is, uh."

Come on. Come on. I just told it to you. Big Al continued to struggle. I went up to the mail truck.

"It is Roscoe Hicks," I said.

"Right. Right. See what I mean, I forget stuff. Don't get old. The Golden Years are fool's gold."

The mailman laughed. "I hear ya. Hold on, I think there's still some paperwork they filled out here." He looked through a folder that sat in a box on his dashboard. "Here you go, Oglethorpe Court, 3751 Pine Barren Place, Pooler. Let me write it down so you don't forget it again."

He wrote the address on a piece of paper and handed it to Big Al. I know for damned certain he wouldn't have given the address to a younger guy.

"I thank you." Big Al tipped his hat in an almost courtly gesture.

"You have a good day, Sir."

As the mailman continued on his route Big Al had a satisfied look on his face.

"I still got it," he said.

"Yeah, I guess you do. I owe you a beer."

"I can't. I got to get home. My mother will be looking for me."

Good lord, I felt like I'd stepped into the cuckoo's nest. I looked at my watch. My new "partner" had been with me for over two hours. That was a long enough break for the staff at the nursing home.

Although he had said he wanted to go home, when we pulled into the parking lot of The Palms my father gave me a questioning look.

"What's this?" He crossed his arms over his chest.

Here we go. I got a knot in my stomach. If he gave me a hard time about going back in as Maryann had predicted I was going to have a hell of a situation on my hands. I skirted the issue.

"I have to go in there for a minute."

"Okay. I'll wait here." No tricking him. In some ways, he was still sharp. He pulled his hat down over his eyes and pretended to go to sleep, as he had done the first day I visited him in the home.

I should have known that things had gone too easy up until then.

"Have it your way. I have to report to some people in the station. Wait here. It may take me a while."

I got out of the truck and headed toward the building. I walked as slow as I could as I tried to figure out how I was going to ask Maryann for help to get him back in without looking like a complete ass. My finger slipped off the call button the first time I tried to press it. The second time I punched it with conviction. I did what I had to do that afternoon and if Maryann had a problem with it I'd face the consequences.

"You're reporting to the chief?" My father was behind me walking fast to catch up. His fancy stick never even touching the ground.

"I guess you can say that," I said.

"I gotta talk to him too."

"It's a her," I said.

"The best chief I ever knew was a woman. I remember one time we…"

Wherever he was going with it I wasn't interested. I knew the next few minutes were not going to be pretty. The buzzer rang and the glass door slid open.

"I know the code to the station, you know," Big Al said to me.

I sighed. That was another conversation I was going to have to have with Maryann. As we walked in she stuck her head out of her door and called down the hall to a charge nurse to help my father settle in. Then she retreated to her office.

The other nurse rushed down the hall with a big smile on her face. She took my father gently by the arm.

"Welcome back, Mr. DeLucia. How was your afternoon?"

"Good. Good. I was working on a case."

The nurse turned toward me. "I'm sure it did him good to get out." She glanced toward Maryann's office and gave a shrug.

"My friend is a detective too." My father looked at me as if he were trying to put a name to my face. "Nice guy." Then he leaned in to the nurse and said in a low voice. "He's got a lot to learn."

The nurse winked at me. "I'll take care of him from here." She waved for me to go.

On the way out, I stopped by Maryann's door intending to tell her that at least one patient had cracked the door code.

She looked up from what she was doing at her desk. "It wasn't a good idea to bring him out. We have our guests' best interests at heart. We have the experience and we know what we are doing." Ouch! Talk about snippy.

She punched the number into a box on the wall. I heard a buzz and the entrance door opened. I snickered and left without telling her about the code.

When I hit the fresh air, I took a deep breath. As stressful as the afternoon had been things actually worked out pretty well. Now that I got to know the old man a little better, I'd come to the realization that I couldn't take everything he said to heart. In fact, I actually enjoyed hanging out with him. It seemed like we were better as friends than as father and son. I was cool with that.

Chapter Eighteen

The GPS led me out Louisville Road to what must have been No-Man's-Land a few years before. Eventually I found Oglethorpe Court, a "village," of manufactured homes plopped in the middle of scrub lands full of fan palms and herds of long horned cattle. In spite of being in the wide-open spaces, the homes, actually trailers on foundations, all with a screened porch and carport, were crammed so close together that you couldn't fart without the neighbors hearing.

I parked in front of 3751 Pine Barren Place, and walked across a postage stamp sized "lawn" of white pebbles that made a crunching sound under my shoes. Nobody answered when I knocked at the door, but I thought I heard movement inside.

"Go away!"

It must have been my day for running into the pissed off of the world. I knocked again.

A woman dressed Wal-Mart chic in a pink t-shirt and leopard print stretch pants finally came to the door and stood behind the screen. I glanced at the picture of Estelle's daughter. It would take a stretch of the imagination to think this was Jill Hicks. The woman was a blond, lean and muscular, as if she worked out with weights, but her most noticeable distinction was her eyes, outlined in heavy black that extended to curves that upturned toward the temples, reminding me of a nightmarish Cleopatra. She stood behind the screen door and seemed surprised when she saw me.

"Oh. I thought you were the jerk next door." She had a hint of an accent that reminded me of my English neighbor Lynch.

"No, I'm another jerk."

At least I made her smile. She softened a bit.

"I'm studying for an exam. Unless you're an expert on randomized algorithms, I don't have time to chat."

I never pegged her for a math major. Shame on me for judging her by her looks.

"Sorry, I can't help you there. I can't even figure out why people watch unboxing videos."

She started to close the inside door.

"I'm looking for Roscoe Hicks," I said.

The door opened wide again. Her mouth twitched.

"May I ask who you are?" she said from behind the screen.

I held out my card. She opened the screen door enough to take it. Unlike Nate Roman she actually looked at it.

"Blue Palmetto Detective Agency?" She closed the screen door.

"Al DeLucia, as you can see from the picture on the card." I looked at the name on the letterbox on the wall next to the door: Hicks/Wharton.

"I take it that you are Ms. Wharton."

"Yes. Marnee Wharton."

"Ms. Wharton, do you know Jill Hicks?"

"I might."

"I'm hoping you can help me." I glanced at the names on the mailbox.

"We were friends. She's dead. A car crash, a little over two months ago."

"So I understand. And Roscoe Hicks. Do you know him?"

She fingered the card and shifted her body.

"My boyfriend."

Boyfriend? Mr. Hicks didn't waste any time in getting back into the game. But that wasn't my business. She must have surmised what I was thinking.

"Roscoe was lonely. What can I say?"

"Does he live here? I'd like to talk to him."

"Good luck with that. He dumped all of his shit here after his wife died and then took off after a couple of weeks. If I had known, I wouldn't have bothered to put his name on the box."

She looked at my card again. "All kinds of investigation," she read. "You know what Mr. Detective? When you find him, tell him to cough up his half of the rent. It's due."

Sorry, sister. I'm not working for you. "One more thing. Can you tell me about the accident?"

"Did I say it was an accident? As I said, I'm studying."

She closed the door.

"I have more questions," I said to the door knocker.

I wanted to ask Wharton if she had a picture of her boyfriend but she didn't respond to my knocking. And how about Hicks taking up with Wharton so soon after his wife died? I guess everyone deals with their grief in different ways.

Chapter Nineteen

The afternoon had been eaten up quicker than a pizza in a frat house and I needed to allow myself a break from work. I was more than happy when Max sent me a text asking if I'd like to walk down to Little Beach and then go for a bite to eat.

Spending any time with Max sounded like a good idea to me.

"Where is this place?" I asked when I met her at her house.

She handed me a nylon bag with a beach blanket in it. "It's not far from the village. There are boulders that form a jetty and you can still see the pilings from an old dock. It's small so tourists never go there, but it's perfect for relaxing and watching the river."

A half hour later, Max led me along a path at the edge of the plume grass, the tall grasses that grow at the end of the water action, until we got to the destroyed dock she had mentioned.

She was right, the place was almost deserted except for some gulls and the little shorebirds at the water's edge that ran back and forth playing tag with the waves. Looking west, the Savannah Bridge loomed upriver.

I took the blanket out of the bag and spread it on the sand then we flopped down on it and watched the sun speed toward the bridge and the hills beyond.

I was writing her name in the sand with a stick when Max smiled at me and moved a little closer. I put my arm around her.

"The sunsets are best when there are a few clouds," she said. "I love clouds. If I painted clouds that look like that with those purples, pinks, and oranges people would say it wasn't realistic."

"But there they are," I said.

"Do you like living here a little better?"

Where was she going with that?

"I don't have much choice."

She looked disappointed and made an exaggerated pout. "That's too bad. I love it here."

"I like being here with you." I wasn't saying that because I didn't want to hurt her feelings. I meant it.

She smiled then quickly went all serious on me. "So why did you come here if you hate Georgia?"

"It's not that I hate Georgia. I hate making plans and then having them changed on me."

"You mean you hate to be told what to do."

I'm far from a teen but since I couldn't rebel against my father back when I was, I make up for the lost opportunity by rebelling against authority whenever I could. At least that's what I was told in the one session of counseling that I had gone to. I never went back, so who knows what else is going on in my head?

"You could say that. I guess. I had plans to move to LA."

"So, I've heard. Several times in fact. Is that when Greenleaf called you?"

I had the feeling that she knew the answer to that. She and Greenleaf seemed to be pretty tight.

"Yeah, you might say I had a bad day at work. I was in an accident on a bridge in New Haven. I got pissed off, and quit."

"You quit because you were in an accident?"

I don't know why I was answering her questions, but I did.

"Maybe that was an understatement. I was nearly polished off by a drug dealer who I probably would have killed if a truck didn't do it first. Then I threw my badge at the chief and the mayor."

"You had a right to be upset."

I sure did, especially after Kim had egged me on by implying the accident was my fault and that I should be more like Donahue. I didn't tell Max that part.

"But I wasn't upset. It was more like I was free. I was coming out of a relationship and had been planning on taking early retirement when I turned thirty-six to go out to LA anyway. I was moving the schedule up by ten months. No big deal."

"Oh? You were in a relationship?"

Max perked up. I think the only thing she heard was the part about me coming out of a relationship.

"According to her, we were more like housemates with privileges. We decided we were both better off going our own way. I sold my half of the house to her at a loss and used the money to buy a condo in Santa Monica. There was no reason to hang around in Connecticut."

"So, the bridge thing was an excuse to go out there sooner."

I was opening up more to Max than to anyone else in my life. "More like the last straw. I had this feeling that if I stayed any longer I would get killed before I got the chance to retire."

"It was time to leave. I hear you," Max said. "A few years ago, I made up my mind that the TV industry screwed me over for the last time. I said goodbye to a hit investigative news spot that I created and goodbye to the misogyny that came along with it."

I wasn't sure if it was exactly the same thing, but I was relieved to know that Max and I were in agreement that sometimes you have enough of a situation and you have to move on.

"Right, it was time. So, like I said, I felt free. I was trying to finish up paperwork on the bridge incident when my cell phone rang. The woman on the other end tells me she's Felicia Greenleaf from the Blue Palmetto Detective Agency. If I learned anything on the force, it was that nothing good comes from dealing with private detectives."

Max looked like she had heard the funniest joke in the world. "What are you smiling about?"

"The irony. Look at you now. Go on."

"I told Greenleaf I had something important to do and didn't have time to talk to a detective. I was about to hang up when she told me my father had founded Blue Palmetto and she was the agency's chief and only administrative assistant. I'm like, No shit? I had figured the old man had died long ago."

"You thought your father was dead all along?"

"Yep, but she tells me Al, Sr. is alive and in a home with dementia. It was weird to be reminded that I was a Junior."

Max put her hand on my shoulder. "I know it must have been a shock. But everything she was telling you was true."

"The way I looked at it he was only contacting me because he needed me. And I told her so. There was a moment of silence. Finally, Greenleaf cleared her throat kind of like I remembered my fifth-grade teacher used to do to get my attention. She told me my father was being well cared for but she needed to know how I wanted her to proceed. I took that to mean she was looking for someone to pay the bills."

"Actually, your father planned all of that ahead. I think she wanted to know about the agency," Max said.

"Right, but I wasn't following the conversation. I asked her why I would care. And she said because I was the owner of not only the detective agency but a house on Ava Island. She even told me it was in Greg Allman's old neighborhood."

Max laughed. "Not exactly. His place was twenty miles from here. But go on."

"Whatever. It's too late anyway for us to become drinking buddies now that he's dead. You want to hear this or not?"

"I'm listening, go on." Max said.

"I asked her if she was sure I inherited all those things, and she got all bent out of shape. You know how Greenleaf is." I imitated Greenleaf's voice as I said, "Not inherited, own. I told you Mr. DeLucia, Sr. is not dead!" Max and I both laughed at my imitation.

"So, you decided to do the right thing and come down to help out."

"No. I told her I didn't want any part of my father's agency or his home. Then I hung up."

"And yet you ended up here." She put her hand on my leg. "That's what

89

happens when you resist a force of nature."

"Or the universe decides to take a dump on you. When I got home I had a letter from a lawyer in Santa Monica. I read the letter three times before it sunk in. The condo would never be finished. The builder ran away with the money. My money was gone and I had no job. I wouldn't even be able to pay the rent on the apartment I was living in.

"I guess nothing good comes from dealing with a lawyer or a private detective."

If she thought I would laugh at that, she was wrong.

"You got that right."

The sun was down now and we were lying on the blanket watching the last rays play on the clouds from beyond the horizon.

"So, finish the story," she said.

"What's there to finish? You know Greenleaf, she called me the next morning and demanded that I tell her what I wanted to do with the agency."

"I hope you were a little nicer to her this time."

I scoffed. "I guess. I checked with several lawyers and found that I was indeed the owner of the home on Ava Island. But what Ms. Greenleaf didn't tell me was that the home was inextricably tied in with my running the detective agency. Thanks loads, Dad."

Max must have liked my story. We grabbed a quick bite to eat in the village and went back to her house where the already good evening took a turn for the better.

There is a law of nature that dictates that a man should fall asleep after sex. Especially after mind blowing, headboard banging, I wished there was a trapeze hanging from the ceiling sex. My problem was that when we finished I broke that law and decided to have a civil conversation with the woman that I cared about very much. When she asked me what was on my mind, I told her.

"I've got to track down Hicks and find out if there is a connection between Estelle's daughter, Jill, and Keller's murder. I'm determined to make some progress tomorrow."

"I could help you," Max said as she made little circles on my bare chest with her finger. "I'm pretty much on schedule with my caseload."

Shit. I should have had a cigarette instead of flapping my big mouth, but it was too late to take up smoking.

"Seriously?"

"Sure, I am the senior investigator in this agency. Or did you forget?"

"I didn't forget," I said before I brought her into my arms and kissed her, ready to start another round of fantastic sex.

She pulled away. "But you don't want me to help you."

"I never got a passing grade in *Works Well with Others*. Sorry."

I truly expected that was the end of the evening, but Max was bigger than that. The loving was more than lovelier in the second go around. But this time Max called all of the shots.

Chapter Twenty

I was walking back to my house when my cell phone rang. It was Estelle. Just the person I wanted to talk to.

"I know it's late," she said.

"It's okay. What is it?"

"I was wondering if you made any progress in finding my daughter."

Only a few months ago I was chasing druggies. I ignored the nonsense that they spewed from their addled brains. It was part of the territory. But confused older people were different. I pandered to Estelle's denial of her daughter's death because no purpose would be served by me forcing the truth on her.

"I'm still looking for Roscoe Hicks," I said. "He's on the run, moving from place to place." That was the truth but it implied I was still looking for Jill.

"I see."

I debated about whether to tell her about Marnee. The woman was obviously under enough stress as it was, being in denial that her daughter was dead. I decided I had no choice if I was to get to the bottom of what happened.

"Have you ever heard of a woman named Marnee Wharton?"

"I never met her, but Jill always mentioned her. They were… they *are* good friends. She works at an auto dealership as a mechanic, but apparently, she is talented with computers and always helped Jill with hers. How do you know about her?"

"You asked me to investigate. That's what I did. Ms. Wharton's name came up. That's all." I didn't think it was necessary for her to know yet that her son-in-law was in some sort of relationship with Wharton, so I didn't tell her about Oglethorpe Court.

"There's something else I have to ask you about." I sounded like a child reaching out to his grandmother. "I think you might know more than you realize or at least more than you are telling me. If I'm going to help you have to share everything you know."

She cleared her throat. "I don't know what you mean."

"My father found a key card from your hotel at one of the places where Hicks had been living."

She made a small gasp. "What do you mean your father found it?"

"He was with me when I checked out where Hicks had been held up."

"I thought that your father had Alzheimer's Disease and was in a home."

"He does. He is. He was helping me. It's a long story."

"Mr. DeLucia, I've been thinking."

I knew from experience that when someone says the words "I've been thinking," there is going to be a problem. But I wasn't prepared for what she said next.

"I've decided not to pursue the case."

"What are you talking about? You were the one who begged me to take on the case. You just asked me if I was making any progress."

"I've changed my mind," she said.

All kinds of thoughts raced through my head.

"Has someone threatened you? Are you frightened?"

"I'm only frightened when you yell."

I lowered my voice. "I'm sorry. I didn't mean to yell. But I'm confused. I know this is important to you. Why do you want to drop the investigation?"

"I'm not totally dropping it. I've decided to let the police handle it."

"The police aren't interested in the case."

"I'll have to take my chances. I'll send you a check for your trouble. Now please drop it."

I had hoped to go to sleep thinking of my good time with Max that evening. Instead, I was trying to figure out what spooked Estelle.

Chapter Twenty-One

I had the feeling that Estelle was holding something important back from me and she really didn't want to drop the case. She had already proved that she didn't always tell the whole story when she didn't tell me that she was notified of her daughter's death. I decided to pursue it a little more even if it was only to satisfy my curiosity. Maybe if I came up with something solid she would change her mind and I would get paid in the end. Several calls to Estelle went unanswered. I found that she had checked out of her hotel.

I was beginning to wonder if Estelle was afraid of Hicks. Maybe there was something to her theory that Hicks was a murdering kidnapper. If he had threatened Estelle, that might explain why she dropped the case and then disappeared. I decided to visit Marnee Wharton again to see if I could get more information out of her. I went back out to Oglethorpe Court the next morning to talk to her.

The last time she slammed the door in my face before I had finished. This time I was determined not to make that possible. I parked three doors down from 3751 Pine Barren Place and walked toward the '98 Honda parked in the driveway. To my good fortune, the car was locked. I looked inside and a small red light blinked on the dashboard indicating the alarm was set. Perfect. I looked toward the house and saw no one. Then I checked out the street. Empty. I gave the side of the car a body slam and the alarm blared as I darted to the side of the house.

It wasn't long before I heard the front door open. Then the lights on the car blinked and the horn stopped. She reset the alarm with her remote without ever leaving the house, not even bothering to come out to see if someone was trying to break into her vehicle. Unbelievable. People have become so jaded.

I waited a while. The heat of the day made sweat pour off my forehead. That same heat apparently kept the neighbors inside because there wasn't a soul in sight. I ran up to the car and gave it another body slam before retreating once more to the side of the house.

"What the hell!" I could hear Marnee yell from around the corner. This time Marnee came out to the car and aimed the fob directly at the door handle. The alarm stopped.

I stood directly behind Marnee. "Well, that's better."

She gave a slight jump, composed herself, then turned to give me a look with those Cleopatra eyes that could have burned down a house. "Did you do this?" She spit out the words. "You did. You set off my alarm."

"Okay. I wanted to talk to you."

Her eyes grew wide. "Watch your step!"

She rushed toward me and gave me a shove that propelled us both into her neighbor's yard.

"You're insane," I said.

"I'm insane? You purposely set off my alarm."

With that the neighbor, a big guy with a Harley shirt and a shaved head came running outside.

"Leave the lady alone. Now!" he bellowed as he ran toward us. I may have let Marnee tackle me, but I wasn't going to take a tackle from that raging bull. I was prepared to deck him when he stopped short and pointed to the white pebbles that made up Marnee's lawn.

"Holy Shit!" the neighbor yelled. "That's a mother of a copperhead."

I looked to where I had been standing where a fat tan colored snake with brown cross bands poised ready to strike.

The big dude darted back toward his place. "I don't do snakes. Pull a gun on me and I'll kick your ass before you can pull the trigger, but snakes... No freakin' way."

"Chicken shit!" Marnee yelled after him.

I heard his door close as I watched the snake slither under a bush.

"That's why you gave me a hit?"

Marnee waved me off.

"I did it for the snake. I thought if you saw it first you might do something stupid like shoot it. You only have to give it space. It's more interested in catching mice than attacking you."

I knew that. "I suppose you think I'm going to thank you. You didn't have to tackle me."

"You didn't have to set off my alarm."

"Did I?"

"Didn't you?"

"I can honestly say I didn't touch your door. I came by to ask you about Hicks.

"I told you, I don't know where he is."

"You must have known that he had a place on Ava Island," I said.

"Well, if you know that why don't you go there and look for him?"

"I did and he wasn't there. But he knew I was coming. He left me a note."

Marnee scoffed. "So, you think I told him you were looking for him. How would I do that? I don't know how to contact him and that is the truth. Like I told you. If you find him let me know. He owes me money."

"Well do you know Estelle Brewer?"

"Jill's mother. I never met her in person, but Jill talked about her a lot."

"Do you know why Estelle might visit Roscoe Hicks?"

"I imagine she's still looking for Jill. But I can assure you. Jill is dead. I went with Roscoe to identify the body."

"Was that before or after he moved in with you?"

Marnee looked as if she were going to explode. She stormed into the house and slammed the door in my face again. I started walking down the driveway to my truck.

"I don't owe you a damned explanation!" She was out on the porch again yelling after me.

I turned and gave her my such-is-life smile, and looked toward where the snake had been. "Right. You don't."

I got into my truck and looked in the mirror. Marnee was standing in the street with her hands on her hips. Then she started walking toward the truck. I rolled down the window.

"I think that his sister has a store up in Hilton Head. It's called the Bantam Gallery," she called out.

"Why didn't you tell me that the first time I was here?"

"I found out afterward with a little creative work on the computer. Don't ask how."

The truth was that I didn't give a damn about what Marnee had to hack to get the information. The only thing I was interested in was finding Hicks.

"Got it," I said.

"Don't forget what I told you."

"What's that?"

"Watch your step."

I didn't need her to tell me that.

Chapter Twenty-Two

I punched Hilton Head into my unreliable GPS and found that it should take less than an hour to get there if I hopped on I-95 North. Excellent, I didn't have to use the freakin' bridge. I wasn't on the highway for five minutes when my phone rang. It was The Palms. At first, I wasn't going to answer it but I did.

"I told you it wasn't a good idea to take your father out." Maryann's voice was shrill. "He's giving us a hard time insisting that "his friend" is going to come to pick him up."

"Are you telling me to come and get him?"

"I'm telling you something has to be done. We are not an Alzheimer's facility."

This was getting old. "And I had nothing to do with you taking him on as a guest. He has a contract with you. I wasn't involved. What do you want me to do?"

Maryann's voice softened a bit. "We have a tour coming through this afternoon with some extremely important people. I'm asking you to take him off our hands for a few hours. Please?"

Please? She actually sounded desperate. My first impulse was to tell her to go to hell, but that might come back to bite me in the ass. I agreed to make a detour to The Palms and pick up Big Al.

* * *

I had promised Johnson that I'd keep him informed if I got a lead on Hicks.

98

I sent him a text explaining that I was on my way to pick up my father and then heading to Hilton Head to check out a place called the Bantam Gallery.

When I got to The Palms Maryann and another nurse had Big Al waiting outside. He was wearing his bush hat and holding the walking stick. It occurred to me that in his prime he was probably a pretty dapper PI.

When I got out of the truck the nurse told me that he was excited to be "working on a case" with his detective friend, a.k.a. me. Maryann was grateful for my help.

Everyone was happy. Except me. Especially after we got on the road and the GPS led me to the entrance of the Savannah Bridge. Apparently, Route 17 was the shortest way to Hilton Head from the Palms. I began to sweat. A few days before, I had heard on the news of a major accident on the bridge involving a logging truck. I thought of the truck that took out Psycho back in New Haven. A sign said there was an exit ahead to avoid the bridge, but it was getting late so I decided I would take the damned bridge anyway. As I passed the exit I gripped the wheel determined to make the best of it.

* * *

"Look at that big bridge!" Big Al said as we got on the long, curved approach to the span. "The damned thing goes straight up!"

"Yeah," I said as we merged onto the bridge. The horizon nowhere in sight.

He was actually bouncing in his seat.

"I mean straight up! Like a mountain. He Yah!"

"Yeah," I said. I could feel my foot tapping the gas. The ride got jerky, but that only made the old man love it more.

"Look at those towers. And the cables. It looks like a sailing ship!" You would think he never saw a damned bridge before.

"Okay." My voice came out like I had a frog in my throat.

"Holy shit. Holy shit. Holy shit! A giant ship is going under us. How damned good is that?" He lifted his hat and waved it in the air.

"Good." Now calm down. You're distracting me while I'm driving. I stole a side glance to catch a huge container ship approaching the bridge. I hoped the pilot knew what he was doing because it looked like it was going to be a close fit.

My hands were feeling numb and I shook first one and then the other to get the blood flowing in them again. I cracked the window open and took another deep breath. The sea air did the trick for a moment. I pushed on. Then with another stolen peep at my father, I could see he was staring at me.

"Are you doing okay? You look pale." Big Al's knitted brow didn't do anything to build up my confidence.

"All of a sudden you're concerned?" The words came out a little harsher than I had intended.

"Shit. I'll drive if you want. I love this. Pull over," he said.

"I'm not stopping on the bridge." We reached the crest of the bridge and the road ahead looked like the downward plunge of a roller coaster complete with a sharp jog in it.

For a split second my vision blurred then came back, like a digital hiccup that loses the signal and freezes up the TV screen. I turned on the air conditioner and dared a glimpse at Al. He was staring at the road ahead. I think he may have been praying. It seemed like an hour, but at last we got to the bottom of the bridge only to find another long, but thankfully low, bridge crossing into South Carolina.

"See no problem," I said. "I'm fine. Why is your seatbelt off?"

Had he been ready to bail out? He re-clicked his belt as we came off the bridge. As he did my cell rang. I answered it with the Bluetooth.

"It's Max. Is that you, Al?"

We both answered "Yes."

"It's for me," I said to my father.

"Where are you?" Max said.

"We're heading to Hilton Head at the moment," I said. "I have my father with me. It's a long story."

"Hi Max. You know my detective friend too?" The old man was getting on my nerves and I vowed never to do a favor for Maryann again.

"I do know him Big Al. Did you go over the bridge?"

CHAPTER TWENTY-TWO

"Of course. It was fine," I said.

"He almost passed out," Big Al said.

"Are you okay?" Max sounded worried. "Did you know you could have taken 95 to 278 to avoid the bridge? It would only take a few minutes longer."

I knew. That had been my plan but the GPS had a mind of its own. "I didn't want to waste time. Besides, I don't have a problem with the bridge."

"I wish you had asked me to go along. I love Hilton Head. It's so artsy."

"I don't need an entourage." Oops. That didn't come out right.

"Okay. You're in a mood. I'll let you work." The Bluetooth went silent.

Damn, damn, damn.

Chapter Twenty-Three

Hilton Head is a "perfect" tourist destination with perfect little shops and perfect restaurants, in case you have any energy or money left after a day on a perfect golf course or a perfect beach. It seemed a little overdeveloped to me compared to Savannah. But I'm the guy who wants to head out to LA so, what do I know?

I spotted a place called the Happy Crab Cafe and we stopped in for a cup of coffee to settle my nerves after dealing with the drive over which took less than an hour, but with my father riding shotgun seemed like several days.

While I was at it we tried the crab cakes: *The best this side of Maryland.* The waiter told me the Bantam Gallery was a block down the street.

We left the truck parked in front of the Happy Crab and walked. The shop, which dealt in antiques and art, was in a well-manicured "village" off Main Street. As we walked in, I smelled the typical antique store scent of dust, mildew, mothballs, and furniture polish.

"I'm looking for Roscoe Hicks," I told the woman at the shabby chic desk. She was dressed in a dashiki and had purple streaks in her long platinum hair.

"He's not hard to find. He's right over there," she said.

I turned to see a guy, who seemed to be a little over forty, by the plate glass window talking to my old man. Big Al was showing him the alligator handle on his walking stick. I couldn't hear what they were saying but for all I knew, Big Al was trying to sell him the cane.

When the younger man saw me approach he seemed to speak more loudly for my benefit. "You should come up again for the Village Art Walk. It takes place twice a month."

My father seemed to have told Hicks that he was interested in art. If he was, it was news to me, but then I'd been finding out that there was a lot I didn't know about him.

My father gave me a sheepish grin. "This is Hicks. He's my son-in-law." And to Hicks he said, "This is my friend. He's a detective."

So, Hicks was his son-in-law and I was his detective friend. What a damned crazy disease he had. Hicks and I looked at each other. I shrugged my shoulders as if to tell him the old guy was out of it.

Hicks took it in stride as he addressed me.

"Mr. DeLucia, I've been expecting you. I imagine you want to ask me questions about my wife," he said.

He was a reed of a guy standing no more than 5'9" with a high forehead and long jet-black hair covering his ears. His unibrow and goatee looked like he had dyed them with pitch and they contrasted sharply with skin so white you would have thought he slept in a coffin.

"You're Roscoe Hicks?"

He had a cocky smile. "You were expecting Salvatore Dali?"

"More like Harry Houdini. What's with the disappearing act?"

He chuckled. "Sorry about the cat and mouse game. I couldn't resist leaving the note at the condo."

"And what about the notes on the car? Kind of childish to be hounding me. No?"

Hicks had a blank look on his face. "What are you talking about? You are the one who is hounding me."

"Am I?"

"You were snooping in my file on the computer where I used to work. Walt Sampson is mellowing out as he gets old. There was a time when he would have shot you and then asked what you were doing."

If that was a threat, it didn't impress me.

"It would have been a lot easier if you had contacted me if you knew I was looking for you. You seem to move frequently."

"I don't think so. The house Jill and I shared was underwater and we had to get out before the bank took it over. We rented the duplex on the Island from my mother but after my wife…" He choked up for a second. "After my wife had her accident I didn't like staying there so Miss Wharton took me in for a while. When my sister gave me this job I moved up here, eventually found my own place and moved my stuff out of the duplex."

Something about the guy's story didn't add up. There are only two reasons why someone moves around like that. Either it's that they are avoiding the law or they're afraid of something. Which was it?

"You still sound like a man on the run," I said.

"So now you found me. Go ahead, ask me about my wife. I know her crazy mother thinks she's alive. She went to my old address and asked Mr. Roman a bunch of questions. He tells me someone else came nosing around too. I'm guessing it was you."

"Afraid so. Is your wife dead or not? Mrs. Brewer tells me someone sent her money. She seems to think her daughter is trying to contact her."

"The woman is delusional," he said.

On that point, I had to agree with him. Every indication pointed to the fact that Jill was dead.

"Maybe," I said.

"She knows her daughter died when her car crashed into the canal. I gave her the ashes. What else was I supposed to do?"

"Did you also give her money?"

"Ha! I'm a starving clerk in an antique store. Where would I get money to send to her? And, why would I?"

"Maybe out of guilt. Why didn't you keep your mother-in-law in the loop?"

"She knew as much as what was good for her," he said.

Was his opinion of Estelle so low that he thought he knew best what she should know? "You seem to have some sort of hold over your mother-in-law."

"What makes you think anyone can have a hold over Estelle?"

"Well, someone scared her into dropping my investigation."

"It wasn't me," he said.

"How do you explain a key from her hotel being at the house you lived in on Ava Island?"

"All right. I did contact her after I moved out. I told her to go to the place and pick up some mementos of Jill that I thought she might want. I was trying to be nice. Maybe she dropped her key."

I'd have to check that out with Estelle. For the moment, I took it on face value. "Ever hear of Andy Keller?"

"I don't recall. Should I have?" He kept taking a sideways glance out of the window.

"You accused your wife of having an affair with him."

Hicks took a step forward. "I don't know how that is any of your business."

"It's my business when the body of the accused ends up at my dock."

"Keller?"

"Yep," I said.

Hicks seemed visibly stunned and solemn, a pained look on his face. "Dead? Can't be."

"Afraid so."

"Whoa, whoa, whoa. You don't think I killed him? I may have had reason to but I didn't."

"Well, someone sure as hell killed him last week."

"He died last week?" He gave a sigh of relief. "You're barking up the wrong tree, Mr. DeLucia. I was on a buying trip in Key West for the shop. Ask my sister. She can show you the receipts I turned in."

I looked toward his sister who was standing at the desk. She held up a folder which I would have suspected contained blank papers had it not been for her confident smile. Meanwhile Hicks picked up a pad from one of the tables and sketched out two pictures.

"What's that?"

"The tattoo on the man you should be looking for. He has a bullet hole tattoo on his shin and an exit wound tat on his calf. Part of the exit wound is still in outline and has to be inked."

I looked down at the tattoo that circled my left ring finger. Kim and I thought it would be a good idea to get commitment tattoos. She got little hearts and I got little x's with a band on each side because it was manlier. Turned out the x's were appropriate.

"A tattoo on his leg isn't much to go on. He could cover that with long pants. What's his name?"

"I don't know his name. But you'll know him when you see him. He's real tall and he's got these weird eyes. The right one is brown and left one is blue. But if you get close enough to notice you'd better watch out."

"What makes you think he killed Keller?"

"One afternoon I came home and he was on our patio talking with Jill and Keller. As I walked up I heard him call Keller a hack. He said he should have known he couldn't count on him; he said Keller would be sorry. I told both men to get out."

"That was the first time you saw them?" I asked.

"The guy with the stupid tattoo, yeah. Keller had been around a few times before. And yes, I was suspicious something was going on."

"Did you talk to your wife about it?"

"I asked Jill why Keller was hanging around so much. She denied having an affair and made up a bullshit story about Keller doing a blog. She said she couldn't tell me anything else, but when it was all over we'd be sitting pretty. Her accident happened the next day."

I swear Hicks had tears in his eyes.

"What did she mean by sitting pretty?" I asked. "Were you having money troubles?"

Hicks scoffed at my remark. "You tell me who doesn't have money troubles these days. I told you our first house was financially underwater. It was those damned crooked bankers."

I couldn't help but notice he had a forlorn look which changed to a flicker of recognition when he looked out of the window.

"Listen, you're going to have to go. I'm busy right now," he said.

I tried to see what he was looking at.

"Is everything all right?"

"Fine. Fine," he said.

CHAPTER TWENTY-THREE

That's when I noticed my father was missing.

I looked around the shop but he wasn't in the place.

"Did you see where the old guy went?" I asked Hicks' sister.

She shook her head.

I couldn't let him wander in a strange town.

"This isn't over. I'm coming back," I said to Hicks.

He walked me out, stopping at the sidewalk by the door.

"No. This conversation is ended."

Chapter Twenty-Four

I didn't have time to argue. All I could imagine was my father on the 6:00 news.

Have you seen this man? Police report an elderly man with dementia missing in Hilton Head, miles away from his home. Authorities blame his negligent son.

Muttering every swear word the nuns taught me not to use, I hurried up the street ducking into every shop to find him. Finally, I spotted a cop in an SUV making a rolling stop at a sign a couple of blocks up from the gallery.

"Yo," I called out.

He came to a full halt.

"My father has dementia and he's lost. Can you help me out?" I asked.

"I'm responding to a call. Go down to the station to give them the information."

The cop took off in a hurry. Big help. I didn't even know where the station was. I worked my way down the other side of the street looking into every shop on that side with no luck. As I approached the Bantam Gallery again, I noticed a small crowd of people on the sidewalk with the same cop I had talked to two blocks up the street. Someone was on the ground.

Was Big Al hurt? My heart started to race. As I ran across the street there were sirens and then an ambulance and two more patrol SUV's pulled up.

Hicks couldn't have been more right about our conversation being over if he had been a mind reader. He was lying inside the open doorway. I could see a red spot spread across his shirt and small bubbles of blood dancing at the corners of his mouth. His sister was hysterical. I tried to go in but the cop I had talked to earlier blocked my way.

"I have to get in there," I said.

"You're not a witness," he said. "You should go to the station to report your missing father."

He was right. I still had to find the old man. Maybe it was just as well that I didn't get involved in this. As I started across the street I spotted Big Al leaning against a building and eating an ice cream cone.

* * *

Talk about a role reversal. I felt like a father who had just found his lost son safe and sound. I was glad to see him but pissed all the same. "Where were you?"

"My son-in-law told me they had good ice cream a few streets over. I went to get one. Want some?"

It was like babysitting a child. "I'm good, thanks."

For the first time, he seemed to have noticed the commotion at the Gallery. "What's going on over there?"

"Someone got hurt. It's nothing for us to get concerned about. Let's go."

All I needed was for him to get involved in what obviously was a murder. I wondered if we had missed a robbery. This might have turned out different if I hadn't left to find Big Al. Poor Hicks. I don't know why, but I had the feeling that in spite of the background on him that Greenleaf had dug up, he was an okay guy.

"Hold on, I'm going to say good-bye to my son-in-law."

"You can't," I said.

"Why not?"

"Mr. Hicks has left the building."

* * *

I spotted the note on the windshield as we walked back to the truck. I snatched it from under the wiper ripping it as I did so. Surprise, surprise the note said; **Some detective you are**.

I scanned the area but saw no one. This meant only one thing. Whoever was leaving these notes had followed me to Hilton Head.

I looked at my father eating his cone, melting ice cream dripping down his hands.

"Do you know anything about this?"

He took a big sloppy lick of the ice cream. "What is it?"

"Never mind. Get in the truck."

I helped him put the seat belt on. Then I got a pen out of the center console. The best I could do for paper was a part of an envelope. I held them out to Big Al.

"What am I supposed to do with that?" he said.

"Write on it."

"What?"

I threw the pen and envelope back into the console. In spite of the fact that he had been missing in action for a while, it was ridiculous to think the note was written by my father.

"Forget it."

And unless he'd risen from the dead, Hicks didn't write it. This was getting old.

Chapter Twenty-Five

Between Hicks' murder, my father wandering off, and another taunting note, I hoped that I had enough adrenalin going to propel me back over the big bridge without losing it.

I purposely waited until we approached the bridge before I started to grill my father so I'd have a distraction. Sometimes distractions are good, even when driving. I rationalized that talking would keep my mind off the span and the water below.

"Why did you wander off?" I asked.

"Don't know."

"You can't do that. Okay?"

"Yeah."

"If you're going to help me I have to know where you are. I don't have time to go looking for you."

"I quit," he said.

"You quit. What do you quit?"

"Working for you. You can't tell me what to do. You're not my father."

At least the "President" of the agency didn't pull rank on me.

"No, I'm not. You're my father. Do you get that?"

"You're my father?" he asked.

If I didn't know better, I'd say he was breaking stones.

"No, I said you. You are my father."

"Ha! You're full of shit. You're older than me. Look at you."

"You never were much of a father. I'll give you that." There. I said it. It didn't feel as good as I thought it would, but at least it was out on the table.

111

"Stop this thing I'm getting out." Al had his hand on the door.

"I can't stop the truck on the bridge. I told you that on the way up."

"Are you taking me back to that jail?"

"You got it."

I thought better of that tack. I was better off if I dealt with him in his own reality. "I'm kidding. I meant to say I'm taking you to the station. You've got to report to the chief."

"Oh."

I knew it wasn't right to pick a fight with my old man, but it got us both safely over the bridge. I breathed a sigh of relief when the truck was back on solid ground.

* * *

For the rest of the ride we listened to the Oldies Station. I'd listen to anything as long as it kept Big Al quiet.

I needed time to mull over Hicks' murder. I kept thinking about how he seemed distracted by something or somebody that was out on the street. I wondered if he knew he was in danger and that was why he cut off our conversation. The more I thought about it the more I became convinced that Hicks wasn't the victim of a hold up, but he was targeted for murder.

When we got back to The Palms one of my biggest fears became a reality.

Big Al gazed at the building through the windshield. "I'm not going in there."

This had the potential to become a big scene. It was getting late and one of the nurses had told me that he was at his most difficult later in the day when he was tired. She called it *Sundowning* and said late-day confusion was common in people with dementia.

Speaking of nurses, I knew that I was going to have to deal with Maryann. Even though she had asked me to take him out this time, while they had their important visitors, I was going to get shit from her. I knew she'd complain that I should have never taken my father out that first time.

112

"You have to go in." I used my deepest and sternest cop voice. It didn't intimidate him.

"Bullshit, I don't have to do anything I don't want to."

Okay. Stay in his reality I reminded myself.

"No, you don't. Tell me what you do want to do."

"Stay with you."

"Don't you want to tell the chief what happened?"

"Nothing happened."

"You don't remember the guy got hurt? There were cops all around."

He thought a while. "Right. I think he got shot. You killed him."

If I'm ever on trial for something, I'll have to remind myself not to call on my father for a character witness.

"I did not kill him. He was killed when someone tried to rob him."

I didn't believe that, but I was beginning to realize that when dealing with Big Al it was best to keep things simple. I was thankful that he didn't remember that at one point he had thought Hicks was his son-in-law. That would have opened up a whole new bunch of problems.

It dawned on me that Big Al may have seen the shooter. Would he remember?

"Did you see anything unusual when you were across the street?"

He twisted his face as if he were trying to squeeze something out of his brain.

"I didn't see anything."

"So, you should tell that to the chief when you go inside."

"Nope. I'd rather go with you."

"Fine you can write up the report."

There's nothing more tedious than writing an incident report and even in his confused state Big Al knew that.

"I think I'll go in and talk to the chief. She's a lady you know."

Chapter Twenty-Six

With that problem averted I went back to Ava Island. When I pulled into the crushed shell parking lot I went straight next door rather than go into the office.

"Yes?" Max said when she opened the door.

"I'm back."

"I'm so happy for you."

Why am I always attracted to women who have attitude?

"If I did need an entourage I would have wanted you in it."

Max huffed.

"Give me a break here, I'm trying for contrite," I said.

Max rolled her eyes and opened the door wider for me to come in. "Did you find the elusive Mr. Hicks?"

"I found him. He claimed he was in Key West when Keller was murdered."

"Do you believe him?"

"I guess I have to. Someone killed him right after we talked. That kind of lends credence to his story."

"Murdered. How?"

"He told me I should be looking for someone with a bullet hole tat on his leg. Then he saw something outside and he clammed up. That's when I realized that Big Al was missing so I went to look for him. When I got back I found someone had shot Hicks."

"You could have been killed! And your father too. Is he all right?"

"Fine. He wasn't even there. I found him across the street after it was all over."

I noticed wrinkles of worry on Max's forehead. "What?"

"I think you're taking this a little too casually. And I don't only mean the fact that you weren't keeping an eye on your father. One murder was bad enough, but now this."

"I hope you're not saying that I should drop the case."

"No, just the opposite. I'm saying you'd better be a little more creative in finding the killer. Starting with the guy with the tattoo."

She's such a great detective. What would she have done?

"Hicks seemed to think the man with the tattoo was bad news and implied that he was the one who killed Keller. Maybe the tattoo guy killed Hicks to shut him up," I said.

"Or Hicks was lying and he did kill Keller and someone, maybe the guy with the tat, killed him in retribution," Max said.

I was surprised to be sharing my thoughts with Max. It was kind of nice.

"I forgot to tell you, Percy Lynch was over here looking for you," she said.

"If he has another offer, I'm not interested."

"I think he always has an offer. But this seemed to be important."

I was thinking about the little brainstorming session I just had with Max as I walked along the sea wall to the Lynch's property.

"Lynch! It's Al DeLucia."

The former ringmaster and his Jane were sitting at a table drinking cocktails. Thank goodness it was too late for sunbathing that day. Monty the Python was nowhere to be seen which didn't make me happy. I want to know where the danger is.

"Yes. Of course, Mr. Santorini, come on up."

"DeLucia." I corrected him.

"Quite. Jane has something she wishes to tell you."

"So, this isn't about buying my property?"

"He's always interested in buying your property, but I'm the one who wanted to see you this time." She got up and took my arm. "Here you sit next to me. Vodka martini?"

"Sure. Leave out everything except the vodka."

She poured me a half of a glass of vodka which I downed. It had been a tough day.

"What's this about?"

"You wanted to know if I saw anything the morning that you found that poor man in the water. Well, I remember now. I was chanting the Sun Salutation out here near the dock." She put her hands together in front of her. "Om Bhaanve Namaha. Om Mitraaya Namaha. Om Bhaa…"

Not again. I was exhausted and I didn't need that nonsense. I took the vodka bottle and refilled my glass.

"Mrs. Lynch, I thought there was something you wanted to tell me."

She shook her head as if to clear it. "Well, there was one bit of an oddity."

I looked around for the snake.

"Mrs. Lynch…What did you see?"

"As I was chanting I saw the detective returning in his boat."

"You couldn't have seen me." I hadn't been out in the boat.

"No, it was not you. It was the elder Mr. DeLucia. I could tell by that silly hat he always wears. And the man who died was on the boat too. He had dreadlocks just like in his picture in the paper."

* * *

WTF? How could my father have been using his boat the morning Andy Keller was killed? Yes, he knew the code to get out of The Palms but even still, how would he get to Ava Island? The Palms was on the mainland over five miles away.

The disagreeable Mr. Lynch walked me to the sea wall and watched as I jumped down and headed along the shore back to my place.

It ran through my mind that he and his wife could have been setting up Big Al to take the blame for Andy Keller's murder as part of some scheme to get the property that the Blue Palmetto Detective Agency sat on.

It still bothered me that Lynch didn't run over to help me get Keller's body out of the water that day. I wondered if he had been watching out of idle curiosity or if maybe his presence on the dock was a case of the criminal returning to the scene of the crime. In my heart, I knew that was quite a leap unless I could find something that linked Lynch and Keller. Between my questions about Lynch's involvement and his wife's accusations about my father, my head was reeling. At that point, what I needed was to go to sleep. All of the events of the crazy day had taken its toll. Maybe I would see things clearly in the morning.

Chapter Twenty-Seven

B ut sleep wasn't going to happen just yet because when I got home I found Johnson on my patio. He was dressed in civilian clothes, khaki cargo shorts and a shirt the same green as his work uniform. I guess he was one of those guys who found it hard to separate his home life from his work life.

"What's up?" I asked him. I wasn't up to shooting the shit right then so I tried not to sound too friendly.

"It's a courtesy call. I had to drop my buddy off at his place down past Turtle Beach. We were at a pre-season charity game at Grayson."

He plopped in a zero-gravity chair without being invited.

I knew Grayson Stadium in Savannah had been the home of the Sand Gnats, an affiliate of the New York Mets. When the team recently moved to South Carolina a new amateur team called the Savannah Bananas made the ballpark its home. I didn't get into it. I had a feeling he wasn't there to talk baseball.

"Beer?"

"Why not?" He glanced down at the way he was dressed as if to say he was off duty.

I went inside and got us a couple of Coronas with lime wedges stuffed in the neck. When I put the bottles on the table, Johnson looked at them and scoffed.

"Problem?"

"No, just that I'm more of a Bud man. That didn't stop him from grabbing one and taking a long swig. When he did, I whipped out my cell phone and looked at the time. I was going to allow him ten minutes before I sent him packing.

"I was surprised you didn't let me know that you got an ID on the guy in the water," I said.

"Hell, you're right I should have done that—professional courtesy at least. Gotta say, I've been pretty busy."

"It's okay. I probably found out his name was Andy Keller about the same time you did."

Johnson's eyebrows lifted the tiniest bit. I wondered if he thought I should have extended him the professional courtesy that he had denied me. Or maybe it was that he was surprised that I got the information on my own. "What else did you find out?" he asked.

"That he was a blogger, but according to the paper you know that," I said.

"Yeah, even though I'm not exactly sure what a blogger does." He genuinely looked perplexed.

I don't think he'd understood that a blogger is usually a person who puts hours of time and energy into writing an online column that nobody reads. But apparently someone was reading Andy Keller's blog and they didn't like what they were seeing. I took a look at the time on the phone. Time for you to go, my friend.

"Hey. Thanks for stopping by. I have to get to sleep. It's been a long day. Call me the next time you take in a game," I said.

Johnson seemed to have a hard time extricating himself from the low chair without falling on his face. He looked down toward the Grady. "Right. You go do what you have to. But mind if I look around a little down there, where you found that ring, as I knock off this beer? I can let myself out when I'm finished."

It was dark. I don't know what he expected to find even with a flashlight. "I thought you didn't think the ring was significant."

"You never can tell. I'd like to see if there is anything else that was overlooked. Even if it's only for training purposes."

What a crock of bull.

"Go ahead. Knock yourself out," I said.

119

Johnson walked down to the dock with me on his heels.

"What are you looking for?"

"I told you. I'm making sure we didn't miss anything." He jumped from the dock onto the boat.

"Your team did a pretty thorough job."

"Nobody's perfect. They can always improve."

I wished I knew what Johnson was thinking. He professed that Keller's death was an accident, yet he was putting an awful lot of effort into the case. If he didn't think the brass ring I found had some significance he wouldn't want to search the yard a second time.

"There's something you aren't telling me. What's the official cause of death?"

"I thought you had to go to sleep," he said.

"I do, but it can wait. How did they say Keller died?"

He hesitated. "I suppose you're going to find out sooner or later. There was no water in his lungs."

That only meant one thing. He was dead before he went into the drink.

"Then what was the cause of death?"

"It was head trauma. Forensics show he was hit on the back of the head."

I guess I was too busy trying to revive the guy to notice any bruise on the back of his head. I was glad that Johnson and I were on the same page. I suspected all along that it was murder. At least now Johnson was sharing this information with me.

"Now all we have to do is find out who killed Keller," I said.

"You mean; all I have to do. But you're right. We're looking at this as a murder investigation now. Was it you who said that in the first place?" He chuckled.

I was too tired to play along.

"Anyway, we know Roscoe Hicks didn't do it," I said.

"You know that for a fact?"

Good, I knew something he didn't know.

"Someone killed him today up in Hilton Head."

"Why didn't you tell me?"

"You're right. I should have done that. Guess I messed up on the professional courtesy front too. As you say, busy."

"Well?"

"I found him. We talked. He claimed he was out of town when Keller was killed. I left. Someone shot him." I felt it important to tell him that I wasn't a witness and the cops had actually asked me to leave so they could conduct their investigation. "Find who killed Hicks and you'll find who killed Keller."

Johnson began to fidget. "Actually, there is a strong suspect."

Now I was worried. Did he suspect me?

"Care to tell me who it is?"

Johnson took a deep breath. "Look, this isn't easy, but things are pointing to Big Al."

Big Al, my Alzheimer's ridden father?

"You're still breaking balls. Right?"

I waited for Johnson to laugh. He wasn't smiling. The laugh never came.

"We were told that he knows how to get out of the facility where he's staying. Did you know that?"

Of course, I knew that. But I certainly wasn't going to tell him. "Where did you hear that?"

"The care coordinator there asked for assistance in finding him this afternoon."

"That's impossible. He was with me."

"In Hilton Head? Until what time?"

"Six o'clock."

"We got the call at 6:15. My officers found him walking down the road and returned him by 6:30. I found out when I called in."

Maryann should have called me to let me know that he was missing. I looked at my phone. Sure enough, I had a missed call from The Palms. I swear I never heard it ring.

"So, you are telling me that because my father apparently knows how to get out of his care facility that makes him a suspect in a murder investigation?"

Johnson didn't look like he was enjoying this conversation any more than I was.

"And there is the matter of your neighbors next door. They have seen him going out on the boat. That stupid hat of his is pretty memorable. And they claim Keller was on the boat the day he was killed."

So that asshole, Lynch, had already reported his trumped-up story to the police before I went over there.

"Look, I don't have any reason to defend my father. But that's pretty circumstantial evidence. Even if he does get out of the place, as you say, there's no real evidence that he has ever been back here. And anyone could have been under that hat."

"I thought the same thing."

"But you don't now," I said.

"I'm not sure what I think now that you tell me he was with you in Hilton Head where you say one of my prime suspects has been murdered."

I knew one thing he wasn't going to hear from me, that Big Al had disappeared a little before Hicks was killed.

"And I might add that I had my father with me only because Maryann Fena wanted me to take him out."

"I'm just checking out the facts," Johnson said.

"Wait a minute, let me see something." I pulled up the charity game schedule on my phone. "The game was at 1:05. It must have been over at what, 4:00? You're not just coming from the stadium. And you knew from The Palms that Hicks was killed. Big Al must have gone back and told them all about Hicks and when they didn't believe him he walked out."

"So, you got me, but it is a courtesy call. I wanted you to know what was in the wind."

"It seems to me that what's up is that the nurse who hates Big Al and the neighbor who wants his land seem to be setting him up."

Johnson cast his eyes downward and frowned. "There's also the brass ring you gave me. It's from the tip assembly on his cane. It hides the gap between the wood and the brass ferrule."

"But this is his yard. He could have lost that before he went into the home."

Johnson shook his head no. "Mrs. Fena tells me that your father got that cane from Mrs. Greenleaf after he entered the home."

CHAPTER TWENTY-SEVEN

"Are you thinking that he hit Keller with the cane?"

"And the ring broke off... It's a possibility," Johnson said.

"This doesn't make any sense. Why would my father want to kill Keller or Hicks?"

"You know Big Al is my friend. I wish I didn't have to do this. I don't know what the motive is yet. Maybe there wasn't a motive. Maybe it has something to do with his disease. He could have acted out of confusion or misplaced anger. I don't know."

"Alzheimer's doesn't work like that."

"Then we've got to work together on this or Big Al is going to spend his last days in prison or in an institution. I'm here to promise you that I'll do all I can."

Johnson has some funny ways about him, but I believed him.

Chapter Twenty-Eight

Johnson told me that they didn't have a motive, or means of how Big Al could get from The Palms to Ava Island. But once that was figured out there wasn't much he could do to help him.

No matter how tired I was, there was no way I was going to be able to sleep now. After Johnson left I went inside and poked around my father's office. It was time that I got a better understanding of him.

The old man was a collector but by no means a pack rat. Everything had a place. Most of his mementos were on a floor to ceiling bookcase in his office that took up one wall of the small room. I looked at his shelves trying to get a hint of who he was. At one point, I couldn't give a damn about knowing, but things had changed.

Judging from some of the things he kept, the guy that I thought was a hardnosed private investigator had a sentimental side. Although I couldn't be sure why he kept some of the things he did. I wondered if they had to do with cases he worked on or something more personal. There was a lump of grey volcanic rock, pretty heavy for something that could fit in the palm of your hand. An eight-inch statue that looked like an Aztec god had me stumped. Maybe he was into Mesoamerican religion. I turned the statuette over and found the word Mexico scratched in the bottom of the terra cotta piece and decided it was a souvenir. In a Plexiglas stand there was a Joe Montana football card. The plaque read Upper Deck Promo Card Limited Edition of 1991. Funny, Montana was a hero of mine in those years when my father was gone. I had the same card. I don't remember who gave it to me. I think my mom said some relative who lived far away sent it to me.

Another small statue, this one of Sherlock Holmes; the one played by Basil Rathbone, my favorite Holmes. The old man's books could have come right off my own shelf; everything from forensics to biographies of Mark Twain, and the Beatles, to mysteries by McBain, Chandler, and Christie.

In a shirt box on the top shelf was a stack of papers about an inch thick. I leafed through them. His PI license and several awards, one from the grateful state of Georgia for finding the Granville kidnapper.

There were also a couple of diplomas and course completion certificates in criminal justice. I had a little more respect for him that he didn't hang that stuff on the wall. Then to my surprise I found a small picture in a plastic frame with no glass. I knew the picture well. It was my sixth-grade class picture—a chubby kid with curly hair and a big smile. How the hell did he get that? He had been long gone by the time I was in the 6th grade.

From the second shelf, I picked up a plastic Magic 8 ball. Was this how he solved his cases?

I held the ball in my left hand and put my right hand on top of it.

"Will I be able to straighten this mess out and get on to LA soon?"

I turned the ball over and gazed down. A blue triangle floated into the window in the ball.

DON'T COUNT ON IT

* * *

Well, I was going to count on it. My goal of closing the office and getting my ass out to LA had not changed even though it seemed to be getting further and further away from me. Now I had to either clear my father of murder or prove that he was a killer. Did he murder Andy Keller or not? Johnson had a pretty good amount of circumstantial evidence that he did. And as far as I knew, he did not know that my father went missing from the gallery a little before Hicks was killed. Could he have gotten hold of a gun and killed Hicks? Did he bring one with him? At this point I was even beginning to doubt that he had Alzheimer's. If he did do it, there was nothing Johnson or I could do to help him. I found myself nodding and decided I couldn't put

125

off going to sleep any longer.

Chapter Twenty-Nine

Early the next morning I was back at the coffee table where I found a list of things that Greenleaf had left for me that needed attention. This stuff wasn't going to finish itself up. I started by writing up a report on a case I had recently finished, a premarital investigation that my father had started for a Savannah socialite's family. The future husband wasn't a gigolo as suspected, in fact, he had more money than she did, which made her father happy. I didn't feel the need to tell them that the future groom was running the same investigation on the socialite through another agency. Who was I to plant a seed of doubt in a romance between two equally shallow lovebirds?

I finished the report just as I heard Greenleaf come in. I went out to the front office and handed it to her.

"One more down. Get it off please so we can get a check," I said.

"I didn't hear from you all day yesterday. I thought maybe you took off for California."

"I wound up in Hilton Head with my father. We found Hicks."

Greenleaf looked pleased. It's not a look that I'd seen from her often. I knew it was because she approved of me bringing my father along.

"So I heard."

Of course, she did. Max must have been keeping her up to date from the time we spoke on the bridge until we got back.

"So, you know Hicks was murdered?"

She bobbed her head. "But, there's something more. I can tell. What is it?"

"Why do you say that?"

Greenleaf sighed. "You must suck at poker. I can read your face like your thoughts are printed there in a Tahoma 14 font."

"Okay, okay. Now that Hicks is dead, Johnson has decided that the Keller case is murder."

"Well, that's what you wanted right along. Isn't it?"

"Yeah, but he's focusing on Big Al."

Greenleaf sat down hard into her seat. Her face was pale. "What are you looking at?"

"Did you know that brass ring that you kicked under the bush was from Big Al's cane?"

"Are you saying I kicked it away to hide it?"

"Did you?"

"No. Of course not. I didn't even know I kicked it."

"But you recognized it when I showed it to you."

"I thought there was something like it on Big Al's cane, but I thought it was impossible that it was from his. I still do. Maybe someone else lost it."

"Do you believe that?"

"At this point I don't know what to believe," she said.

For once Greenleaf and I agreed on something. "Are you all right, Greenleaf? I have to go check something out."

The color returned to her face and she sprung from the chair like a superhero. "Do what you have to do and clear your father. I'm holding down the fort here."

I didn't want to get into it with her but I was going out to see what I could find out about the guy with the bullet hole tat. If it implicated my father further or cleared him, I wasn't going to worry about it.

Chapter Thirty

How hard could it be to find a guy with such a ridiculous tattoo? The tattoo still had some outline that had to be inked in so I assumed that the guy was working with a local tattoo shop. There was no guarantee, but it was a place to start.

I thought I'd seen a sign for a tat studio in the Village Plaza when I had gone to the Post Office. I never noticed the actual studio, but then the Post Office wasn't easy to find either. That was conveniently tucked in the back of the drugstore next to the pharmacy counter which struck me as a clever way of tempting tourists to buy Ava Island Beach T-shirts and beach towels when they came in to mail postcards. For all I knew, the tattoo studio was tucked into the Post Office too.

I pulled into the Village Plaza on Ocean Boulevard to find the only available parking space blocked by a plastic sandwich board with the warning that the lot was reserved for plaza customers only. It seemed counterproductive to waste a space like that and I was about to get out and move the sandwich board when I caught a glimpse of a guy in a green shirt coming out of Cafe Garbanzo at the far end of the shopping center. I saw him get into a boat of a car, a white '61 Pontiac Catalina convertible. The car was older than I was, but even from across the lot I could see it was still a sweet vehicle with a huge hood and trunk.

I drove over and grabbed the space. Once parked, I noticed the lot attendant, a little guy in a fluorescent safety vest, writing down my plate number. He must have been no more than five six, but with his aviator sunglasses and the cock of his cap he carried himself as if he were a foot taller. I walked over to him.

I got the impression that he took his job of keeping the lot open for the store customers seriously.

"Where's the tattoo shop?"

"Inside the drug store," he said with a deadpan look on his face.

"Are you kidding me?"

He broke into a grin. "Of course, I am. You're standing right in front of it."

I looked at the covered walkway that ran the length of the U-shaped shopping plaza. The tattoo parlor was marked by a small wooden sign that hung from the rafters: The Golden Osprey Tattoo Studio.

"Right."

"I'll bet you're one of those guys who needs his wife to find the mustard for him because he's too lazy to move things around in the refrigerator."

Yeah and I'll bet he wasn't. "If I was married, maybe I would be."

As I walked up the steps to the walkway I could feel his eyes on my back. I'm sure he thought I was parking illegally in the lot and going someplace other than to the tattoo shop.

When I went in The Golden Osprey, it seemed more like an art gallery than a tattoo shop. A large open space with light oak floors and upholstered benches situated so you could sit and admire photos of tattooed bodies as if you were in an art museum. I walked around the room admiring the pictures. There was one of a female back with the Mona Lisa. Another showed someone's shoulder decorated with the Hands of the Creation. Then there was a beautiful woman's breast inked with a depiction of Starry Night, an ankle with Picasso's Peace Dove, a Monet on an instep, a Dali on a thigh, an Andy Warhol Soup Can on a butt.

A man with graying temples dressed in an expensive looking blue suit greeted me.

"Take your time and look around. If you find anything that interests you, or if you have questions feel free to ask," he said.

"I do have a question," I said to the man. "Do you do bullet holes?"

"If you're asking if can I do bullet holes, the answer is I can do anything. Will I do them?" He glanced around the room at his neatly framed works of art. "I'm afraid bullet holes would not be suited to my clientele."

An uppity tattoo artist. What do you know?

"So, if someone had such a tattoo it would be safe to say he didn't get it here."

"As I said, not my clientele. Could I interest you in something perhaps a bit more enlightened? Maybe Munch's *The Scream*." He pointed to a photograph of an upper arm with the faithful representation of the painting. "That's actually my arm. I had that done to celebrate firing my shrink and opening this business."

Why didn't I think of that when I fired my shrink? I passed on the tat. I already had a ring on my finger that brought back nothing but bad memories and that was enough body art for me. "I'm looking for a guy with a bullet hole tattoo. So, I take it you don't know who I'm talking about."

"Afraid not."

"Any ideas where someone might get the type of tat I'm talking about?"

He wrinkled his nose as if he were smelling low tide. "You can try Beach Inks down by the UPS store on Beach Street. But I'm telling you now, you won't get the quality you'll get here."

* * *

I left the Golden Osprey irritated, and when I'm like that I get hungry. I saw a kid walking by with a donut and the power of suggestion made me crave one of the great cinnamon sugar donuts that Max had told me they sold across the street at the Mini Donut stand.

I didn't think it would hurt to make a quick dash over and grab a half dozen for the road and maybe bring one to Greenleaf too. I hadn't counted on a long line. I must have waited all of ten minutes but it was worth it. Bag of donuts in hand, I headed back to my truck in the lot across the street.

When I got to the parking lot the guy in the fluorescent vest was standing behind my truck and writing in his pad. He didn't say anything but apparently my time in the parking spot was about up. As I drove out of the lot I noticed a small folded piece of paper under my wiper blade. My first thought was that it was from whoever had been taunting me about being a lousy detective. I drove through the village until I found a parking space on the side of the road down by Ava Island Beach. I got out and read the note. *Friendly Reminder. The Ava Island Village parking lot is for customers of the plaza only.* It was signed D. Weeks.

Busted for getting my donuts. Technically I was a plaza customer since I went into the tattoo shop. So I spent a little time across the street at the Mini Donut stand. What's the big deal? I balled the note up and threw it on my seat. Then I ate a donut as I drove toward Beach Street.

The ride should have taken five minutes but because of the beach traffic, bicycles, pedicabs, and jaywalkers it took almost twenty minutes. I could have walked it faster.

Beach Ink was a small storefront place with a dusty parking lot that it shared with three other businesses.

When I opened the door to the shop a bell rang and I walked into a room with walls covered to the ceiling with paper diagrams of tattoos to choose from—not unlike one of the many T-shirt stores on Ava Island but instead of cute sayings and pictures of anchors and palm trees these were mostly Gothic representations of bloody knives, skulls, dragons, and bats. I was sure I was in the right place.

I could hear talking and a buzz from a machine in the backroom. It seemed to be a one-man operation so I took one of three chairs by the window to wait.

"I'll be done in about ten minutes." It was a female voice that came over a speaker. It was obvious that I was being watched on CCTV. Almost exactly ten minutes later a young woman came out of the back room. The first thing I noticed besides her orange hair was that she had a full sleeve of tattoos on her left arm. I got up as she walked toward me.

"Hi, I'm..."

"Lo," she said and walked out of the door.

Realizing she was a customer, I sat down and thumbed through an *Inked Magazine*. The next person who walked out of the back was a tall woman with jet black hair. As far as I could see, there wasn't a tattoo on her. I lowered my head and went back to the magazine.

"Are you here to read or to get a tat?"

"Neither. I need information. Are you the owner?"

She took a step back and her eyes narrowed.

"Yes…"

"Al DeLucia." I put out my hand.

"You a cop?"

"Private Investigator."

"Ah. A cop without a health plan. Malaysia Streetbridge." She took my hand. She had a grip like a longshoreman.

A college age kid came in. He had a tattoo on his neck that said *Tina Forever.* There was a line drawn through the name Tina that looked like it was done with a ballpoint pen.

"Am I late? I'm psyched about the next session."

"You're fine," she said. "This won't take long."

Malaysia turned to me. "Now what's this about?"

"I'm trying to get a lead on a guy. I don't know his name but he has a distinctive tattoo; a bullet hole."

"No exit wound?"

"Yeah, that too. Have you done one like that?"

"More like twenty. Where is it? Shoulder, stomach, groin, all of the above?"

Groin, who the hell would get a bullet hole there?

"On his shin. This is a young guy. Know him?"

She thought a moment. She stuck her hands in her pockets. "Look, I'm a licensed tattoo artist. I do everything by the book and that includes keeping my client's confidentiality. Nice talking to you, Mr. DeLucia." She glanced at the customer as if she were looking for approval.

He grinned.

"I'll be right with you. Let me go in the back and set up," she said to him.

First a tattoo artist with a stick up his ass and now one with high ethics. I would never guess it was such a noble profession.

As I was about to get into my truck the customer with the neck tattoo ran up to me. "Yo Dude, wait up. Couldn't help hearing."

"You know the guy I'm looking for?"

"I could give you a hint if I could remember."

I reached into my pocket and took out a twenty. "Memory coming back?"

"Another twenty might do it."

"Not for a hint." I took out another ten.

"Okay. I was here when a dude was getting a tattoo like that."

"A bullet hole?"

"Yeah. He had these powerful legs like he was a cyclist. And I heard him complain about how he hoped the pain wouldn't give him a problem at his job."

"And his name?"

"Who did you say you were looking for?"

"A guy named Davis," I said.

"Yeah, Davis. That was his name."

I folded up the money. "Listen, wanker. I don't have time for games."

"No, no, no, no, no! All right, okay. I'm sorry. I didn't get his name. But he sounds like the guy you're looking for."

"Where can I find him?"

"No idea." He was holding up his hands palms out. "Straight talk. I'm sure he bikes. I wouldn't lie."

"That's it?" I took the ten and stuffed it in his shirt pocket. The twenty went into my own pocket. "Tina is a lucky girl to be rid of you. Get out of here."

The little twerp went back into the tattoo parlor without another peep.

Chapter Thirty-One

I pulled up in front of the porch at the Blue Palmetto and was about to bring a donut in to Greenleaf when the note on the seat caught my eye. Mr. D. Weeks seemed to see everything that goes on in that parking lot. I wondered if he ever noticed a bicyclist with an inked bullet hole on his leg. I started the truck and ate two more donuts as I drove back to the village.

A huge white 4-wheel drive was pulling out of a spot shaded by a tree draped in Spanish moss in the center strip of the Village Plaza parking lot. The guy behind the wheel was trying to back out while holding a cup of coffee in one hand and a cell phone in the other. I waited patiently. The laid-back Georgia lifestyle must be taking the edge off of my attitude. Back in the northeast I would have called him a jerk or worse and given him the finger. Maxine would be proud of my new-found self-restraint. When he left I took the parking space.

I spotted the parking attendant's fluorescent vest. He was by the bicycle rack discreetly watching to see if I was going to go into one of the shops or I was going to leave the plaza.

"Mr. Weeks?"

A glimmer of recognition crossed his face for a second. Then he set his jaw. "I know. The note; it's my job."

"Forget it. It's good to see someone who takes their job seriously."

He visibly relaxed his shoulders as he allowed a faint smile to appear.

"Forget the Mr. Weeks business. It's Demarco all the way."

"Al. Blue Palmetto Detective Agency" I said. "I'm trying to find someone.

I'm hoping you can help."

He actually looked impressed. Most people don't realize what a boring job being a PI is.

"If I can."

"I'm looking for a cyclist."

Demarco gave a little laugh and waved his hand in an arc around the village.

"Take your pick. With the limited parking situation in the village a lot of the tourists rent bicycles."

"I'm pretty sure this guy is a local." I gestured toward the bike rack. "So I think the chances are pretty good he's come here to go to the Post Office or whatever. He's a young white guy. He's inked on his leg with a bullet hole and exit wound. And if you got a close look at him he has one eye that's brown and the other that's blue. Sound familiar?"

"Yeah I've seen someone like that. But he doesn't ride a bike. At least not a regular one. He drives a pedicab."

A pedicab. Why didn't I think of that?

"The bike cab company is a few blocks down from the plaza," Demarco said. "Why don't you go ask them?"

I looked from the parking lot to Ocean Boulevard, the main street through the village was jammed. Driving through the village can be an exercise in patience with the number of cars, scooters, and bicycles on the streets. I turned back to my new-found friend Demarco.

"Do you suppose I could leave my truck here for a few minutes while I run down to check out the cab company?"

Demarco smiled. "No can do. As it is, you parked without going into one of the shops."

"Right." I wasn't happy, but good for him I thought. You don't find too many people who are serious about their jobs like that.

Chapter Thirty-Two

The office for the Sunrise Bike Cab and Scooter Rental company was located a block down from the Village Shopping Center between a pizza restaurant and a souvenir store.

Besides offering rides in peddled vehicles that looked like the front end of a bicycle attached to a hansom cab they rented the three wheeled cars that I had often seen tourists use to troll around the town. Made of fiberglass and painted jellybean colors, those vehicles had two wheels in front but only one in the back.

A pretty mechanic looked up from one of the vehicles she was working on and wiped her hands on a rag.

"Interested?"

I smiled my answer back to her.

She pointed toward a guy up by the office. "My father will take care of you." She bent back over the machine. The guy was already headed my way.

"They're disguised scooters, but they're a lot of fun. I can get you into a rental with just your license and a credit card," he said.

"Not today. What I'm here for is information," I said.

"Sure. Besides these bad boys we have bike cab rides, and island tours. You like history? We have a history tour that takes you over to Fort Pulaski National Monument."

I shook my head no.

"Then there are the sailboard and kayak rentals. We even have a surf and turf combo that combines the kayak and bike cab tours. What are you interested in?" He took a step between me and his daughter's backside.

"A guy with a tattoo."

He gave me a perplexed look. "Hey, that's cool. Whatever fills your sails. But maybe you should try one of the bars."

I handed him one of the business cards Greenleaf had made for me. He looked at it. "Blue Palmetto, huh? I know the old guy. Same name. He your father?"

I nodded. "I'm looking for a specific guy. He's got a tattoo that looks like he was shot in the leg and he has one eye that is blue. Word is he peddles a cab. Does he work for you?"

"We've got ten drivers and none of them fit that description."

"You're the only bike cab company on the island. Aren't you?"

"We were for five years. But lately a couple of independents have cropped up. One-man operations."

The mechanic stood up from the three-wheeled car she was working on.

"I'm the owner," she said. "The guy you're looking for sounds like Tanner. Dave's the worst. He'll offer our customers a better price and steal them right out of our cab."

"Sounds like a nice guy."

"It's fine with me. We've got more than enough business. But it's the idea. You know?"

"Where I can find him?"

"Try down by the pavilion at the beach. The indies usually hang out there."

I decided then and there that one of these days when I had some time I was going to come by and rent one of those little cars.

* * *

It was late so I finally gave up and went home to do a computer search on David Tanner. I was surprised to find how many David Tanners were out there; over two hundred David Tanners on Facebook alone.

None of them were the one I was looking for. I wasn't surprised. I don't use Facebook myself. Most guys my age don't. I had to open an account to do the search and I hoped none of my friends got wind that I was on it. Too uncool.

I tried Instagram and Twitter. There were almost as many David Tanners on those sites too, but none of them were the dude I was looking for.

An Internet Phone search gave me a listing for David Tanner Photography in Savannah. No. Then there was a David Tanner electrician. Nope. David Tanner waste management, and David Tanner blacksmith. No and no.

I was surprised that I couldn't find anything on the David Tanner I was looking for. How could someone not have an Internet footprint? Unless he was a ghost.

Chapter Thirty-Three

Sunday morning was overcast, but the local news channels made a big deal out of promising that it would clear by noon. I think the weather people work hand in hand with the Chamber of Commerce to reassure the tourists that their Georgia vacation will be the best ever. At any rate, it was no morning for visitors to be taking rides in a pedicab, so I didn't bother to go out and look for Tanner.

I spent the time going over other cases that had to be wrapped up. Every once in a while, I'd take a break to hop on the Internet to look at rentals in the LA area that were in close proximity to the ocean.

A one bedroom in Venice Beach ranged from 1,950 bucks a month for a closet sized 300 square feet to $3,300 for 800 square feet. In Santa Monica 59 hundred big ones got you all of 900 square. Still not a huge place.

It may not have been the most productive use of my time considering how much work had to be done, not only on the cases my father left open but also getting to the truth behind the Andy Keller and Roscoe Hicks murders. But keeping the California dream alive was the only thing that stopped me from throwing up my hands and walking away. That and the fact that having a viable agency to sell, plus the money I would get from the prime location of my father's house was the only way I could afford to make my move to LA.

As the morning wore on I started to think about how I hadn't been nice to Maxine. I know she thought I resented she was my boss. But I've had woman bosses before. I think my real problem was that I was out of my comfort zone finding myself in the situation of taking care of my parent. Not exactly a traditional role for a guy. And as much as I prided myself in being enlightened, I think I was taking it out on her. I decided that I should make amends. I sent her a text.

Me: *Dinner?*

I waited fifteen minutes and didn't get a reply. This wasn't a good sign. Finally, I decided to do it the old fashioned way. I punched her number into my phone.

I hate actually talking on the phone, probably because I don't always filter what I say in a direct conversation. It rang several times and I was almost ready to hang up when she answered

"What do you need?" Her voice sounded less than warm.

"Is that any way to talk to someone who is going to make you dinner?"

"I'm sorry. I didn't catch your name. Is this Bobby Flay or Todd English?"

"Very Funny. No, this is some jerk who made a mistake and wants to make it up to you by making you my special balsamic chicken."

"I don't usually eat with jerks."

"But you'll make an exception this time?"

"Only because I want to see if you can cook."

Max was making me work for this. Couldn't she see it was my way of apologizing to her?

"Good. What time can I come over?"

There was a pause on the other end of the line. "I thought you were making dinner for me."

"I will. But I thought it would be better if I made it at your place. I know you've got that nice kitchen and the oven doesn't work over here."

There was an audible sigh. "All right! Be here at four. But I'm not lifting a finger. And you're bringing over all of the food."

The lady drives a hard bargain.

I spent another couple of hours or so working on paperwork with the periodic Internet apartment hunting breaks. Then I went over to Max's place carrying a bag full of groceries and two bottles of wine. It was only 3 o'clock.

"You're early," she said.

"I thought we'd have a drink before I started." I made us each a rum and ginger beer using the liquor at her pool bar. I handed one to her.

"You didn't even ask if I like ginger," she said.

"Do you?" I sniffed my drink and took in the spicy sharp smell of the ginger beer.

"Yes."

"We're good then." I clinked her glass.

We chilled for a while and she never mentioned Hilton Head. Better yet, she didn't mention wanting to help me.

"Don't you think you should start dinner?"

"I like being out here by the water with you," I said.

"Are you reneging on your promise?"

"No. No, no, no, no. I never break a promise. You know that."

I went inside and tried to figure out her induction stove while she sat out on the lawn by the water reading a food mystery set in Key West.

The plan was to have a nice dinner, some good wine, and then go down to Ava Island Beach to attend the drum circle. Following that we would go up to the village to have some ice cream at the Creamery followed by whatever felt right. I was hoping that after all that attention her idea of "right" would be the same as mine.

I put the chicken in the oven, set her table with some dishes and silverware that she had left out expecting me to use. They seemed a little fancy and more suited for the northern lifestyle, but if that's what made the lady happy, who was I to question?

Then I went outside, stopping at the bar to make two more drinks, threw in some limes, and brought them down by the water. We spent a good fifteen minutes talking and watching a Great White Heron strut over the lawn.

The drum circle started about 5 o'clock and ended after the sun went down, which at that time of year would be about 8 o'clock. Sound carries easily on the island and we could already hear the drumming from down at the beach as we were finishing our drinks.

"If we eat now, we should still have an hour or so at the celebration," I said.

When we went in the house she seemed happy that the kitchen was totally clean and I had set a perfect table right down to candles.

"Maybe I underestimated you," she said.

"Don't worry about it, everyone does. But I'm full of surprises. Wait until I serve you my special chicken."

She sniffed the air. "Funny. I don't seem to smell it."

I pulled out her chair for her. "You will. Sit here and I'll be right back."

I was back at the table in a flash. "Heh."

"Where's the chicken?"

"I kind of was rushing around setting the table and making the drinks and all."

"And?"

"I forgot to turn on the oven."

Max lowered her eyes to look at her empty plate. I couldn't read if she was trying to stifle a laugh or if she was trying not to explode.

"I'm not hungry yet anyway," she said. "Let's leave the chicken to cook and go to the circle. A friend is going to be down there. It's time you meet some new people."

I must have done something right in a past life to meet a woman as understanding as Max.

Chapter Thirty-Four

The hollow sounds of the drum circle in the distance seemed to be drawing people out of their hotels and condos as if they were under a spell. Instead of driving, Max suggested that we walk the two blocks up to the beach along with the others.

As the parade of ramblers approached the crosswalk on Beach Street I knew walking was the right decision. Ava Island Beach claims to be the #1 Beach in the U.S.A. From my previous visit there with Max, I'd say that could very well be true. There was certainly lots of white powdered sand that stretched in each direction. Still, a better claim would be Busiest Parking Lot in the U.S.A.—especially for the Sunday night drum circle.

If we had driven, we would have been in one of the hundreds of cars that were inching along bumper to bumper on the road trying to get in the parking lot as the rhythm of the drums called to them. I was glad I had listened to Max.

A sign on the side of the road marked the street as an evacuation route. If traffic was this bad for a drum circle it would be impossible to get off the island in an emergency. With only two bridges to the mainland, if a hurricane struck, my advice would be to stay put, get drunk, and kiss your ass goodbye.

"I've never seen it this bad," Max said. "I should warn my friend. Can I borrow your phone?"

I handed her my cell and I could hear her telling someone about the traffic.

"When you get here, call back at this number and I'll tell you where to meet us," she said. When she hung up she tried to give the phone back to me.

"Hold on to it until you get your call," I told her as we navigated around cars illegally blocking the crosswalk.

We finally made it to the picnic benches on the other side of the street and started walking toward the music.

Far ahead I noticed a bike cab, with two flags bobbing on fiberglass rods behind it; one American and the other black, red, and gold. I'm not that up on current events, but I'm pretty sure those were the colors of the German flag.

The cabbie had managed to enter the lot by riding up on the grass to cut around the log jam of cars. It stopped near the pavilion. The passengers got out and headed up the steep sidewalk to the modern concrete structure built on stilts.

Instead of driving away the cabbie pulled his rig under the building. I could only guess that he was told to wait for his passengers. When he got out I could see that he was a tall guy, but from that distance I couldn't see his eyes or if he had a tattoo. He headed toward the beach.

I grabbed Max's hand to hurry her along but I didn't tell her about my hunch that Tanner was going to be at the drum circle.

"Let's go this way," I said.

We marched along one of the beach accesses that kept people from trampling the seagrass on the dunes. Once on the beach, we could see a crowd of frenzied dancers on the beach side of the pavilion. We trudged on unable to resist the beat of drums.

Unlike drum circles I had seen on visits to LA where there might be a hundred or more players pounding on every type of drum imaginable, this circle had no more than a dozen players mostly on goblet shaped djembes, barrel congas, with a few Native American hand drums thrown in. As expected, the sound was deafening but more amazing were the hundreds of people of every age doing their thing. Some danced and others chanted. Still others sat in chairs and drank wine as they picnicked. Many took video with their phones. Every once in a while, a whiff of pot attested to the mellowness of the party.

The guy I suspected was Tanner was standing near the drummers and talking to a young woman with a long red scarf. Suddenly she started to dance as she wound the scarf in a suggestive way around her body. She grabbed his hand and pulled him into the dance on the sand. I had to get closer to the couple.

"Let's dance," I yelled to Maxine.

"Seriously?" she said.

"Definitely. We have to get in touch with our inner hippie."

I'm not sure if she understood what I said, but we got into the merry crowd. At one point, Max held the phone to her ear as we danced. How she heard it ring, with all of that noise, I don't know.

I tried to move closer to the couple, but a large woman wearing gossamer wings got between us. She grabbed my hand and Max took the other and before I knew it we were in a circle of people dancing around the girl with the red scarf and Tall Guy. I couldn't see if his left eye was blue but the infamous bullet hole tat on his leg was clear. It was even uglier than I had imagined. I had found Tanner at last.

A muscular guy with a toothy smile broke in and grabbed Max's other hand. Max mouthed something in the way of an introduction, but I didn't catch it. My concentration was on Tanner who seemed embarrassed by being in the center of attention. I broke away from Max and her friend and stood next to him. I tapped him on the shoulder.

"Tanner?"

The guy glanced over. "Who's asking?"

"Al DeLucia, I'm a detective. We need to talk. I have some questions for you."

He seemed to have a hard time understanding with all of the noise.

"What?"

"I want to talk to you about Keller," I said.

He seemed to catch the word Keller if I read his expression right. At that moment, the winged woman grabbed my hand and pulled me away.

Tanner stopped dancing with the girl with the scarf. Then he burst through the dance circle and made his way through the fringes of the crowd. I broke from the circle too. The last I saw, the lady with the wings had grabbed

Max's hand and brought her into the center of the dance as Max's friend with the teeth clapped his encouragement.

I tried to follow Tanner through the crowd. Someone yelled at me when I got in the way of a picture they were taking. Then a girl swinging a lighted hula hoop on each arm hit me with one of the spinning rings. I made my way around her and pushed my way through the crowd. I could see Tanner far ahead running up the ramp to the pavilion.

"Hey." I called out.

He had a good lead on me and I lost sight of him in the crowded pavilion where vendors were set up selling everything from food to souvenirs.

I ran out to the parking lot which was still in massive gridlock, now from cars leaving the drum circle early to "avoid" the rush. One by one they made their way toward the single exit that funneled them out to the street. I spotted the pedicab with the flags which once again jumped onto the grass to cut the line.

He bolted out onto Beach Street. I heard horns beeping and the tires screeching. The pedicab made a violent lurch when a car clipped its back end but remained upright. Tanner maintained control and headed in the direction of the village.

"Hold up," I yelled as I ran on the path that paralleled the street. I weaved around people hauling coolers, umbrellas and surfboards until the path ended at a crosswalk.

A lady with a walker had already pressed the button and was halfway across. In spite of the flashing lights on the poles and blinkers in the road lining the crosswalk a car barreled up the street. I could tell it had no intention of stopping. I put my hand on the lady's walker to hold her back.

"Jerk!" I yelled at the car. It sped up the street toward town and honked at the bike cab and cut around it. By this time the cab with its two flags bobbing behind it was too far away for me to catch. I learned something that day: in spite of being in pretty good shape for age thirty-five I can't run as fast as I used to.

I jogged about a mile until I got to the village where I checked every restaurant and side street for the bike cab.

* * *

Ava Island Village in the evening is as glamorous as South Beach, as outlandish as Key West, and as packed as Daytona yet, all contained in a three-quarter mile strip of souvenir shops, dive bars, exclusive clubs, and restaurants of every caliber. I checked every place I could think of but couldn't find a trace of Tanner or the cab.

I found a white Ava Island Police car with a bold green stripe and a big yellow five-pointed star on the door parked in front of the hardware store. When I walked up to it the cop behind the wheel rolled down the window.

"Did you happen to see a bike cab flying an American flag and a German flag behind it?"

"Is there a problem?" the deputy asked.

"Only a minor one. My girl thinks she may have left her phone in the cab earlier in the day. I'm trying to help her find it."

"Gotcha," he said. "It's kind of late. Most of the cabbies are off of the street. Try tomorrow."

I pressed on.

"I thought you might know him since this is his route, from here to the beach. I noticed that he had an awesome bullet hole tattoo on his leg."

The cop gagged a chuckle.

"Tanner. I didn't see him. But good luck getting the phone back."

"It's worth a try," I said.

I ducked into a bar blaring country music where the singer was lamenting losing his girl and then getting drunk. I approached the barkeep.

"I'm looking for a tall guy with one blue eye. Do you know him?"

"No. Shouldn't be hard to find though."

"Really?"

"Well yeah. How many people are walking around with a patch over their eye?"

"I didn't say he had one eye. I said he had one blue eye. The other one is brown."

"Well he'd be harder to spot then, wouldn't he?"

I moved on to the club next door. The woman behind the bar was decked out in hot pants and a well filled out tank top. "What can I get you?" She asked with a husky voice.

A large woman in a skintight red dress sashayed by the pool table in the middle of the room as she belted out a song about it raining men. People were passing her money which she stuffed into her bra which was already overflowing.

I spoke loudly to the bartender so I could be heard. "I need some information. Have you seen a tall guy with one blue eye? The other one is brown. He has a bullet hole tat on his leg."

"Gee, could you be a little more specific? That could describe about anyone."

I couldn't be more specific if I gave her Tanner's DNA map.

"I take that as a no."

"Lighten up. I'm pulling your chain. You're looking for Tanner."

"That's right. Where can I find him?"

The woman by the pool table with the bra full of money finished her song and the music changed. The bartender I was talking to picked up a wireless microphone. "Excuse me. It's my turn. Got a request?"

I shrugged. "Surprise me." I put a fiver on the bar. She looked at it skeptically and tucked it into her pants. Then she hopped up on the bar and started belting out a song.

The big lady chimed in from the other side of the room like it was some kind of battle of the microphones.

"Aren't they wonderful?" The woman on the stool next to me must have been pushing sixty. The guy she was with seemed to be her husband, who looked totally confused and more than a bit uncomfortable. She leaned in toward me and shouted so I could hear her. "You would never know. Would you?"

"Never know what?" I asked.

"That they aren't women. You knew that. Right?"

No shit? "I did. I certainly did," I said.

The song ended and the bartender hopped down. She put the microphone behind the cash register before coming over to me.

"So, what's Tanner done?"

"I need to talk to him. That's all."

She scratched her cheek with two long multicolored fingernails as if she were considering if I could be trusted or not.

"You're a cop?"

"Nope. PI. I couldn't arrest him if I wanted to. I want to talk to him. Do you know him or not?" This time I threw a twenty on the bar.

"You insult me," she said as she slid the bill into her pocket. "I know him. He does odd jobs around here sometimes."

"How do I find him?"

"I don't know. The maintenance company hires him once in a while. Do you fish?"

"What's that got to do with anything?'

She pointed to a poster on the wall. "There's a fishing tournament at the pier the day after tomorrow. I hear he entered. You go down early. I'm talking ungodly early, and you'll find him."

I put another ten on the bar. "Nice song," I said.

It was late, I was tired, and Max and I still hadn't eaten. I decided to forget Tanner for tonight. I headed to Max's place almost tasting the chicken I had made for dinner but didn't get a chance to eat.

Chapter Thirty-Five

When I went into my pocket to check my phone for the time it wasn't there. I remembered that I had given it to Max so she could take her friend's call. At least I had an excuse for not letting her know where I disappeared to. Most likely, her toothy friend with the muscles had given her a ride home.

It didn't seem to be that late, but I decided to call it a day. With my stomach growling, I headed back to Max's place. I couldn't wait to share with her over dinner how I almost caught up with Tanner and about my lead that he might be at the pier for the tournament. Things were finally falling into place.

To celebrate I decided to duck into the Creamery to bring her a quart of homemade ice cream. That on top of the dinner I made for her should score me some extra points.

The line in the Creamery was a little longer than I had expected, but Max would understand. I never knew a woman as patient as she was. What a contrast to Kim who always complained that I was late, inconsiderate, self-centered, and on, and on. When I finally got up to the counter to place my order I noticed the clock hanging by the menu board. It couldn't be 10:45 already. I hoped that after the drum circle Max went straight home and took the chicken out of the oven or it would be burned to a crisp.

"A quart of chunky chocolate. Could you kinda step on it?"

The guy must have been the Ice Cream Despot because he took all his blessed time. Then halfway through filling the quart took another order before finishing mine.

With the ice cream in a bag I hoofed it down Canal Street toward Max's place. As I got away from the village center the road lighted only from the homes that ran along one side of the street gave me a sense of peace, the quiet punctuated by the sound of an occasional fish jumping in the canal on the other.

The few cars that went by put on their high beams and gave me wide berth. I passed Hicks' duplex house where my father had found the hotel key.

I wish I had asked Hicks what mementos he had left behind for Estelle. I was thinking that I had to ask her about it, when headlights from behind made me turn around. The car was big and barely creeping down the street. I thought of the old Pontiac I had seen around town, but in the dark, I couldn't tell if was the same vehicle. Probably someone looking for a house number.

I reached for my phone to call Estelle while it was on my mind. I patted my pockets then I remembered once again that I didn't have my lifeline. The car passed me. I watched as the car turned in a driveway, and headed back. If they were going to ask me for directions, I wouldn't be much help. I didn't know anyone around there.

When the car picked up speed I thought, good they're not going to stop. Then it seemed to be going way faster than it should on that street. The lights blinded me. I thought I was going to get hit. I dropped the bag with the ice cream and dove to the shoulder. I went down, tumbling in the grass. I tried to stop but couldn't and I landed in the canal.

"Asshole!" I yelled, but there was no one to hear me but the jumping fish.

I climbed out wet and muddy. I picked up the bag with the ice cream and pressed on down the road looking over my shoulder every few seconds. I kept telling myself it was just a drunken tourist, or someone texting while they drove. I wasn't doing a good job of convincing myself.

* * *

When I knocked at the door, Max answered it dressed in a robe. She didn't say not to, so I walked into her kitchen.

"The chicken was good," she said. I caught a tone in her voice that reminded me of my ex.

I felt something sticky under my shoes. The melted ice cream leaking through the bag had puddled at my feet.

"I got you some ice cream," I said, "but it…" I looked at the mess and threw the bag into the sink. "I can explain."

"I'm sure you had a good reason to abandon me," she said.

"I spotted Tanner and tried to follow him. You weren't exactly abandoned. You had your friend there."

"His name is Jeff. I introduced you."

"I couldn't hear at the time. Did he take you home?"

"I didn't feel like walking alone. He enjoyed your balsamic chicken. I saved you some." She started to walk out of the kitchen. "Good night. I'm going back to bed."

It was kind of early to be sleeping but I was in no position to question. She went down the hall to her bedroom and closed the door. Something told me that her idea of doing what "felt right" and mine were not going to be the same that night.

I grabbed a piece of chicken and headed home. Halfway across her lawn I remembered that she still had my phone. I went back in and called to her from the kitchen.

"I'm back. I forgot to get my phone." Silence. "Max?"

"What is it?" I heard from her bedroom.

"I need my phone."

"It's in my beach bag. I left it in the hall bathroom."

I found the beach bag hanging on the knob of the linen closet door. I rummaged through it but couldn't find the phone so I dumped the tote on the vanity. Found it. I started stuffing things back into the bag. As I picked them up I noticed that along with Max's hair products there was men's deodorant, men's shampoo, and shaving cream on the vanity. Jeff's? I was pretty sure he didn't live there. A frequent visitor? Apparently, I didn't know Max as well as I thought I did. I was going to confront her but I knew I had no right to. I was about to leave when Max came out of the bedroom in a short white robe.

"Are you still here?" she asked.

Was Jeff in there? I wasn't about to ask.

"I'm leaving," I said.

Chapter Thirty-Six

As tired as I was I couldn't go to bed after that. I went home and worked on case files at the coffee table until I eventually drifted off in the early hours.

I woke up hungry. I hadn't eaten anything since the piece of chicken I had grabbed before I bolted from Max's place the night before. I'm not the most pleasant guy when I wake up. I'm even less pleasant when I'm hungry. Combine those two with the lingering effects of being pissed off that I messed up my chances with Max and this had the makings of a lousy day even if the early morning sun over Ava Island promised otherwise.

If I was going to change the course of the day for the better, I needed food and fast. I drove down to the Double Yoke, a greasy spoon without the grease, and had a double stack of blueberry pancakes topped with a fried egg.

I spotted an older guy down by the end of the counter who reminded me of Big Al, but looked a little more down and out. I caught him eyeing my meal.

I was just about finished when he asked the waitress for the check. When she walked by me I signaled to her to stop.

"How much is it?" I asked.

"I'll get your check in a minute," she said.

"I mean his."

She looked at the old guy's check. "Two-fifty. He only had an English."

"Put it on my bill and then get him what I had. Tell him he won a free breakfast for being the millionth customer or something."

I paid her and left.

The old guy in the restaurant reminded me that I probably should see my father at some point. If I could catch him in a lucid moment I might be able to learn something to help clear him.

With all of the work that Big Al left unfinished that I had to wrap up, I knew I wouldn't have time to visit my father later in the day. Instead, I headed to The Palms at 7:45.

As I had predicted, it was another beautiful morning in Savannah but still cool enough for me to drive with the windows open. Finally feeling better now that I had a full belly, I had high hopes that I would have a productive day ahead of me.

For a change, I practically had my choice of spaces in the parking lot. Obviously, most people don't visit early in the morning unless the patient is in bad shape. I sat for a minute wondering if Big Al was awake. If he wasn't... duty served and I'd have a clear conscience. I just hoped that he wouldn't insist on tagging along with me for the day.

Thinking I might as well get it over with, I straggled from the truck. As I walked around a medi-transport parked by the entrance I caught a glimpse of a woman going around the other side of the vehicle toward the parking lot. In my mind, I developed a scenario in which she had been summoned in at this early hour to deal with a husband in crisis. Could the transport be for him? That's the problem with my line of work. You always look for the negative.

As I got to the door I noticed I had left my cell phone on my console and turned around. When I approached my truck, I recognized the woman I had passed at the van.

"Estelle?"

At first, she didn't seem to recognize me. Her face turned red when she realized who I was.

"Mr. DeLucia. You surprised me."

"Do you know someone here?"

She dug through her pocketbook and found a pair of sunglasses which she plopped on her face before she answered.

"Uh, why yes. An old friend. This is one of the better facilities, but it's still a horrible place." She sighed. "When the time comes for me, just shoot me."

At that moment, I felt sorry for her. She must have been sharing her biggest fear. I tried to make light of her remark.

"No can do. I'd go to jail. Besides, you're way too young to worry about that."

"Well, aren't you the silver-tongued devil," she said as she got into her car.

I put my hand on the door so she couldn't close it. "Would you mind telling me what mementos Hicks left for you at the empty apartment?"

Estelle frowned. "I wasn't kidding when I told you that I want you to drop the case."

I don't think Estelle grasped that now it wasn't just about finding out what happened to her daughter, Jill. I had to clear my father before Johnson decided he had enough evidence to press charges against him.

"Right, I understand. I'm not working for you now. But I'm curious. Can't you humor me?"

She huffed. "I'll bet you get that stubborn streak from your father. All right, I'll tell you. He left Jill's phone for me in the apartment. The mementos he was talking about were pictures she had on it. My son-in-law wanted me to have them. I guess he did have a heart after all. And before you ask, you can't see them. They're personal."

She must have been reading my mind because I would have loved to have gotten my hands on that phone. There might be all kinds of things I could learn from it.

"I get it," I said.

Tears started to well up in the corners of Estelle's eyes. "I wish I had never asked you to investigate."

What? Now she was laying a guilt trip on me?

"Oh?"

"Now my son-in-law is dead and while I didn't care for him, I'm sorry that he was murdered. And, I'm no closer to finding out where my daughter is."

I wanted to yell and tell her that her daughter was dead. But she'd heard that before. Like my father, she seemed to have her own reality and it was probably best to let her live in it.

"Okay, Estelle. But if I can do anything to help you out, you know how to reach me."

"No. I don't need anyone else getting hurt. Now if you don't take your hand off of my door I'm going to close it on your fingers."

I had no doubt that she would have. She drove off without even asking me what I was doing at The Palms. Odd. Although I think she knew my father was in a home, I never told her which one. Maybe she assumed that was where Big Al was. Or, maybe she didn't give a damn what I was doing there.

When I finally got into the building I was somewhat surprised to see that the facility had a completely different vibe at that time of day. Not that it was ever a cheerful place, but later in the day when visitors were likely to come in, there seemed to be an attempt to lighten the mood. I saw no groomed patients sitting in the solarium, no bingo games, no music. This was the business of daily life and in some cases death—bedridden patients receiving meds, dimly lit hallways with only the caregivers darting between rooms wheeling racks of covered breakfast trays. I noticed that every TV was tuned to the same channel, probably so the staff wouldn't miss a beat of the morning shows as they moved from one room to another. I understood why Estelle seemed down after calling on her friend. If the facility felt dispiriting during visiting hours, it was downright morose in the morning.

I stopped by my father's room. Al Roker was talking about the weather to an empty bed. My first thought was that my old man had kicked off. Shit. I didn't have time to deal with something like that. I put it out of my mind because I had mixed emotions about Big Al. I was sticking with my conviction that the day was going to get better, not more complicated.

I walked up to the nurse's station and spoke to an LPN that I did not recognize.

"I'm here to see Al DeLucia but I don't see him in his room. I'm his son."

"Oh, I think they are giving him a shower."

See. Simple explanation. "Okay. I was in the area and thought I'd drop in."

The nurse frowned. "Too bad. You missed your mother by a little bit."

"My mother?"

"Yes, she had breakfast with him. She's such a dear to help out every day. Mornings are so hectic around here." She picked up on the confusion that must have been plastered all over my face. "I'm sorry. I assumed Mr. DeLucia's wife was your mother."

Maybe I heard wrong. But she definitely said Mr. DeLucia's wife. I started to laugh.

"No. His wife…" I was going to go into the story about how he left, how my mother was dead. Then I decided it wasn't worth it. "I think you've got it wrong. My father isn't married."

The nurse frowned and looked at her chart. "Who did you say you are again?"

"Al DeLucia." She still wore her frown as if it was a badge of authority so to clarify I added, "Junior." I think it was the first time I actually used the word in reference to myself.

"I'm sorry if I spoke out of turn Mr. DeLucia."

"The woman you are talking about. Is her name Estelle?"

"I'm sorry. HIPAA. You understand."

No, I didn't understand. HIPAA my ass. Maybe she should have thought of that before she hit me with the news that my father had a wife.

"I uh, got to go. Maybe I'll get back later."

Somehow, I made my way out to the parking lot and into my truck. Estelle? Wife? WTF! I sat staring at the front door of The Palms thinking that at any moment Maryann Fena was going to come running out to tell me that the nurse was mistaken and Estelle Brewer was not married to my father. She was just a kind lady who visited every morning to help him with breakfast. Maryann never came out.

Estelle had struck me as being a caring person from the first minute I met her. Maybe she was a friend of the old man. On the other hand, the people at the nursing home wouldn't list Estelle as my father's wife without verification. Besides, she told me she lived up in Augusta. How could she live up there and visit my father every morning?

I could imagine asking Big Al's Magic Eight Ball if Estelle had some ulterior motive in asking me to find her daughter. When I turned over the imaginary ball, the little triangle floated into the window and read, "You can rely on it, Chump!"

Chapter Thirty-Seven

I t may have been cool when I arrived at The Palms but as the heat of the early morning sun intensified the truck became unbearable. Along with it, my disbelief turned to hot rage. I turned on the ignition and jacked the air conditioner to high then headed to the office.

When Greenleaf came in she caught me pouring vodka into a water glass. "It's only 8:30," she said. As if I needed to be reminded.

"I know what time it is. I've already been out and about. You're here early today. There's plenty to do. I'll pay you for the extra time."

"You know I'm on salary. I'm referring to that." She pointed to my drink.

"Beef Jerky Bloody Mary. My second breakfast today. Want one?"

"I don't see any tomato juice."

She was using that mother's martini voice—two parts disapproval and one-part worry.

I pulled the piece of beef jerky I was using as a swizzle stick out of the glass and took a bite out of it. "I don't like tomatoes. But, I can get you some and add a celery stick so you'll have all of the food groups covered."

She didn't seem amused as her eyes jumped from my rumpled clothes to the coffee table littered with papers.

"Did you sleep last night?"

"I worked late. I guess I forgot to go to bed."

"Your father used to do that too."

I wasn't sure if she was talking about staying up all night or drinking early in the morning. I suspect she meant both. I took a swig of vodka and turned on my laptop.

She picked up on my body language right away. "What's wrong?"

"When you gave Estelle Brewer my cell number…"

"That again? Move on."

"I'm trying to move on. But the more I try, the more I get sucked in. It's as if this agency is built on quicksand."

"Skip the melodrama, I told you I was sorry that I gave her your private number. Didn't you ever make a mistake?"

"Yes, my mistake was coming down here instead of going to LA. When you gave Estelle my phone number did you know who she was?"

Greenleaf's face was so tight I could hardly understand her when she spoke. "I might have seen her around."

"With my father? Is she a friend of his?"

She shrugged. "I guess you could say that."

"A close friend?"

"There's no law that says Big Al can't have friends. I'm his friend too."

I took that as a yes. "How close?"

"Define close."

"The staff at The Palms seems to think Estelle and my father were married. Is that correct?"

"Not exactly."

"You mean they were living together."

"No. I mean they are married."

So, it was true. "She told me she lost her husband."

"She did. Her first husband died years ago. He was a friend of your father's. The man didn't give any more of a hoot than a dead owl about Estelle. She had a major crisis in her family and she turned toward your father."

That didn't make me happy since my father had abandoned his own family. "Before or after her husband died?"

"I don't gossip."

That answered that question. So, my father was cheating with his friend's wife. I wasn't surprised.

"She told me her name is Brewer."

"She's a progressive woman. What can I say? That's the name she was born with. She didn't want to use either husband's last name."

"How long?"

"That they've been together? Twenty-five years."

Twenty-five years. Was I hearing things? That would mean that Big Al and Estelle got married right after he disappeared.

"Was he even divorced from my mother at the time?"

"I said they've been together twenty-five years. They got married a couple of years ago just after Big Al realized he was getting dementia."

"That's crazy." Or was it? As my father's wife Estelle would get everything that my father had.

"And if you're thinking that she married him to get his money, think again. He turned everything over to you first, at her suggestion."

I hate when Greenleaf does that to me. Hey, I didn't think it through. So what? It was a private thought that she had no right to snatch from my head.

"It's still crazy to marry someone who is losing their memory. Why didn't they get married before?"

"Estelle's husband died years ago, but your father was married."

"He could have come out of the woodwork and asked my mother for a divorce. At least we would have known he was alive."

"Look this isn't for me to say. Ask your father for the details." Greenleaf started to walk toward the office.

That would be fine if he could remember them. Or if I could catch him in the right frame of mind.

"You know that isn't going to work."

Greenleaf cast her eyes down. "Maybe it is time for you to know. Who can get hurt now? Your mother couldn't give him the divorce. She would lose his pension and she needed that in addition to what he sent every month to raise you."

My brain was bouncing around like a tennis ball at the U. S. Open.

"Are you saying my mother knew Big Al was alive and didn't tell me?"

"Don't blame her. It was a decision they came to together. They thought it was best for you to think he had died."

So that explained how he had my school picture and knew what teams I followed. "What about Estelle? She said she lived up in Augusta."

"She did until recently. Her first husband had a horse farm up there. She would make frequent visits down here or your father would go up there."

"You knew this all along and you never told me."

"It wasn't my place. Still isn't. But I think you have a right to know. And now you do."

I still wanted to know why he left in the first place but I doubt if Greenleaf would tell me.

"I'm kind of busy here." I didn't mean that to sound as bad as it did. Even though Greenleaf was a pain at times I shouldn't take my problems out on her. What I was trying to say was I couldn't wrap my head around everything that was going on.

"I'm busy myself." Greenleaf started for the door then turned. "You're not going to find your father in a glass. And the killer isn't in there either." She went back to her office.

"If you're going to lecture, me tell me something I don't know," I said under my breath.

She didn't leave me alone for long. In a little while she returned and threw a stack of folders on my desk.

"Some old cases I picked at random. Whenever your father had a mental block he would go over old cases. It usually gave him an idea."

I caught myself short of telling her to take the rest of the day off so I could have some space to think. She meant well, and I knew she was the backbone of the agency, but I was tired and in no mood to be treated like a kid.

"Maybe later if I get a chance."

"Suit yourself."

She didn't mean suit yourself at all. It was clear that she thought she knew what was best for me.

Chapter Thirty-Eight

I needed some air. When Greenleaf went into her office I took my drink and went out on the porch. I purposely didn't hold the screen door so that it slammed behind me.

I sipped my vodka and watched the live oak rain leaves. If Greenleaf had known about my father being married to Estelle she should have told me. I was sure I was right about that. Yet somehow, she managed to twist everything around until she was pissed off at me.

My phone rang.

"Mr. DeLucia, this is Maryann Fena." Her voice was so shaky that I hardly recognized it. Had my father died after all? Damn.

"What's wrong?"

"Your father is missing."

Well, that was better than dying. Not much, but better.

"He probably just went for a walk. He'll come back."

"No, it's been a while."

"I was just there this morning. He was in the shower."

"I'm afraid that whoever told you that was mistaken."

Mistaken, or they were lying to me in hopes of finding him before I found out?

"What else aren't you telling me?"

The rest of the conversation was a blur. I told her I was headed right down but she said it would be better if I waited for word from her.

I sat down on the porch swing and tried to process the whole mess. The father that I didn't know I had was accused of murder and now he'd gone missing. The woman who hired me to prove her daughter wasn't dead turned out to be my stepmother. On top of that my new girlfriend, who was my superior in the agency I owned, had obviously been hooking up with another guy.

What was I doing wrong? Nobody could have such a run of bad luck and not have some responsibility for it. This had to be the lowest point in my life of low points. As I got up to go inside to tell Greenleaf about my father, a mail truck pulled into the lot. Good. Even a shitload of junk mail would be a diversion.

I was surprised when the letter carrier got out of the truck and approached the porch.

* * *

"Registered letter." She handed me a clipboard and pointed to where I had to sign. I looked at the sender's address: a law firm in Santa Monica. My heart began to race. At last. I was getting my money back from the condo. I scratched my name on the form. "Thank you!"

"Must be good news," she said when she saw my smile.

"Oh yeah. And I could use good news in more ways than one."

"You have a good day." She handed me a fist full of junk mail, most of which were credit card offers, got into her truck and drove off.

I threw the junk mail on the swing and sat next to it as I ripped open the envelope from the attorney and pulled out a three-page letter. California here I come. I began to read out loud.

"Dear Mr. DeLucia."

I shook the pages to see if a check would fall out. No. I read some more, silently now. I stood up and the whole yard was a blur as the world spun even worse than it had on the big bridge. I balled up the letter and threw it on the swing with the junk mail. Not only didn't I get my money back but I owed taxes and attorney's fees on the condo I would never live in.

"Damn!"

"Who's Dan?" Greenleaf called out from inside.

"I didn't say Dan."

"Who then?

"Forget it."

I didn't need an eight ball to tell me that this sucked big time. I drew in my breath and held it a few seconds; repeat, repeat, repeat. I felt calmer and my vision cleared. Okay, so I had one more thing to deal with. I'd find a way.

I told my phone to call the Ava Island Police Department. When they answered, I asked for Johnson. When they connected him, I had to stick a pin into his cheery hello.

"Hey, I don't know if you heard. My old man went missing from The Palms. As far as I know, they notified the department."

"This is news to me. But I'm going to look into it right now."

"Yeah. I'm not worried yet, but you know."

"Like I said… and I'll get back to you."

I could only imagine what was going through Johnson's mind. In light of the fact that my father was a murder suspect I didn't want to tell him that someone from The Palms had been allowing Big Al to go on his little jaunts on a regular basis. Friend or no friend, Johnson had a job to do, but I didn't have to give him any more ammunition to use against the old man.

* * *

As I was about to go inside I spotted a familiar red Mustang parked across the street. Too familiar in fact. It was an exact duplicate of the car I had wrecked on the Pearl Harbor Memorial Bridge back home. Leaning against the hood and leering at me was Psycho's clone. It was freakin' Batshit.

Batshit watched as I jumped off the porch and sprinted across the lot toward the Mustang. If that jerk was looking for trouble he had come to the right place. When I got almost to the street Batshit held up his phone and took a picture to taunt me and then hopped into the car. The Mustang's engine roared as its tires peeled. Then he made a sudden U-turn. The car fishtailed and he almost sideswiped me. I tried to jump out of the way and felt my hands pushing off from the rear fender in an effort not to land under the wheels. My face almost made nice with the bumper before I bounced to the pavement. As he raced down the road in the direction of the bridge to the mainland two things registered in my noggin: the car had Georgia plates and there was a barcode on the bumper. It seemed Batshit got a rental to almost exactly match the Mustang I had wrecked on him back in Connecticut. Either he liked that car a great deal or he was trying to send me a message.

Well, that opened up a whole new set of possibilities to explain what was going on. The notes, Andy Keller's murder, Hick's assassination—Batshit could have been involved in all of them. So far, I had nothing to connect him with Keller's murder, but Hicks' was a different story. Assuming Batshit was the one leaving the notes, I couldn't overlook the fact that the note on my truck proved that Batshit was in Hilton Head when Hicks ended up dead. For all I knew he could have even somehow aligned himself with Tanner. On the other hand, he could have only been playing some kind of mind game with me. If he was, the drug dealer was smarter than I had given him credit for because he was getting to me. Or, he could have been exactly what his name implied: batshit crazy.

Chapter Thirty-Nine

Seeing Batshit threw me even more off my game. The last I knew he was on vacation courtesy of the Connecticut State Prison System. So how could he have been watching my place?

I gave Charlie Moss a call. He must have seen my name on the caller ID because he knew it was me.

"Al, how's it going, man? I know you didn't call me to rub in how nice the weather is down there in Georgia."

Charlie is always upbeat. It may be because he's from the Midwest.

"You're right. But since you brought it up, it's 79 and sunny here today; and every day."

"Loser."

Charlie was breaking balls but little did he know that I was feeling a bit like a loser.

"Up yours," I said. "Talking about losers what can you give me on our friend Batshit?"

"Funny you should ask. He was released from Enfield two weeks ago. Some lawyer got him out on a technicality. The asshole actually said right on the news that even though Batshit was most likely guilty, upholding the law was more important."

I didn't have to guess. "The attorney is from the Yale Law School."

"You must be a genius, Bro. You want a good laugh? Listen to this. Batshit's real name is Poindexter Cockburn."

Imagine Charlie making fun of the guy's name. I guess even happy people from the Midwest are politically incorrect at times.

"Well I'll let you go," I said.

"Do you know where he is?"

"Me? No. Why?"

"It took him all of three days before he violated his parole by not checking in."

Was Charlie surprised by that? "Maybe he'll get off on a technicality for that one too," I said.

"Why are you asking about Batshit anyway?"

"I was thinking of life up in the frozen north and he popped into my mind. I thought I'd ask. Hey, someone is at the door. Peace, man. Keep in touch."

I hung up. I knew that if I told Charlie that Batshit was on Ava Island he would contact the police department and things would get complicated. I didn't need cops coming around mucking things up when I had to find Big Al. Things were already complicated enough.

Charlie confirmed what I wanted to know. Batshit was out of jail so that could possibly have been him that I saw watching the place.

If it was, what the hell did he want? It wasn't an accident that he was parked across the street from the agency. It could be that he had dropped by to satisfy his curiosity. Fine. Now get lost. One thing was certain, if he was here to get even with me for Psycho's death he was messing with the wrong guy. Whichever the case, I had too much on my mind to waste time on that dickwad.

* * *

I started looking at the files Greenleaf gave me even though I couldn't see how looking at old cases would help. Still, Greenleaf seemed to think that doing so would allow me to see things more clearly. I slid the stack of folders closer. It wouldn't hurt to give it a try.

The first file was the back-injury case that I had just worked on. I knew more than I wanted to know about that case. No sense in looking at that one. I picked up the second folder, a divorce case my father worked on ten years before. It involved two couples who split and then traded spouses in a double wedding. Interesting but I'd seen that situation before.

I had the feeling eyes were on me. Every once in a while, I'd look up and catch Greenleaf glancing toward me through the open door.

"Thanks," I yelled.

"There's no reason why you should shout," she called out.

"But then you'd have nothing to complain about."

The third file caught my attention. The thick packet was yellowed and had coffee rings and frayed edges from years of handling. I read the label on the tab: Granville. Random my ass. It was obvious that she wanted me to familiarize myself with my father's magnum opus because she thought it had something to do with Keller's murder. If she knew something helpful about the case, which I was sure that she did, I wished that she would come out and tell me.

"Granville?"

"Are you reading it?" she said from the other room.

"No."

When I looked up Greenleaf was standing in my door. "Do you know anything about the case?" she asked.

Greenleaf tended to repeat stories not because she was senile but because she wanted to drum them into your brain.

"You told me about it, remember? I don't see what this has to do with anything," I said.

Other than what she had told me, I had not been interested in finding out much more about Granville. Maybe it was time that I became familiar with what the old man did back in the day.

At first, I thumbed through the pages, then I began carefully reading every word.

I knew that there was something in that file that she wanted me to find out for myself because in her opinion I was stubborn and that I most likely would ignore anything that she told me. That wasn't necessarily correct. On the other hand, it wasn't necessarily incorrect.

I perused my father's long-closed case wondering what Greenleaf thought I could learn and how it would help me locate my father. I wasn't getting a damned thing out of the exercise.

I tossed the file aside and reviewed the fourth folder in the pile—a background check on a chemist who was going to do some sensitive work for a local company. Tedious stuff. Every once in a while, when my eyes grew tired I'd catch myself glancing at the Granville file that I had thrown aside.

Screw it. I decided to take another quick peek to see what was so damned special about Granville. An hour and a half later I was still reading. Finally, I put the file down and rested my neck on the back of the couch. As I stared at the ceiling I asked myself what the hell I was doing. It was an interesting case without a doubt—a small child kidnapped from the home of a local racecar driver. So what? I had once helped find the missing wife of Yale University's president. It turned out she wasn't actually kidnapped. She was having an affair with the president of Harvard. Still, I did find her on a private island in Long Island Sound. Of course, that story never hit the papers and I never got a citation.

I was wasting my time. No more. I gathered the pages of the file together and as I tapped them on the table to put them back into the file, a napkin from Old Salty's, a restaurant in the village, fell out. Written in a chicken scratch that I had seen on other papers my father had written was A.K. with D.G, 4:00. If A.K. stood for Andy Keller it could be that my father had a connection with him after all.

"Greenleaf!" I called.

She was in the doorway in seconds. "If you insist on working back there, maybe you should invest in an intercom."

"We're closing up. Remember? No sense in investing in hardware now."

She scoffed. "So, what is it then?"

"Did my father know Andy Keller?"

"Not that I know of. But I don't know everyone he is acquainted with."

"Could you look through his appointment book to see if he ever had a 4:00 with Andy Keller?"

"What date?"

"That's what I want to know. Go back as far as you have to. You only need to look at 4:00 p.m. appointments."

She sighed and walked back to her desk.

"Greenleaf." I called after her.

"What?"

"Thank you."

I heard a distinct mumble which I didn't care to have her repeat.

An hour later Blue Palmetto's indispensable administrative assistant was back at my door.

"I didn't exactly find Andy Keller's name but your father had a four o'clock with an A.K. a little over a month ago. In fact, it was on the 16th, the day before he signed himself into The Palms. I didn't find it in the appointment book. If it had been in there I would have put it in and I would have used the full name. I found the initials penciled in on his desktop calendar. If they met here at 4:00 I would have been gone for the day."

"Al wrote the note on the napkin and again on his calendar. It must have been important."

"Don't talk of him as if he's dead. Al realized, and still does, that his short-term memory isn't good so he writes everything down sometimes in multiple places so that he won't forget. My guess is that Big Al was at Old Salty's when he made an appointment with Andy Keller for 4:00. He wrote it on the napkin and then came back here and put it on the calendar to double ensure that he would remember."

"I don't remember mentioning Old Salty's. You knew the napkin was in that file, didn't you?"

Her face grew red but she held her ground and looked me square in the face. "Maybe."

I stood up. "Come on. I'm taking you to Old Salty's for lunch."

I could tell that she was wondering if I was kidding.

"I'm not paying," she said.

Chapter Forty

Ava Island Village was hopping with tourists and there was hardly a parking space to be had. Not good news for the residents of the island but damned good news for the business owners. The few off street spaces directly in front of Old Salty's Bar and Grill were filled, as I had expected. As I drove past, I glanced at the parking lot at the Village Plaza. There might be a few spaces there due to Demarco's diligent eyeballing of who parked in the lot, but I knew that our new-found friendship did not come with parking privileges. I hung a right to get to the town parking lot—full to capacity as expected. I turned and drove along a residential street a block behind the business district and found a place to park along the street.

"I guess I could park here and hope I don't get a ticket."

Of course, that wasn't good enough for Greenleaf.

"I'm not walking all the way back to the restaurant. It's too hot. Can't you drop me off?"

It's not like she was out of shape or too feeble. She rode that Schwinn of hers all over the island every day. I inhaled deeply and counted to five. The space would probably be gone when I returned, but she was right, it was a walk. I drove back to Ocean Boulevard, this time approaching Old Salty's from the opposite side of the road. Demarco spied me as we drove past "his" lot and gave me a tip of his hat, but didn't motion for me to drive in.

"Stop!" Greenleaf practically jumped out of her seat belt as she screamed out.

Tourists are always crossing outside of the crosswalks. I hit the brake looking for someone in the street. "What?"

"Some people are going to their car."

I spotted an older couple walking down the steps from the deck of the restaurant, the woman carrying a doggie bag. "You don't expect me to hold up traffic until they get ready to leave do you?"

"Why not? It will give the cars behind us a chance to look around at the stores instead of zipping down the street. You'll be helping business."

I don't know if the old guy was being territorial or not but he was taking his sweet time about getting out of the parking space. Meanwhile the guy behind us in a white BMW convertible was honking his horn.

"Let me pull up to the crosswalk and let you out then I'll find a spot."

As I pulled ahead a few feet the geezer pulled out of the space in front of the restaurant and the white BMW behind me took the parking space.

"See," Greenleaf said.

Frustrated and eager to see if anyone in Old Salty's remembered Keller and my father being there, I pulled into the parking lot at the real estate office next to the restaurant and parked. I'd keep an eye on the truck while we ate and if they called a tow truck, as the sign threatened, I'd run over and move it. Even if I had to pay the tow charge it would be worth it if only not to hear Greenleaf complain.

We chose to sit at the picnic tables on the deck. As luck would have it, the hostess sat us across from the Beemer Guy who was soon joined by a woman half his age. He glanced toward our table and smirked at us.

I turned toward Greenleaf. "I'm having the grouper sandwich."

"I don't eat endangered fish," she said.

"If this was an endangered variety it wouldn't be on the menu. But don't let me force you. What would you like?"

"I'll take the alligator," she said with a straight face that quickly broke into a smile. "Don't look so shocked. I'm kidding. I'll have the catfish and chips."

Who would have guessed that Greenleaf had a sense of humor?

The waiter came and she gave him our order before I could open my mouth. I didn't expect anything less from someone who ran the office with the efficiency that she did. "He'll pick up the check." She pointed to me.

When the waiter left she leaned in to whisper to me. "Do you mean you came here just for lunch? I thought you'd ask about your father."

"I was going to." I should have told her that she never gave me a chance, but she was actually pleasant to be around when she was in a good mood. I didn't want to break that spell.

The waiter brought us two beers. I grabbed mine and took a swallow.

"We didn't do cheers," she said and held up her glass. "To Blue Palmetto!"

"To Blue Palmetto." As we clinked glasses I silently amended the toast. *To closing Blue Palmetto.*

"Eye contact!" she yelled. "If you don't make eye contact it's seven years' bad luck." She made her eyes big and stuck her face in mine. "You like Max?"

She caught me off guard. "Yeah. Why?"

"I mean do you l-i-i-i-k-e her?"

"I don't know." I gave my shoulders a quick shrug. I knew Greenleaf thought that I meant I didn't know if I cared for Max or not. But what I meant was that of course I liked her, but what I didn't know was how everything fell apart between us.

"What do you mean you don't know? You're acting like a teenager. Either you do or you don't."

No. I was definitely not a teenager and I didn't like being treated like one. I was a grown man with grown man problems.

"It's not a good idea for me to get involved with Max."

"Why not? For heaven's sake? You enjoy being around her. I can see it."

"When it's time for leaving, what then?"

I had no idea how much I inherited from my father. I cared too much for Max to someday just up and leave her, either aggressively by walking away or passively by losing my memory.

"You'll figure it out."

I hoped Greenleaf didn't think that now we were best pals and that I was going to share my sex life with her. She had already goaded me into saying too much. I was about to ask her why she wanted to know when the waiter arrived with our order.

He was about Keller's age and dressed in a pirate outfit.

"Do you remember serving a young dude with blond dreadlocks and an older man who wore a khaki bush hat? Say about three weeks ago," I asked.

"Man, you don't realize how many people come in here every day. Three weeks ago may as well be three months ago."

Greenleaf took the waiter by the arm and pulled him close to her. "The guy with the bush hat probably asked for a special order; grouper head stew. With the eyes. You remember now?"

"I'd remember that if it were three years ago. Sorry."

I took out a $20 bill and handed it to him.

"I didn't give you the check yet."

"It's an extra tip. Ask some of the other wait staff if they remember. If I get what I'm looking for you'll get another one."

Greenleaf was tackling her catfish and chips like she hadn't eaten in a month. In between bites she kept looking in my eyes as if she were going to hypnotize me so I would spill to her how I felt about Max. I wasn't going to tell her that it didn't matter since Max had other interests.

I was getting creeped out by Greenleaf's behavior so I was relieved when the waiter came back with a co-worker, a twenty-something in a lady pirate outfit who could fire a cannonball across my bow any day.

"Phil says you're looking for someone who remembers the old gent in the khaki bush hat."

"Do you?"

"For sure. He ordered the grouper stew and paid for it with a hundred-dollar bill. He told me to keep the change. It had to be my biggest tip ever."

Yeah, my father the big spender. You would have thought that he could have sent some money when I was a kid. Or did he? I was going to have to reevaluate what I knew about our "relationship" during that time of my life.

"What about the guy he was with?"

"You mean Andy? I knew him from the beach." Her face tightened. "He's dead you know. I saw on Twitter that someone killed him."

"Yeah. That's the one."

"Do you remember what they were talking about?"

"I work my feet off serving these people. I don't have time to listen in on the customer's conversations."

After thinking about it, I could have phrased that question in a different way.

"Fair enough. Is there anything else you remember?"

"Only that Andy was recording with his phone as they were talking. I figured it was an interview. He was a blogger, you know.

Her voice cracked.

"You don't think the old guy did it, do you? Killed Andy, I mean."

Greenleaf stirred a bit in her seat.

"No. He's my father." I said it as if it explained it all when in fact it explained nothing.

"Ah," the waitress said leaning inward. "When I gave them the check Andy mentioned to me that they were going to Waycross after they had lunch," she said. "I don't know if that means anything to you."

I gave her a twenty. The same as I had given the first waiter.

She looked at it in her hand and put on a weird smile.

"You're not your father."

"I appreciate that," I said as she went about her business.

Greenleaf mumbled something under her breath about no respect.

"What do you know about Waycross?" I asked.

"It's a small town about two hours from here. They call it the gateway to the Okefenokee Swamp," Greenleaf said. "You know, where Pogo comes from."

"Who?"

"Forget it."

"You seem to know a lot about the place. Why the heck would my father go to Waycross with Andy Keller? And who was their 4:00 meeting with?"

Greenleaf stopped chewing and was rolling her tongue over her teeth. I couldn't help to notice that the eye contact that was so important to her a few minutes before was missing.

"Humm," she said finally. "Big Al knows people out in Waycross."

"What people?"

"I remember the name Givens from way back in the Dark Ages. They're a couple, Daryl and Avalou. Your father married them."

Now that was a shocker. "Don't tell me he's a minister." If he was, no doubt it was the mail order variety so that he could scam people.

Greenleaf laughed out loud. "Oh, Sweet Jesus save us! No. But he is a justice of the peace. Still, I'm not sure if it's legal or not." She shook her head.

First, I learned that my father eats fish eyes and now that he can marry people. I wondered what else I didn't know.

"Who are these friends?"

"Daryl and Avalou Givens. They used to visit once in a while then at some point they stopped. I don't remember why or when. I thought maybe they had died."

"You must have a theory why he'd bring Keller out there."

"I may." She looked away as if she were trying to find a safe place to hide.

"Care to share it?"

Maybe she found that safe place to hide deep inside of her because she came back with an emphatic, "No."

"Why not?"

"If I did that, I might be spreading something that wasn't true and that could cloud your entire vision of the case. But if you come to the same conclusion, I'll be sure to let you know."

I whipped out my phone and did a little research. It wasn't long before I found an address for Daryl Givens in Waycross.

"Okay then. I'll bring you back and I'm heading out to Waycross. I always wanted to see The Okefenokee Swamp."

Chapter Forty-One

In my perfect world, I would find not only my father at the Givens place but the answer to who killed Keller and Hicks.

I was hoping for that perfect world as I put the F-150 through its paces while Batshit's untrustworthy GPS lead me down I-95 south.

Now there was a thought. Maybe Batshit showed up because he wanted his navigation system back. I laughed and jammed the pedal to the floor. Damn him, I had enough to deal with without him stalking me and leaving stupid messages on my windshield.

With that out of my system, I brought the truck down to ten miles over the speed limit until I got to the double bridge to Champney Island. With lots of adrenalin and luck, I got over the span with a minimum of head spin and a lot of clutching of the wheel only to find I had to cross a similar bridge to get off the island.

With the bridges behind me I exited I-95 at Brunswick to U.S. 82 west. That last sixty miles to Waycross, the flat terrain hosted little more than farmland and the occasional tin roofed house with the requisite car on blocks and barking pit bull on a chain.

Two hours after dumping Greenleaf off at the office, I reached the humid little burg of Waycross, a railway center on the edge of that giant drainage pond called The Okefenokee Swamp. I parked at a Wendy's in sight of a white water tower painted with the words Welcome to Waycross. I went in and got some food and brought it to an outside table. An African American couple with a little girl was seated at the next table. The little girl, about two years old, waved at me.

"How are you today?" I asked between bites of hamburger.

The child pointed to the water tower. She seemed to be fascinated by a cartoon painted on it.

"Pogo," she said to me.

"Let the man eat," the father said.

"Pogo."

"You mean the teddy bear on the tower?" I asked.

The father put a straw in the child's milk carton. "That's not a bear. Pogo's an opossum from a comic strip."

"He lives in the swamp," the mother said.

"Right, Pogo." So, Greenleaf was talking about a comic strip character.

When I got in the truck, I held in the home button and spoke into my cell. "How big is The Okefenokee Swamp?"

The little lady that lives in my phone gave me a quick response. "Checking my sources for you." There was a slight pause. "Here is information from the web."

According to my phone, The Big O is a shallow, 684 sq. mile, peat-filled wetland straddling the Georgia–Florida line. In addition to alligators and snakes, it is home to the black and orange warmouth, a tough hitting pan fish.

Johnson had talked about going fishing someday. When all of this mess was over maybe we could organize a fishing trip. We could bring the old man along too, if he showed up by then.

My cell rang and Max's picture appeared on the face of the phone. I hit the accept button on the second ring.

"Did Greenleaf tell you about Big Al taking off from The Palms?" I asked.

"She did. That's why I'm calling. I just got off the phone with Major Johnson. Big Al's been spotted in several places around Chatham County and even here on the island, so he's okay. It's just a matter of them catching up with him."

"How hard can it be to find an old man with a shot memory?" Ouch, that needed a disclaimer. "I'm not taking it out on you, I'm just saying."

"I know Big Al better than you…" Now it was Max's turn to backpedal.

181

"What I mean is I'm confident that even though he has his problems he knows what he's doing on a professional level. I think he can take care of himself, but I'm still worried. Like you."

"Call me if you hear anything else."

With my short rest all but ruined, I headed to the Givens property on Swamp Road about a half hour outside of the Waycross town center. The narrow road went on through lonely forest for so long that I concluded that Daryl and Avalou were people who valued their privacy. I wondered how welcome I would be to come knocking out of the blue.

My gas gauge was showing that my fuel was getting low so I was happy when the finicky GPS told me to turn down what seemed to be a poorly paved driveway. If Batshit's GPS was wrong, and the Givens' house wasn't ahead I might end up out of gas in the most desolate place I had ever seen. I was relieved to eventually come up on a weathered little woman in old-fashioned pants that stopped just below her knees. She was using a small blow torch to strip paint from an old chest of drawers. Behind her stood a one-story ranch style house of concrete block that, judging from the out dated jalousie windows of narrow glass slats, seemed to have survived at least fifty or sixty scorching summers. It looked as inviting as a kiln.

She switched off the torch when I parked. "Can I help you?" Her tone gave no hint of welcoming.

"Are you Avalou Givens?"

I got out and was standing at the front bumper of the truck when she put up her hand to halt me.

"That's right. Are you a salesman? Because if you are, there's a clearly written posted sign at the foot of the driveway." She put her hands on her hips. "That goes for bill collectors as well."

"I'm not selling anything, honest. And I don't like collection agents either."

"Well then." She seemed to relax a bit.

In the distance behind the house a huge black cloud rose up against the blue sky. Tornado was my first thought.

"What's that?" I asked.

"It's smoke. The Okefenokee is burning again. You get used to the ash, the smell not so much."

"Can't be good for the environment, or your lungs either."

"Tell me about it. Now they want to build a titanium mine next to the swamp. Daryl and I are fighting it with the Sierra Club. It doesn't make us popular with the people who say the mine will bring jobs. But then we never were all that popular around here. What did you say you want?"

"I'm here to talk about the Granville kidnapping."

"Oh." She turned on her torch and continued to bubble paint from the chest and scrape it off with a putty knife. "I think you should leave."

"I just have a few questions," I said. There was a feeling in my gut that this little lady could be dangerous. I told my imagination to keep itself in check.

"Don't say I didn't warn you." Then she screamed, "Daryl!"

With that a shot rang out and ricocheted off the driver's door of my F-150 just a few feet behind me. Avalou dropped the torch and ran into the house as the flaming canister spun wildly on the driveway.

What the hell just happened? In hindsight, I should have introduced myself; maybe mentioned my father. But no, not me. I had to come right out and announce that I wanted to question them about Grandville. All of this went through my mind as I lunged forward and rolled as I hit the ground before scrambling around to the passenger side of the truck.

"Do you want every cop in the county down on you?"

I chanced a peek above the passenger door toward a steel barn about 200 feet away. The bullet must have come from there.

I opened the door and hugging the floorboard, I managed to get my hand in the glove compartment to retrieve my Glock.

"Is that you Daryl?" I shouted as I crouched beside the truck. I was answered by another gunshot.

"There's no need for this, Daryl. I only want to ask a few questions. But I'm warning you. I am armed and if I have to shoot back I will. You should know, I don't miss."

I guess Daryl wasn't impressed because another shot rang out and the driver's side front tire of the truck exploded.

With one eye on the house, in case Avalou started firing from there, I got off a warning shot that, if anything, proved that I could hit the broad side of a barn.

Daryl answered by destroying the back tire on the driver's side. The truck lowered itself with the awkwardness of a kneeling camel. I smelled gasoline and watched it puddle under the chassis. As it formed a rivulet down the driveway toward Avalou's torch, I scrambled to my feet, fired off one shot in the general direction of the steel shed to gain time before I ran like hell. There was a slight pop and a whoosh like when you start up a gas grill. My truck was soon engulfed in flames.

As I dove away from the fire and heat, I felt like Ivan the Great shot out of a circus cannon. My arms and legs spread as I flew. I realized too late there was no net.

Chapter Forty-Two

The next thing I remember was waking up on a couch with two women standing over me. One of them was Avalou. "Don't get up," she said.

My eyes darted around the room.

"Stay down," Avalou ordered.

I tried to sit up anyway. There was another woman too. My eyes darted looking for Daryl and his gun. My head throbbed and I put my hand to it. I felt a damp bandage and when I pulled my hand away I saw blood on my fingers.

"Every cop in the county will be here," I said to Avalou.

"We're country. Nobody pays a mind to gunshots." The other woman was matter of fact.

"Who the hell are you?"

"Daryl. I'm afraid it's all my fault. I didn't realize you were Big Al's son, or I wouldn't have shot at you."

She handed me my wallet.

"You should rest a bit." Her voice was anything but that of an armed assassin.

"I don't need rest. I needed answers." I tried to get off of the couch but my head had ideas of its own. I plopped back down. "Maybe I'll just sit a minute."

Avalou frowned and sat in a wicker rocker. "Yes, you rest. Daryl will get us something to drink."

Daryl disappeared and soon came back with three cans of Dr. Pepper.

She handed a soda to me. "You said you had questions. Shoot."

Avalou giggled at the expression. I didn't think it was that funny.

"I need to know about my father. Did he come out here with a young surfer type named Keller?"

"Andy. He's such a nice boy. Your father brought him by about a month ago. Andy was writing about the Granville Kidnapping to put it on the Internet. Why are you asking?" Avalou clutched the rocker as if she were worried that the answer would make her fall off.

"Keller was murdered and my father has disappeared."

"What!" Tears formed in Avalou's eyes.

"You're not saying your father had anything to do with Andy's death. Are you?" Daryl asked.

"I'm not. But the police think he might." I would think that the Granville Kidnapping had been covered to death in the papers back in the day. "Why would my father want Keller to bring the kidnapping up again after all of these years?"

"That surprised me too," Daryl said. "Your daddy never wanted a lot of publicity about it. But he said it was time, and that the boy could be trusted to do a fair report. But he also warned us that some people would be upset and to watch out if strangers came around. That's how the misunderstanding with you happened. I thought you were one of those strangers who he warned us about."

Misunderstanding. Is that what she called almost killing me?

"Mr. Keller was mostly interested in learning about Georg Gerber," Avalou said.

"Why the focus on Gerber?"

"He's the man who was accused of kidnapping Christmas Granville." Avalou's tone seemed to question why I wouldn't know that.

But I did know that. I had read the name Gerber in the file. "Still, in all of the times someone brought up the Granville kidnapping to me since I arrived in Georgia, no one ever talked about the kidnapper."

"But that's the thing," Daryl said. "We never believed it was a kidnapping even though Georg confessed to having the child stay with his family for a while. Georg worked as a handyman on Granville's estate in Augusta. He and his wife had rented the cabin from us in June of that summer so their little boy could do some fishing. They planned on staying three months. We got to know the family a little before the troubles started.

"Then toward the end of July, the Granville toddler disappeared. The police named Georg as a suspect. Their evidence was based mostly on a ransom note written by someone who might be German, and tools that were used to open the window to the nursery had Georg Gerber's fingerprints all over them."

"Martin Granville hired your father to find him. Big Al traced Gerber to our cabin," Avalou said.

"Was the girl there?"

"No, just the little boy, their own son." Avalou held back from tearing up again.

"After he was arrested, Georg insisted that Martin Granville had paid for the cabin and asked the Gerbers to watch the girl," Daryl said.

"So, Georg Gerber admitted that he took the girl?"

Avalou clasped her hand over her heart as if she were pledging allegiance. "Not exactly. He claimed the Granvilles were having marital troubles and Martin was worried that if they divorced, his wife would never give him custody of the child. Georg claimed Granville sent his daughter to stay with them for a few days until he could straighten things out with his wife."

"Of course, nobody, especially not the jury, believed him."

"I believed him," Avalou said.

Daryl touched Avalou on her back. "Yes, you always did, my dear. You were the only one."

"If Granville was behind his own daughter's disappearance, why would he hire my father to investigate?"

Avalou became so agitated that she sprang from her seat. "Because he had an agenda, that's why. He wanted to destroy his wife."

"So, he hired your father to make it look good." Daryl was turning the can of Dr. Pepper in her hands.

"Your father and Martin Granville had a mutual friend, Gil Johnson.

Johnson was a cop and when Martin insisted on hiring a private investigator Johnson recommended Big Al. You know the rest," Avalou said.

"Maybe he doesn't know all of it, Avalou. I'll tell him." Daryl continued. "Big Al started tracking Gerber north after Granville gave him a roadmap that he said he found in one of his barns. The markings on the map indicated a route to Ohio where Georg had family. But your father didn't find any trace of someone who had seen them along the way; no stops for gas or food, no motel stays, nothing. Big Al got almost to Charlotte, North Carolina when he realized that maybe the map showing the route to Ohio was left behind to throw everyone off the track. He started heading south in the opposite direction."

Each woman was so eager to share the story with someone hearing it for the first time that I could only imagine how many times the two of them had discussed this between themselves over the years. Avalou took over again.

"He found a gas station attendant in Waynesboro who said that a tall light-haired man with a little dark-haired girl came in to get some snacks after pumping gas. The attendant thought them an odd pair. He looked out the window at their white truck. It was dark and he couldn't make out who was in it but he assumed it was the child's mother. He remembered the man asked directions on how to get back on the highway headed south. The gas attendant noticed fishing gear in the vehicle. Al searched every gas station and restaurant on the road headed south for three days, finding several people who remembered the man and the truck. By that time, he was close to the Okefenokee and he had a hunch based on the fishing gear the attendant saw. He went place to place looking for someone who fit the description of Georg Gerber and Christmas Granville. When he got here we told him that we never saw the little girl, but of course we knew Georg was our tenant." Avalou was shaking as she told the tale.

"Please, Avalou. You're getting all upset. Let me finish the story." Daryl turned to me. "We told him that a man named Gerber and his family were renting a fishing cabin from us about two miles from here."

"Was the Granville child there when my father found Gerber?"

"Georg's wife swore that a lady with an English accent came to take the girl back to Granville," Avalou said. "They found a sweater that belonged to Christmas on the clothesline. That sealed poor Georg's fate. The wife said she had washed it and forgot to give it to the woman who picked up the child. I believe the story. If Georg did kidnap the child, why would they leave the sweater in plain sight?"

"People do strange things," I said. "I understand the child was never found."

"The ransom was left at the drop-off spot by the water tower with the picture of Pogo that reads *Welcome to Waycross.*"

I had to laugh. "Until recently the only Pogo I knew was a phone game. But I know the tower you are talking about."

"Game? No, the cartoon possum. How old are you anyway?"

I shrugged. "Tell me more about the ransom."

"It was never picked up. The police assumed that Georg panicked. The little girl was never found." Avalou looked to the distance. "That is a swamp out yonder. Who knows where she is?"

I knew Georg was convicted of kidnapping and went to prison. He wasn't in jail long before another inmate killed him. "What happened to the wife?"

"They were going to arrest her as an accessory but she insisted that her husband told her Granville wanted them to watch the girl until someone could pick her up," Daryl said.

"I'd like to see that cabin."

"You can't. It burned down not long after the kidnapping. The insurance company claimed that somebody torched it and they wouldn't pay a penny."

Avalou couldn't keep out of the conversation in spite of Daryl's plea for her not to get over excited. She went into a drawer and came out with some papers.

"I have the contract that Georg signed when he rented the cabin for the summer. He rented it under his real name. A kidnapper would not do that. He would use a false name."

She handed the contract to me. It was a standard lease. There was also a note from him inquiring about renting the cabin. The last lines were written in German. *Ich bedanke mich bei Ihnen im Voraus. Hochachtungsvoll, Gerber.*

"Do you know what this means?"

"I looked it up once. I think it basically means thank you. I don't recall exactly, but I know it wasn't anything significant," Avalou said.

"Would you mind if I scanned these?"

"I don't know what good it would do now. Georg Gerber is long dead. But go ahead if you want."

I took out my phone and scanned the contract and then the note as well.

"I'm surprised that my father didn't think that something was up with Granville."

"I think he was too close to the situation. Your father and Martin Granville became friends for a while. It wasn't until later that they had a falling out." Daryl took a long sip of her Dr. Pepper.

That shouldn't have surprised me. I could imagine that in his younger days my father made a lot of enemies.

"What did he have against my father?"

Avalou sighed. "It's not my place to say."

"But she will," Daryl said.

"Well, I'm only telling you facts not gossip. We learned all of this after we became friends with Big Al."

Daryl fidgeted in her chair. "Tell the story or I will."

Avalou cleared her throat as if she were about to give a speech. "I'm getting to it. As you know, your father found Gerber but not the child. Eventually, Martin Granville divorced his wife and was feeling pretty low. He started doing drugs and would have gotten in deep if Big Al and Officer Johnson hadn't stepped in. The three of them became close. They were like the Rat Pack of Chatham County. Ringa Ding Ding. You know what I mean?"

"Not exactly." Rat Pack? Ringa what? It was like she was speaking a foreign language.

"There were parties, and drinking, and girls, and who knows what else. The famous racecar driver and the hero private eye were like local celebrities. The cop partied right along with them, but because of his position, kept out of the limelight for the most part."

"The falling out, Avalou. Tell me about that."

"That happened when Martin married one of the young ladies who worked in your father's office. Your father felt his friend stole the woman from him. Martin's point of view was that he felt the woman married him on the rebound after your father didn't marry her."

Holy shit. I didn't have to be a detective to see where this was going. "Estelle was married to Martin Granville?"

Both women nodded.

If I had this right, when my father didn't divorce my mother so she could keep his pension, Estelle decided not to wait and married his friend Martin Granville.

"I'm getting it, go on."

Avalou was clearly the bigger gossip of the two. "So, Martin moved his bride up to Augusta to put some distance between Estelle and Big Al. It wasn't long before Estelle realized she had made a mistake but she stuck with the marriage and had a baby."

"Jill?"

"That's right. But until the day he died in that crash at Daytona, Martin suspected Estelle was cheating and suspected that the child was not his."

"Was Jill my father's daughter?"

Daryl leaned in as if someone might hear the secret.

"What do you think?"

Chapter Forty-Three

That was way too much for me to process all at once. If what they were telling me was true then not only was Estelle my stepmother, but her daughter Jill was my half-sister. "I should see my truck now," I said.

"It's fine," they both said.

Fine? Maybe I was dreaming, but I seemed to remember that it had been engulfed in flames. I stumbled to the door. Daryl and Avalou looked at each other.

The F-150 was a burnt-out shell sitting on its rims. I couldn't speak. In fact, I didn't want to because if I did I'd spew out a string of profanity in front of the two old women that I would only regret later.

"Well, there is some good news," Avalou said in a mock cheery voice that cracked on the word news. "Show him, Daryl."

Daryl went to a basket on an old kitchen table that was repurposed for use on the porch. She picked up Batshit's errant GPS and handed it to me. "It was blown out of the truck before it burned."

I actually lost my vision for a second. I'm sure it was from anger more than the head wound. When I could finally see, I tossed the GPS into the yard with a grunt.

"Daryl…" My voice was a little above a whisper and so calm that I actually frightened myself.

Fear covered both of their faces. Daryl managed a tentative, "Yes?"

"Return my gun please."

"You're not leaving yet, for sure," Avalou said. "Rest a while and then have something to eat before you go."

"My gun please."

"Oh Lord! He's going to shoot us, Daryl."

Daryl went back to the repurposed table and took the gun from the same basket.

"Don't hurt Ava. I take full responsibility." Daryl stood in front of her love and handed me the gun. Her hands shaking.

"Thank you." My voice was a little less psychotic, but not by much. I took the gun.

"Stop!" Avalou screamed.

I pulled the trigger and put three bullets right through that mother lover and the GPS danced on the dusty ground as pieces of plastic and electronic innards flew through the air.

When the dust settled I felt as if I was finally rid of what I realized was Psycho's curse, and all of the shit that went along with it.

"Thank you, Daryl. That thing has been nothing but a pain in my ass since I got it."

"Well, if we had any doubts that you were your father's son, that proved it. You are as impetuous as he is."

I didn't want to hear about how much I was like my father. Not then. Not ever.

"I need to get a vehicle to get back to Ava Island."

They wanted to drive me but I assured them that I could drive. Then they insisted that I take their Prius. After a little while of back and forth, I agreed to borrow their car.

The whole way back I thought about Keller and Hicks and my father. Things started to fall into place. When I finally got back, I took the higher bridge to Ava Island. No more waiting in traffic on that lower little drawbridge.

Chapter Forty-Four

As I congratulated myself on my triumphant crossing of the bridge and my new outlook on life, Greenleaf called.

"Where are you?"

"I'm on Midnight Pass. I just got back to the island."

There was a pause on the other end of the line. Greenleaf didn't say it, but it was obvious that if I was on Midnight Pass I had taken the high bridge. I could sense her surprise.

"I wanted to get you before I went home. The Palms has been trying to get you. I told them you were probably in a dead zone out in the middle of nowhere and that I'd let you know that you had to call them. That was an hour and a half ago."

"What did they want?"

"They said they would only talk to you. I left you several voice messages but of course you never bother to check."

One of these days Greenleaf was going to have to come into the 21st century and learn how to text. Nobody uses voicemail anymore.

"I'll call them," I said and hung up. I didn't have time to deal with their complaints. If they had found my father, they would have told Greenleaf. I was sure that they were going to tell me that in light of Big Al's most recent disappearance, they were going to put him out of their facility. I'd call them later after I got home and rested.

* * *

I was curious about the German phrase at the end of the note from Gerber inquiring about the rental of the cabin.

When I got back to the Blue Palmetto I sat in the Prius for a few minutes and typed the German words, *Ich bedanke mich bei Ihnen im Voraus. Hochachtungsvoll, Gerber*, into an online translator on my phone.

As Avalou had recalled, it simply meant *I thank you in advance. Sincerely, Gerber.*

That seemed like a lot of words to say so little. I decided to try another translator. I found one and typed in *Ich bedanke mich bei Ihnen im Voraus. Hochachtungsvoll. Gerber* to see if I got the same translation.

To my surprise I saw the words *I thank you in advance, Sincerely. tanner* on my screen.

By mistake the second time I typed it in, I put a period instead of a comma after that long German word *Hochachtungsvoll.* That made all of the difference and translated the name Gerber into the word tanner, as in a person who works with animal hides.

Before I could process what I had discovered, Max came into the yard through the opening in the bamboo hedge.

"Where did you get that?" she asked as I got out of the Givens' car.

"I had to borrow it."

"What about your fancy truck?"

"I don't have it anymore. The GPS either."

Max followed me up onto the porch and sat on the swing. "Is everything okay?"

Wondering why she cared would have normally been my first reaction, but I think I was finally beginning to understand that she genuinely cared about my wellbeing.

"I have never been better. I feel like a curse has been driven from me. Did you know that Estelle was married to Martin Granville before she married my father?"

"Yes, Greenleaf told me. But she figured you'd be more willing to believe it if you heard it from somebody else. So, she asked me to keep my mouth shut."

She was right. I did have an irrational tendency to disregard what Greenleaf told me.

"Well, I have one up on the two of you. Do you know what the German word gerber means?"

"Tanner."

"You knew that?"

"I lived in Germany when my father was in the army."

"I had to use an online translator." I showed her the note Georg Gerber wrote inquiring about renting the cabin.

"Georg Gerber and David Tanner must be related." Max was thinking exactly what I was thinking.

"That makes sense, and it gives us a motive. Georg Gerber went to jail for kidnapping the Granville child. Let's assume that David Tanner is his son. If the son didn't want Andy Keller to do a blog piece dragging up the kidnapping, that would be motive to kill him."

"I don't know. What about Hicks? Why would he want Hicks dead?" Max had a good question.

"Hicks was married to Estelle's daughter. I assume Jill was Granville's daughter as well." I watched Max's face. Maybe she was a better poker player than I was, but she gave no indication that Jill could be my father's daughter. "Hicks told me that Keller was interviewing Jill when Tanner had an argument with him. All of the facts link to the Granville kidnapping and point to Tanner as the killer."

When I heard the dirge ringtone from my phone I knew it was Maryann from The Palms again. My first reaction was to ignore the call. Then I remembered that Greenleaf said they had tried to call me when I was out in Waycross. If anything, they were calling to cover their asses about my father going missing. I decided to answer anyway in case they had some news that he had been found.

"DeLucia." My voice was less than friendly.

"This is Maryann Fena. I've been calling all over hell's half acre trying to find you."

"Well consider me found."

CHAPTER FORTY-FOUR

"I have some information about your father."

"Which is?"

"It seems this isn't the first time your father has left The Palms without our knowledge."

I could have told her that. But I knew that if I did she would use it as a way to absolve herself and The Palms of any wrongdoing. I wasn't going to give her the satisfaction of doing that. Besides, Big Al wasn't at the point where he was a danger to himself. I'm sure that when he signed himself in he didn't think that they were going to hold him prisoner.

"I see."

"I have to tell you I had no knowledge of what was going on. If I did I would have creamed somebody's corn."

It was typical Maryann mucking around in the bullshit instead of coming out and telling me what she had to say. Maybe if she had allowed him a little more freedom he wouldn't have had to sneak out.

"Exactly what was going on?"

"It came to my attention through one of the guests."

"What did?"

"That one of our staff had been sneaking Mr. DeLucia out early in the morning at the end of their shift."

Staff? Now that was news. I thought my father had been going out on his own. I played along to hear her squirm.

"How was that possible?"

"The staff member worked until 4:00 a.m. and would leave with your father, bringing him back before the staff change at 7:00 a.m."

I guess Maryann didn't run as tight of a ship as she had thought.

"Who is this staff member?"

"I can't say, but be assured I kicked them into the middle of next week, and they won't be back."

"I think I have a right to know. This staff member might know where he is."

"I'm sorry. I can't say."

"And what about my father?"

"As you know, the authorities are looking for him. You did say that you didn't want any alerts in the media."

"You realize that you're going to be held responsible."

"Look, Mr. DeLucia. I know we got off on the wrong foot. I'm trying to make that right by giving you this information which the police do not want made public yet."

I was about to give her an argument when she hung up the phone.

Maryann had carefully avoided giving me any clue as to whether the person working at The Palms that was taking my father out was a man or a woman. Could Tanner have gotten a job at the nursing facility knowing that Big Al was there? Then the even creepier notion of Batshit being the culprit crossed my mind.

Chapter Forty-Five

Of course, the person who was taking my father out of the nursing facility could have been just about any one, and maybe their reason for doing so was not as sinister as it appeared. But on the other hand, if it was Tanner he could have been trying to set Big Al up for Keller's murder. That could explain how the Lynches thought they saw my father on the boat with Keller. Then there was the possibility of Batshit. His beef was with me. He probably blamed me for his brother's death and for wrecking his Mustang. It was getting late but I decided I had to find Batshit and see if either of my theories was true.

The Mustang Batshit was driving when he almost ran me over had Georgia plates with no frame. Most privately-owned vehicles have a vanity frame or at least a frame with the car dealer's name. Even more telling was the barcode sticker I noticed when I almost spilled my brains on the bumper. The car was a rental but it wasn't the usual Chrysler 200 or Camry. You didn't get a car like that at an airport counter. Batshit obviously went to great lengths to find a Mustang exactly like the muscle car I destroyed on him. It didn't take me long to find the only place in the area that would rent a car like that—Fantasy Car Rental in Savannah. I gave them a call hoping they were open late. They were.

"Hi, this is Poindexter Cockburn." I had to choke back a laugh at the thought of his name. No wonder he and Psycho became criminals. They must have been in a schoolyard fight every day of their childhoods. "The 'stang I rented won't start."

The female on the other end gushed sympathy, as she had been trained to do.

"I'm so sorry for your inconvenience, Mr. Cockburn. We'll get someone right out there. Are you still at the Surfside Motel on Tybee Island?"

Okay. Just what I had hoped for.

"Hey, wait a minute. I got it started. No need to come out."

I was still hanging up the phone as I ran out to the truck. Then I remembered my truck was a pile of burned out metal at the Givens place out in Waycross. I certainly was not going to take their hybrid. I ran back inside to get the keys to my father's Mercedes.

With the top down and the wind whipping at my hair, I decided that I had been a dumbass to refuse my father's wheels. Sweet.

If Batshit wasn't at the Surfside Motel when I got there I'd wait all night if need be. He started this harassment but I was going to end it and if he had anything to do with my father's disappearance he was going to wish he had stayed in Connecticut.

When I got to the motel I didn't see his car until I drove around to the back of the building. It was parked by a lawn reserved for guests who needed to walk their dogs.

I got out and inspected the Mustang. It was almost identical to the ride that got Twizzlefied on the bridge back home, except this one had a built in GPS. Good choice in upgrades in my opinion.

"Well, if it isn't the PI. I have to take back my words. Maybe you are some kind of detective." Batshit was standing at the back entrance of the motel. "The lady from the car rental called and said she thought something was afoot," he said. He started to walk across the driveway toward the car.

"The notes are going to stop, Poindexter."

"I think you are correct."

There was something black in his hand. He pressed a button and a flash of metal flicked out. He continued to advance.

I willed myself to stay calm and made eye contact.

"Put the weapon down," I said in an even voice as I maneuvered myself out of his range.

Batshit kept coming toward me. When he got close enough, I grabbed his arm while kicking out my leg and hooking it around his. I could have tossed him if need be, but waited for him to make the next move.

"Tell me what this is about so I can fix it," I said.

"Man, what is the matter with you?" He yelled as he dropped what was in his hand.

"That's better," I said. I relaxed my grip, but remained ready in case he tried anything.

"Dude, I was only going to open the door to show you the leather. The battery in the fob is dead and the car joint told me to use the physical key until I bring it in."

I silently thanked whoever had approved our retraining when I was on the force. At one time I might have taken a more offensive approach to disarming him and one of us might have ended up dead.

"My mistake. But what did you expect? You've been leaving threatening notes on my truck."

"Can't you take a joke? That was nothing compared to what you and my asshole brother did to my wheels."

"Murder isn't a joke. Not even in Georgia," I said.

"Murder? It was a note... or two."

"Three to be exact."

"Still. The notes didn't harm anyone. What are you talking about murder?"

"You've been following me. You were even in Hilton Head."

"So what? I was only trying to find a way for us to come face-to-face so I could tell you thanks, and not to worry about the car."

"What are you talking about?"

"The car. My Mustang. It was a small price to pay to get away from my brother. It was because of him that I ended up in the state college system."

I hadn't heard that euphemism for jail in a while.

"When the lawyer from Yale got me sprung I got a new chance on life and that would not be possible if my dear departed brother were still walking this earth."

"You serious, Batshit?"

"Did I shoot you when I had the chance?"

"You didn't have a gun."

"Well, there you go. I'm a reformed man. And do not call me Batshit from this day on. My name is Poindexter."

With a name like Poindexter Cockburn, it wasn't going to be easy for the guy to go straight, but I believed he meant to try. I helped him up.

"Tell me one more thing," I said. "How long have you been down here in Georgia?"

"A little over a week. You know. When the notes started."

"Of all of the places in Georgia, you happened to pick Savannah?"

"No. I knew you were here. It's all over the street back home. Hey, I hear you threw your badge at your chief. Well. Done. Sir!"

Like I needed Batshit's approval. Someone had been helping my father leave the nursing facility for quite a while. It couldn't have been Batshit if he just arrived a week ago. I asked anyway.

"Have you ever been to The Palms?"

"A restaurant?"

"A rest home."

"Like with smelly old people? No way." He looked at the Mercedes. "You came in that sweet machine? Where's your truck?"

"Probably in the scrapyard by now."

"You wrecked another vehicle? Dude! Where did you get your license, at McDonalds?"

Chapter Forty-Six

So Batshit admitted responsibility for the notes but apparently, he was not the one who was helping my father sneak out of the nursing facility. The only thing I could do was turn my attention back to finding Tanner.

The drag queen had said I'd find Tanner down at the fishing tournament at an ungodly hour. There is no hour more ungodly than 4:00 in the morning, so I set the alarm on my smartphone to go off at 3:30. A quick shower and a cup of black coffee shot some life into me and I drove down to the pier.

Ava Island Fishing Pier sits beneath the black and white iron lighthouse on the island's southernmost point. According to the sign on the beach, the deep channel that runs in front of the pier is a pathway from the Atlantic for spotted trout, striper, tarpon, and the sharks that follow them into the mouth of the Savannah.

The sky was still dark but already fifty or so people had claimed their fishing spots. They stood in silence toying with their rods amid the smell of bait, beer, and tobacco smoke. The light of several Coleman lanterns cast a faint glow over the whole scene while every fifteen seconds the sky above brightened with the flash from the lighthouse.

Down at the end, a chubby guy in a tropical shirt with matching shorts got a hit.

"It's a nice size tarpon," someone next to him said. "There ya go. Keep pressure. Rod down. Down."

"Hammerhead!" Someone yelled.

The fisherman started to panic and tugged at the pole in a useless effort to pull the tarpon away from the shark.

Someone dropped a lantern tied to a rope down close to the water. The attacking shark was a good ten feet long and I could see its eyes set at the ends of its mallet-shaped head. Several people gathered around.

"Keep it low," someone from the crowd said.

"I need some help," the fisherman said as the shark almost made him lose his rod over the side.

A young guy grabbed the rod just in time. The light from the lighthouse flashed as if to remind me that I wasn't there for the fishing. I took a good look at the guy. It was Tanner.

"You take over," the chubby guy said to him. "I'm too out of shape."

The hammerhead kept hitting the tarpon until the injured fish swam under the pier in an effort to escape. The rod bent as Tanner fought to bring in the fish.

I maneuvered next to him. "We're going to talk sooner or later," I said to Tanner.

The tarpon swam from under the pier and the line screamed out.

"What's this about?"

The giant hammerhead hit the tarpon again. The injured fish leaped from the water.

"Andy Keller," I said.

"I'm a little busy here. The Cottage Restaurant…7:30 tonight… I'll be across the street."

Only a jerk would ruin someone's fishing experience of a lifetime. "Sure. And give that line some slack," I said and walked off the pier.

I'm not the most trusting guy in the world but I had a gut feeling that Tanner would show up as promised at the Cottage restaurant. And if he didn't I'd find him again, but the next time I wouldn't be as easy on him.

* * *

You won't see a Netflix detective spending hours poring over real estate documents at the Hall of Records. But to prove a local businessman was investing in land with money that he skimmed from his partner, that's what I was doing. There were no lights, no cameras, and definitely no action to keep my mind on task. My mind kept drifting to Max. I had no reason to think that things were ever going to be the same for us but I decided that I should ask her to dinner anyway. It was my way of showing her that I still wanted to be friends even if she had hooked up with the guy from the drum circle. I sent a text to Max.

Me: *Dinner at the Cottage tonight?*

It took a while for her to get back to me. I was thinking either she didn't want to bother or she had something going with Jeff.

Max: *Okay. 8:30.*

That wouldn't work with the window Tanner had given me.

Me: *7:15 would be better.*

Again, a delay.

Max: *Fine.*

I could almost hear the huff through the text message.

* * *

The restaurant was one of the more upscale on the island, decked out as if it had been a fisherman's cottage, with a huge blue marlin on the sign over the entrance. Fake pilings that ran along the sidewalk and up the steps were strung with heavy rope.

Max seemed to be in a good mood. "Let's sit out back in the open air by the band. I love it back there."

Yeah, it was nice, even kind of romantic, back there all right. But it was too secluded. I wouldn't have been able to see when Tanner arrived for our meeting across the street.

The hostess greeted us and asked where we preferred to sit.

"Hey, out here on the front porch would be great," I said.

She led us to a table by the railing with a splendid view of the street. When we sat, Max had a disappointed look on her face.

"What?"

"I asked to sit out on the patio."

"You did? I'm sorry. I guess I'm a little nervous. I'm so excited to be here with you. I'll get the hostess."

"It's fine. There's a nice breeze out here."

Crisis averted. I passed on the basil mojito that Max ordered and took a craft beer instead. We both agreed on the Cottage's famous lobster sushi roll.

While we waited for our food, I kept an eye across the street as I drank my beer. I was trying my best to make small talk, but Max could tell I had something on my mind.

"You seem a little distracted."

If I told her that I was actually working she would not have understood. This was supposed to be a nice dinner between friends, not a stakeout.

"No. Not at all."

She took another sip of her drink. I could smell the basil from across the table. I much preferred my malty IPA and ordered another when a waiter went by.

"You polished that off pretty fast. What's bothering you?"

"Nothing. You like that drink?"

"It's good."

"I hate the smell of basil. It smells like cheap aftershave."

She raised her eyebrows. I should have left it at that.

"Speaking of aftershave. When I got my phone from your beach bag I noticed you had my shampoo on your vanity, along with deodorant and a bunch of other stuff."

Maybe I should have gone for subtleness but they didn't teach subtle at the police academy.

Max pulled back a bit as if she thought I was going to bite.

"Your?"

"Well, I don't mean mine. I mean stuff like I have. You know men's stuff."

"Your point?"

"I'm not sure if there is one anymore." After I blurted it out, I wished I had told her I was distracted because I was waiting for Tanner to show up.

Max started to giggle which was not the reaction I had expected.

"So, you think those products belong to another guy?"

"I don't care who they belong to."

"Maybe someone who stays over. Jeff maybe?" Max was truly trying to set me up. I felt like a skunk in a catch-and-release trap, but she had no intention of releasing me. At least not until I squirmed and begged for a while.

"Not my business." And it wasn't.

Her giggles turned into a full-blown laugh. I looked around to see if people were looking at us. I downed a gulp of beer.

"You never heard of the Pink Tax. Have you?"

I shook my head.

"Well, like so many other things, it's a ripoff for women. We spend 50% more for products aimed at us that sometimes have exactly the same ingredients as those made for men. So, I tried the men's products."

"They were in the guest bathroom."

"Because I decided I didn't want to smell like a man, so I put them there."

I tried to make a joke of my stupid assumptions. "I'm glad you didn't like them. The price of men's products would probably go up."

The waiter came with the food in time to save me from putting my foot further into my mouth. He served Max a rectangular plate with a huge lobster tail shell filled with lobster and rice rolled in seaweed. I snatched some wasabi from her plate with a fork. As he put my plate in front of me I spotted Tanner's bike cab with the flags on the fiberglass rods pull up across the street by the Double Yoke Breakfast Bar.

I hopped up. "I'll be right back."

"Again?" Max sounded as if she had almost expected me to abandon her once more.

"This won't take long. I promise."

Chapter Forty-Seven

I dashed down the porch stairs and ran across the street toward Tanner. He looked as if he were about to say something when the expression changed on his face. I heard a car roaring down the street from the direction of the water. It seemed like the car was aiming for the bike cab. A second later, there was a loud crash and the bike cab rolled sideways pinning me against the trunk of a parked car which absorbed most of the impact. Tanner was thrown from the cab, scrambled to his feet, and ran down Main Street.

I was stunned but lucid enough to realize that the car took off speeding through the traffic circle and passed the gazebo on the opposite corner. I recognized it as the 1960 Pontiac that I had admired in Demarco's parking lot. In my mind that pretty much confirmed that it was the same car that forced me into the canal.

Some people pulled the bike cab away freeing me, and I took off after Tanner. He was about 200 feet ahead when I saw him force a tourist off a motor scooter and take off with it. I stopped running when I got to the bike cab company and watched as he turned down a side street. He'd shaken me off before; I wasn't going to let it happen again. The owner of the pedicab place was sitting at an umbrella table up by the office door.

"I need one of your cars." I pointed to the weird little vehicles with three wheels that I had seen her working on a few days before.

"I need a copy of your license and credit card info," she said.

I ran up and threw my license and AmEx card on the table.

"Hold these. I'll be back to settle up."

"How do I know the card isn't stolen?"

She had to pick now to get technical. I held my license next to my face to show her my picture. "Look, it's me. Look at the card. Same name. You know me from the other day, for crying out loud." I reached in my pocket and pulled out $75. I put it on the table. "It's all the cash I have on me. Trust me."

"I need paperwork."

"This is an emergency. You can find me at the Blue Palmetto Detective Agency if I don't bring back the vehicle."

She shook her head. "I don't think so."

"Please. Your father knows my father."

Funny I should play that card. Even I wouldn't trust someone who used my father as a reference.

She threw me a set of keys.

"You'll have to take the pink one. I shouldn't do this."

"Trust me," I said as I jumped into the tiny scooter car that looked like an egg on three wheels.

"Wait." She ran down to hand me my license. "You'll need this. And I'm keeping the credit card until you bring it back."

I peeled off down the street zipping around cars until I took the same street that I had seen Tanner turn down. I followed the street until I got to the end where I had to make a right turn on a one-way road that headed west along the Savannah River. As I putt-putted past the last high rise, to one of the few undeveloped areas on the island, I realized he was headed toward Little Beach, the same beach that Max and I had walked to. Just ahead I spotted Tanner. He took a left and I followed. The road ended abruptly at the beach. He ditched the stolen bike and ran along the sand. I jumped out of my three-wheeler and followed. We passed the pilings that marked the long-gone dock. I chased him along the small beach until he got to a point where the beach was no longer passable. He tried to scramble over the rocks that formed the jetty out into the water. As he struggled to climb over the rocks I tackled him dragging him down to the sand. As I pinned him, he grabbed a piece of driftwood and whacked me on the side of the head.

Stunned for a minute I let up on my hold and he scrambled from under me. I rubbed my head with my hand to ease the pain.

"What the hell are you running for? We had a meeting," I said.

"You set me up. That car almost killed me. Of course, I took off." His voice was shrill and his face pinched with fear.

"I was almost killed too. Think about it. Someone doesn't want me to ask questions about who whacked Andy Keller and Roscoe Hicks. I know Georg Gerber was your father."

He laughed.

"You see, that's where you're an asshat. I didn't kill anyone. Keller was going to help me clear my father's name."

"You mean you were okay with Keller digging up the past?"

"I was angry that he wasn't doing more," Tanner said.

"Ha! He called you an asshat!" The voice was all too familiar.

I know that the real inheritance I'm going to receive from my father isn't a detective agency but the dementia he had already started to exhibit. At that moment, I thought maybe I had already lost my mind. But I wasn't hallucinating as I watched my old man climb like a crab over the rocks from the other side of the jetty. Damned, freaking, aggravating, obnoxious, frustrating, old fart. First, he went missing and then he decided to show up at the worst possible moment. This was no time for a family reunion.

"Where the hell have you been?" I gave him a hand to get off of the rocks.

"To tell you the truth, I don't recall."

I would have said he was playing head games, but the people at the Palms House assured me that the lapses were real and would get worse with time.

"You don't recall. Yet you show up way out here on a beach that even I didn't know I would be on."

"You were in that stupid little car. I followed. I'm a better detective than you. Good thing you didn't have to go over the big bridge to get here." He would never win any awards as Mr. Personality. That was for sure.

"That you remember! Well, I have news for you. I'm over that."

"You don't have to yell at the old guy," Tanner said.

I was about to tell the ear jacker to butt out, when Hicks' girlfriend, Marnee, climbed over the jetty. I guess it was reunion time after all. The party was getting bigger. And uglier.

"Who the hell are you?" Tanner's eyes were fixed on a gun in Marnee's hand.

"My friend is with me," Big Al said. "We're going fishing."

"She's not taking you fishing today, Pop."

"Sure, she is. She's my friend from the station."

"Yeah, but no fishing with your friend today."

Who was I to question my father's reality? To him, she was Marnee, his friend from The Palms, who snuck him out early in the morning to take him fishing. It was a better reality than mine who saw her as the danger she was.

"Who are you?" Tanner asked again.

Talk about renewing old acquaintances.

"Mr. Tanner or Gerber, whatever you want to be called, I'd like you to meet Marnee Wharton, the grownup version of the kidnapped girl, Christmas Granville," I said.

Tanner's jaw dropped. "Granville. Are you shitting me? My father went to jail because of you." I thought Tanner was going to go after her but he didn't.

Marnee squinted her Cleopatra eyes. "Yeah, well life sucks. It hasn't been a picnic for me either being sent off to live with relatives in England who changed my name and didn't tell me who my real parents were. So, don't tell me your troubles."

I don't know about Tanner, but I understood about being abandoned. "Well, I get it. Parents can do a head job on their kids. But at some point, you have to take responsibility for your actions and stop blaming your upbringing."

"What would you know?"

"I know you resented that Jill was born as the replacement child for you. You came back to Savannah to befriend her. Then you took up with her husband and killed her, all out of resentment."

"I thought Jill was killed in a car accident," Tanner said.

"Jill's body was found in her submerged car but it wasn't an accident."

212

"What do you mean?" I think Tanner needed a scorecard to keep up. I tried to explain.

"I couldn't understand why Jill's car would crash into the canal. She wasn't impaired, the weather was good that night, and no other cars were involved. I read speculation in the newspaper report that she may have been texting, but Hicks gave Jill's phone to Estelle. Jill had forgotten it at home when she went out so she couldn't have been texting. Then it struck me that we don't drive cars anymore. We drive computers. Anyone with the technical skill can hack into a car and control all kinds of things including acceleration and braking."

"That's science fiction," Tanner said.

"It's not. Car manufacturers remotely update vehicle software all of the time. All someone needs are a laptop and the know-how."

"You make it sound easy," Marnee said.

"Ah, there you go again. From day one you couldn't resist bragging how you were taking an online computer course from Stanford."

"A lot of people take online courses," Tanner said.

I don't know why the guy was sticking up for Marnee. Maybe he empathized with the underdog. Although, judging by that heater in her hand, we were the underdogs.

"But only extremely intelligent people take courses in advanced computer security," I said.

"You mean they teach you how to kill people by taking over their cars?" Tanner didn't get it.

"The course is designed to protect networks and prevent attacks but that isn't the way Marnee used it. She used it to cause Jill's accident."

"Better dying through technology," Marnee said. The callousness of her remark made me realize how sick she was.

If you Googled an image of sad, it would come up with a picture of my old man at that moment. He stepped forward between Marnee and me.

"My wife had an accident?"

"Not your wife, your daughter did, Dad. Yes, Jill had an accident." The funny thing was that he was right when he said Hicks was his son-in-law.

I wondered if that came out of his confusion, or if in a lucid moment he remembered who Hicks was.

He shook his head. I gave him time to process it on his own. I had a more immediate problem to deal with. I wanted to be sure that the woman with the gun processed it as well. From the look of realization on her face, Marnee got it right away.

"That's right. Jill was my father's daughter. When Estelle dies your father's estate would be yours for the claiming. You didn't have to kill Jill or go through the elaborate charade."

"It wasn't only about money."

Her voice had a chilling flat affect, but somehow, I understood exactly what she was talking about. The feeling of being abandoned leaves a lasting impression on a kid.

"You blame everyone who had anything to do with the kidnapping for your screwed-up childhood. That's why you tormented Estelle by sending her money and the candy, making her think Jill might still be alive."

"If that woman didn't come along, my father would have stayed with my mother and I wouldn't have been sent away. I wanted her to know what it felt like to be abandoned, to not know for sure if your family is alive or dead. I knew about the chocolate kisses from Jill. I thought it was a nice touch."

I knew that Big Al couldn't tell you what he had for breakfast, but his long-term recall was amazing. I wondered if he was on the ball enough to shed some light.

"Big Al, listen to me. You remember Martin Granville?"

"The race car driver. Yeah. The bastard married one of my secretaries."

"Yes, Estelle. How did he know her?"

"He met her when he hired me to find his daughter."

I studied Marnee's face. I think she understood that Estelle didn't hook up with Martin Granville until after he divorced his wife. But it was too late to undo all that had been done.

"There you go," Tanner said. "Keller must have discovered that she was alive and in Savannah so she killed him before she could be connected to Jill's murder. And she must have killed Hicks too. Now she's going to kill us all and make it look like a deranged old man murdered two people and then killed himself."

Marnee looked at Tanner as if he were an idiot. She started to say something but Big Al's hero instinct kicked in at that moment. As Johnson had said, the disease doesn't change what's inside of a person.

"Holy shit, holy shit," my father said as he jumped in front of me. "You're not killing my friend." He reached for her gun and it went off. My father fell at my feet.

"No!" Marnee screamed when she realized what happened. I think she genuinely had a soft spot for Big Al and that was why she used to bring him on outings.

Seconds later, Johnson appeared with Max beside him. He shot his firearm and Christmas/Marnee fell. The little beach was beginning to look like a slaughterhouse.

I ripped his shirt and applied pressure to a gaping wound in Big Al's shoulder.

"Max, what are you doing here?" I managed to choke out.

"Johnson showed up at the accident scene and I told him you went chasing the pedicab driver. We followed you."

Little did I know I had been leading a parade with everyone following in on the chase.

"I'm glad you did." I could hear Johnson calling in for medical assistance. I kept the pressure on my father's wound. He was breathing but wasn't conscious.

Max went over to Marnee and checked for a pulse.

"Nothing," she said.

Chapter Forty-Eight

Max left to get Greenleaf. I rode in the back of the ambulance with Big Al. The old man took a bullet for me. That shouldn't be confused with *my old man* took a bullet for me. Big Al was protecting his friend, not his son. But it didn't matter anymore. He was a hero no question about it.

From what the emergency responders told me, Big Al had a good chance of making it. I felt bad that Marnee wasn't so lucky, but Johnson couldn't take the chance that Marnee would shoot anyone else. He had no choice but to kill her.

When we got out of the ambulance I ran alongside the gurney as they wheeled my father toward a swinging door. A hospital guard stopped me and pointed toward a counter in the waiting room. "You have to check in over there. They need information."

I watched as they pushed the gurney through the door and it swung shut. The guard stood in front of the door and gestured toward the reception area as if I couldn't figure out where I had to go for myself.

From Big Al's previous visits to the emergency room, they already had his name and other essential billing information.

"Has his insurance changed?" seemed to be the biggest concern of the woman behind the desk.

I was going to give her a hard time and ask if they were going to deny treatment if he wasn't insured. As far as I knew that was against the law and the Hippocratic Oath as well. Instead, I decided that being an asshole wasn't going to help Big Al so I lied and said everything was the same as it had been. For all I knew, it was.

"Can I go back there with my father?"

"Right now, they are evaluating the situation. Take a seat and I'll call you as soon as you can go in."

The woman pointed to the waiting room, which was crowded with people whose concern about their own loved ones was certainly as major a deal to them as Big Al's dilemma was to me. Loved one: now that was not a term I ever thought I'd use in the same sentence with the name Big Al.

I was irritated but I think that was because I knew I had to have a conversation with Greenleaf which I did not want to do. I knew Max would tell her what had happened, but I felt she should hear it from me. I went old school and gave a call instead of texting her.

She was pretty upset and I realized why texting is so much better than talking on the phone. If I had texted Greenleaf I wouldn't have had to deal with emotions—hers or mine.

Through her sobs, Greenleaf kept asking, "What about you? Are you okay? What about you?"

On my end, I kept mumbling, "I'm fine."

"As soon as Max gets here, I'm coming down," she said.

I saw Johnson walking my way and I had the excuse I needed to tell her that I had to go.

Johnson stood over me and put a hand on my shoulder. I slapped my hand on the stained seat next to me.

"May as well sit down," I said.

"How's he doing?"

"They're not telling me anything."

"From what I saw back there at the beach, at least the bullet missed his heart," Johnson said.

"Yeah, small target. Right?"

Johnson didn't seem impressed by the gallows humor. Maybe I should have said it caught him in his shoulder and left it at that.

"That was the Al I remember. He'd take a bullet for a friend any day." He pointed to his head. "This may go, but what's in here…" He made a fist and tapped it against his chest. "What is in here stays with you always. No disease can change a man's character."

"Yeah." I didn't agree with him as far as my father's moral qualities, but I wasn't going to argue. It didn't matter if Johnson's perception of my father's character was the same as mine or not.

"What about you?" Like Greenleaf, Johnson felt it necessary to ask. And I answered him the same way I answered her.

"I'm fine."

Unlike with Greenleaf, my answer sufficed for him.

I got up and went to the reception desk.

"Can I see Mr. Al DeLucia?"

All that got me was a polite, "We'll call you as soon as you can go in. Please have a seat."

"Can you at least tell me how he is doing?"

"I'm afraid I don't have any information. Please take a seat and we will get right to you."

Apparently making a pest of myself wasn't going to move things along any faster. I went back to sit next to Johnson. He was sitting slouched over with his elbows on his spread knees and his hands on his head. I thought he might be praying.

"It's ironic, isn't it? I had to kill the girl that your father and I thought we had lost twenty-five years ago."

So that was it. The old cop needed a little sympathy for himself.

A few minutes later Johnson hopped out of the seat. "At least it's over."

"Is it?"

"Damned right, it's over. I have the motive, I have the means, and I have the confession. Case closed."

So that's how it was in his mind. He had. I was waiting for him to acknowledge that I handed him all of those things, but it didn't happen. Something told me it was the same thing twenty-five years before when my father handed Gerber over to him. Johnson took the credit.

"Case closed," I said.

"Damned right!" He said it strong and loud enough for everyone in the room to look our way.

"As soon as they get Big Al back to new and settled in The Palms we got to go fishing. I know this spot on the Ogeechee River where the striper run twenty pounds."

"I don't think he's going back to the home. They don't want him. He's too hard to handle."

"Who said that?"

"Maryann, the Care Coordinator at The Palms."

"You stay here and worry about your daddy. I have to talk to someone."

Johnson walked off into the bowels of the hospital and I waited for word on Big Al. I was going stir crazy so to fill my time I played solitaire on my phone. It was better than trying to watch the endless court shows on the TV that hung on the wall with its volume off. About a half hour later I spotted Max and Greenleaf at the reception desk. I was never so happy to see two friendly faces. I went up and tapped Max on the shoulder. She turned and realizing it was me threw her arms around me.

"I guess I ran off on you again," I said. Something about the hug told me that everything was good between us. I held on to her taking in the delicious smell of her hair. It beats me what it reminded me of, but it was good, and thankfully it wasn't the scent of Irish Spring. If she paid a Pink Tax to smell that good it was money well spent. I made the hug last as long as I could before I let go.

"How is he?"

"They said we could go in to see him in about five minutes," Greenleaf said before I could answer. "I told them I was his wife."

It wouldn't have surprised me if she was his wife too. At that point, nothing at all would have surprised me.

Finally, a nurse called us and led us down a hall lined with patients in beds waiting to be seen.

"He's under sedation," she said.

When we got to his cubicle I let Greenleaf and Max go in first. I took a breath and followed.

Al's eyes were closed and he had no color.

"Is… he dead?"

Greenleaf glared at me.

"No. Didn't you hear her say he's under sedation? And he can hear you, by the way." Greenleaf said.

The way she put her hand on his I wondered if maybe there had been something between them at one time.

A young guy with bloodshot eyes came through the curtain and introduced himself as Dr. Nash.

"If all of you could step outside for a minute," he said and one by one we ducked through the curtain and went back to the waiting room so the doctor could conduct this examination. Johnson was waiting there with a tall woman in a business suit.

"This is my friend Danielle Jenkins. She's a social worker here."

Danielle put out her hand. "As soon as your father is better we'll have to move him out of here."

I started to get defensive. "You can't put him out in the street."

Johnson held up his hand to stop me.

"That's true." She moved a little closer to me and pretended to whisper. "But a hospital is no place for sick people." She winked at me. "I've been on the phone with The Palms. We're transferring him back there as soon as he's well enough."

"Did you talk to Maryann Fena?" I asked.

"I did. And I think that she understands the law a little better now."

Danielle gave me her card with her number circled before leaving.

"I've got to go too." Johnson pointed an invisible gun at me. "Fishing… when you're ready. Don't forget."

"A hospital is no place for sick people. Here's my card," Max said in a sweet voice. She probably would have gone on mimicking Danielle if Dr. Nash hadn't come to talk to us. He explained that the bullet didn't do any major damage and had been removed.

"But he's getting up there in years and he's not in the best of health. I'm not going to tell you that it's not serious," Dr. Nash said.

CHAPTER FORTY-EIGHT

He agreed it would be a good idea if I stayed for the night.

Chapter Forty-Nine

There's nothing creepier than a darkened hospital room with only the bar on the wall shedding an eerie blue light that would make even a relatively healthy patient look beyond sick. In Big Al's case, the odds that he was about to go on his final caper were pretty good.

Dr. Nash had explained that while the bullet didn't strike a major organ, my father's age and health were against him. I sat in a straight-backed chair by the side of the bed listening to his shallow breathing.

I could only watch the bag on the pole drip into the tube that snaked into his arm for so long before my imagination took over.

I started to think that every movement of the sheets marked his last breath. Every sound became a death rattle. Though I'd never heard a death rattle. I wasn't there when my mother died, and when Psycho was obliterated by the truck all I could hear was screeching brakes.

The monitors did nothing to ease my mind. The lines on the screen went up and down like the graphing of a crazy day on Wall Street. After an hour or so I had to divert my mind so I wouldn't go nuts. I turned off the sound on my phone and played video games until my head drooped forward to rest on my chest. I don't know how long I was sleeping before the phone fell to my lap and I woke up.

The drip still kept up its steady rhythm and the monitor continued its cycle of highs and lows.

Big Al rubbed his tongue over his cracked lips. I took a sliver of ice and touched it to them as the nurse had shown me to do.

"If you think you're going to die without answering a few questions you're wrong," I whispered.

He moved.

"Don't worry, I'm not going to ask where the hell you were for all those years. It doesn't matter anymore. But you have to tell me what I'm missing about Granville."

The machine beeped. I guess I hit a nerve. The machine beeped again. Damn. Maybe I went too far. I headed to the door to find a nurse, but one was already headed to the room.

"It beeped," I said realizing I sounded like a three-year-old.

"He probably moved and a lead came loose. No need to worry."

"Oh. Okay. Should his heart rate be going up and down like that?"

She smiled. "You're looking at his respiration pattern. He's fine."

"Sorry for freaking out. I don't understand all of this equipment, you know?"

The nurse gave me a sympathetic look. "Relax. If he was truly near death, he would be intubated and on a ventilator in ICU. You go take a break," she said. "I'm going to clean him up a little. He'll be here when you get back."

I got up and walked into the hall as she pulled the curtain around the bed to do whatever she had to do.

I walked out of the room into the blinding light of the hallway. A nurse took a slice of pizza from a box on the counter. She held up the slice and pointed to the box offering me one. I declined. Another nurse looked up from her computer and asked if I needed any help. It struck me what a thankless job it must be taking care of sick people in the middle of the night as you grabbed a bite between rounds. Special people nurses are. And if I were to be honest, I'd have to include my nemesis, Maryann from The Palms, in that assessment too.

I took a walk to get some water in the lounge. As I made my way down the hall, I noted the names by each door; a habit of observation I picked up when I was a cop. Gifford, de Lafontaine, Johnson; I stopped to look closer. Clair Johnson; I wondered if she was a relation to my father's friend. I continued down the hall. Owens, Dwelt, Stewart, Wisehart, another Johnson; this one was a David. It's a common enough name so I wasn't all that surprised that there were two in one hallway. I probably wouldn't have even noticed them if I hadn't seen Major Johnson earlier when he tried to help out my old man.

When I got back to the room the nurse was gone and the curtain was open. I sat in the chair beside the bed.

I was still wrestling with the fact that I didn't know what I wanted that line on the monitor to do. Everybody has to die sometime but I needed time to figure out how I was going to react if that line went flat and the beeping sound went on until a nurse came along and turned it off. I still had questions for my father.

"You did finger Gerber as the kidnapper, right?"

No response.

"Did you get the wrong guy?"

I may as well have been talking to the pillow for all the response I got from Big Al.

"I noticed a couple of patients named Johnson here," I whispered. "It got me thinking. The major has been a good friend to you. He's old school; loyal to people he goes way back with. Do you and your buddy know something I should know?"

He began to stir and I remember how agitated he had become the day I first saw him at The Palms when I told him I had met Johnson. Was he trying to tell me something?

The machine beeped again. This time I knew that it was from the movement, but I wanted it to mean that the old man was trying to pass some information on to me.

The monitor beeped again. I jumped up from the chair. "You hold that thought."

A nurse poked her head into the room.

"Keep him alive. At least until I get back."

It was early morning. If I hurried I'd get home in time to go fishing with Johnson.

* * *

224

It was only 6:30 in the morning when I pulled into the Blue Palmetto driveway. When I got out of the roadster a stream of morning sun found its way through the canopy of the live oak tree. It reflected off of the hood creating little ripples of light on the porch ceiling. Once again, I appreciated what a cool car my father had chosen.

I found Greenleaf on the couch and Max on a recliner in the main office. They were both sleeping, but woke up when I walked in. They looked at me as if it were a home invasion.

It was the first time I had ever seen a hair out of place on Greenleaf's head. They both looked rumpled.

"Oh no!" Greenleaf cried out.

I know that seeing me walk in without calling ahead led her to think the worst.

I shook my head no. "Not yet," I said. "But it's not looking good right now."

"Then why are you here?" Max rubbed at her eyes.

"I'm going fishing with Johnson."

"Fishing!" Greenleaf shot off the couch. I thought she was going to deck me.

Of course, Max had to jump in with her opinion. "Just when I think you've changed, you go right back to your old selfish ways."

A vote of confidence would have been nice, but I probably deserved their low opinion of me based on my past resentment of helping out with the agency. Although, this time they were leaping to unfair conclusions.

"Johnson said the stripers are huge on the Ogeechee. I have to see if he's telling the truth."

Greenleaf's face was red. "Well you do what you want. I'm going back to the hospital. That man doesn't deserve to be left alone at a time like this."

I never thought I would agree with her but I did. I wasn't going to tell her though.

"And I'm going with her," Max said. "I hope you enjoy your fishing trip."

"I know you don't mean that," I said. "But yes, do go. If he says anything let me know."

225

They both left in a huff as I bolted to the storage closet to get my father's heavy tackle.

Chapter Fifty

After I found Big Al's fishing rod and tackle box in the supply closet, I called Johnson and told him I couldn't take hanging out in the hospital anymore and that I'd like to take him up on that fishing trip.

"Nothing like a little fishing to calm your nerves and help you forget your problems," Johnson said.

I had the phone on speaker and while he gave me directions to a boat launch on the Ogeechee River, I took a stainless-steel diving knife from Big Al's tackle box and buckled its sheath a little above my left ankle. As he droned on about how much fun it was going to be, I practiced whipping the blade out of its holder and jabbing at some pretend monster of the deep. After I got off the phone, I threw on a pair of long fishing pants that hung in the closet, and then headed out. I was ready for anything.

My father's 300 SL didn't have a GPS and that was fine with me. I used the maps app on my phone to follow US 17 to State Road 144. Forty miles and almost an hour later I crossed the causeway to Savage Island. I soon found the boat ramp on the Ogeechee River not far from Civil War Era Fort McAllister.

The place was deserted except for Johnson who was leaning against his ancient white pickup truck in a lot surrounded by giant oaks covered in Spanish moss. He looked at his watch when I arrived. I wondered how he got out there before me. Did he already have the boat on the trailer and hitched up in anticipation of my call? As soon as I parked he jumped into the truck and started the motor. I guess he was afraid the striper wouldn't wait for us.

"Guide me back," he said.

I stood off to the side and waved him along as he backed the trailer down the ramp until the twenty-footer hit the water. Johnson left the driver's door open when he jumped out of the cab.

"Are you sure there are stripers way out here?" I gestured toward the narrow river that slunk through the salt marsh.

"You just wait, my friend. Those bad boys love it here. They face the current and let the river bring their food to them and they get bigger and bigger."

I threw my gear into the boat and undid the safety straps as Johnson installed the drain plug.

He released the trailer winch. "We'll probably see a school or two once we get upriver."

He threw me a tow rope and I wound it around a cleat near the bow of the boat. "I hear it's awesome when they clear the water."

Johnson raised his eyebrows. "So, you know about stripers?"

"Not a thing. A guy at the gas station mentioned it." The knife sheath was jabbing into my leg and I rubbed above my ankle with my right foot.

Johnson noticed. "You'll be sweating like a whore in a church in those long pants on."

"It's better than mosquito bites. I can do without the Zika virus." I took a can of bug repellent out of my knapsack and sprayed my clothes. Then I offered him the can.

"I'll take my chances." He pretended to cough and wave away the spray fumes. He gave the bow of the boat a shove to get it off the trailer and I guided the boat into the water with the tow rope.

While he parked the truck and trailer under the trees in the parking area I waited, standing in the shallow water and holding the lines so the boat didn't float away.

"Hop in," he said when he got back.

He started the boat and we pulled away from the boat ramp.

"Ever seen an alligator up close and personal?"

My eyes followed his gaze to the other side of the river. A dark form almost indistinguishable from the water floated motionless just below the surface. Its nose and eyes above the water, it seemed to be watching us.

"You mean I was in the water with the mother of all alligators and you didn't tell me? Let's get the hell out of here."

Johnson snickered. "Why?"

"This place must be crawling with them. What if they attack the boat?"

"I doubt it. A bigun like that got to be a bull. He don't want anyone else in his territory."

"Yeah, well, we're in its territory."

"That old boy is more interested in a turtle, or a fish than you. If you fall in, just you don't go drawing attention to yourself by flailing away in the water. He might think your arm or leg is a fish."

"I plan to stay in the boat, thanks."

"Good, because once he gets you in a death roll and pulls you under you're a goner. The old folks used to say that if a gator brings you under you need to stick your hand down his throat. There's a flap back in there that keeps it from drowning, you gotta pull on it."

"I'll keep that in mind."

"Can't say I ever tried it myself." He laughed as he put the boat in gear and slowly headed away from the gator.

It was the first time I'd ever seen Johnson relaxed and happy. I could tell that boating was his element.

We were just a little upstream when he cut the engine and anchored. He pulled a mullet head from a bucket and tossed it to me. "You know how to bait a hook?"

"Sure." I caught the bait which immediately slipped out of my hand. I picked it up and stuck a hook up through its lower jaw.

Johnson smirked until I pulled the hook straight up out of the top of the Mullet's mouth and then pushed it through the soft spot on the top of the head.

"Well I'll be damned. Where did you learn that fancy baiting?"

"I fish for blues back home. Baiting a hook is pretty much the same."

I rubbed my ankle.

"I know you're here for a little R and R but I was wondering about Al," he said.

So was I. For all I knew he was a goner already. If so, I'd have some regrets to deal with concerning my decision to go fishing. "It doesn't look good."

"Damn it all. That's not right." Johnson hung his head in respect. "At least we cleared his good name."

I shrugged. "I guess we did." I couldn't resist putting a bit of emphasis on the word "we."

Johnson, picking up on my sarcasm, stood brandishing a paddle.

"Son you must think I'm dumber than a truckload of bricks. Stand up."

"I was kidding. Okay?"

"The hell you were." He bared his teeth. I had the feeling that I was getting to see the real Johnson.

"What bug got up your ass?" I reached under my cuff to feel for the knife. Johnson knocked my hand away with the paddle.

"I said stand up. And don't touch that leg again. I'm guessing you got a gun under there."

"It's a fishing knife. No big deal." I hiked up my pants cuff. "Why all of the suspicion?"

Johnson wasn't as dumb as I thought. I kept an eye on the paddle in his hand. He knew I had the knife so that element of surprise was out. I'd have to keep my options open for another way of overpowering him if I needed to.

"If your daddy is so bad off you wouldn't be out here fishing unless you were up to something."

"Okay, so you got me. Let's put it all out there. Marnee had confessed to killing her sister but you were a little too quick to shut her up with that bullet. That's because you were on the boat with my father and Keller that morning and you killed Keller. Maybe you hit him in the head with a paddle?"

"Now why in frozen hell would I want to kill that boy?"

"Because he was digging too deep into the Granville kidnapping. You thought he'd find that you were working with Granville to pull off the kidnapping hoax. Did you plant the evidence that led my father to Gerber?"

"You should write books, boy."

"Well, dude if I wrote a book, do you know what I'd write about? A cop who tried to frame a man for kidnapping. The ladies in Waycross said that Gerber and young Christmas were seen in a white pickup truck by a gas station attendant. The attendant thought there was someone else in the truck. It wasn't Gerber's wife, it was you. You've got that old white pickup right there in the parking lot. Plus, I saw it in an old photo in your office so I know you had it back then. And you know what? I'm willing to bet that you own an old Catalina too."

"You're a little too nosey like your daddy." Johnson's face was getting red and he started this crazy tic of lifting his shoulders up and down.

"What I can't figure is why you needed Hicks out of the way."

"Hicks was a useless piece of money hungry shit. He started this whole mess. He took up with Marnee thinking he was cheating with his wife's friend. He never knew that Jill and Marnee were step-sisters. Or that Marnee murdered Jill."

"So, Keller found out the kidnapping was a hoax. How could he connect you to it? Granville died when his racer crashed years ago. He couldn't finger you," I said.

"Keller found Granville had transferred a large amount of property to a certain corporation. It was Hicks who figured out the company was in my wife's name. Hicks wanted money or he would tell Keller the meaning of what he found."

Hicks had claimed that Jill had hoped to be sitting pretty when it was all over. Someone was bending the truth.

"Did you pay him?"

Johnson laughed and grabbed a mosquito out of the air with his free hand. He threw the insect's body onto the deck.

"Does that answer your question? That's what I told him I'd do to him. When I took care of Keller, Hicks took off because he knew he would be next. I didn't know where he was until you tipped me off about Hilton Head."

Without warning Johnson swung the oar. I ducked and could feel the whoosh of air a little above my head. Again whoosh/duck, whoosh/duck, whoosh/duck like we were doing some sort of perverted Cossack dance.

Finally, I lost the rhythm and the paddle caught me square on my upper arm. I went down landing against the gunwale. He came at me with the paddle as if he were wielding a harpoon. The stinging and throbbing in my arm reminded me that I couldn't write him off because of his age. I grabbed the paddle when he swung it again and whipped it overboard. Then I launched at him like a pit bull going after a raw steak.

Chapter Fifty-One

I hit him a little too hard and before I knew it, we were both in the murky water. Below the surface, I grabbed on to Johnson who was doing his best to get away. When we broke back to the top, I could hear yelling from the shore. Max stood at the boat ramp, waving her arms. I didn't have enough time to wonder why she was there.

"Alligator!" she screamed.

On the opposite shore, I could see the bull who was still keeping an eye on his territory. Attracted by the commotion in the water, it rose on all fours keeping its belly high and began an awkward flat-footed walk to the water. I let go of my grip on Johnson and dove, remembering what the cop had said about attracting a gator. I swam below the surface until I saw the hull of the boat. I came up behind the motor.

Johnson seemed to be following his own advice. It was too late for him to dive without disturbing the water, so he floated on his back as still as if he were a corpse. The old guy was ballsy as hell. The image of Psycho getting taken out by the truck popped into my head and I didn't dare breathe.

When the alligator got to within ten feet of Johnson, it stopped. The beast turned around and headed back toward the bank. Had something else caught its attention? Johnson still floated unmoving and I wondered if maybe he had had a heart attack and died, until I spotted the slightest flap of his feet to propel him toward the boat.

I was still in the water behind the motor as I coaxed him on silently in my mind.

Come on. You can make it. Take it nice and slow.

He was maybe ten feet from the boat now. I planned to hop into the craft at the last minute to haul him in. Any sooner and I'd chance alerting the beast. Johnson got bolder and moved his feet and arms a little more to get to the boat quicker. The gator snapped around and raced toward him again.

I watched the beast's powerful jaws clamp down on Johnson's leg then release it. It snapped again and held on this time. In spite of his injuries, my father's old friend fought for his life, going for the monster's eyes with his fingers. I remembered what he had said about the death roll. If Johnson went under the surface there would be no chance.

I scanned the shore. Where was Max? I know I wasn't imagining that she had been on the shore when this all went down. She was nowhere in sight. I was going to have to do this myself.

What had Johnson said? *Stick your hand down the alligator's throat and pull the flap that keeps it from drowning.*

No freaking way. Instinct told me to get in the boat. Peering over the side, I saw the paddle that had gone overboard between the boat and the battle royal. Johnson's only hope was if I could beat the monster about the eyes and snout with it. With any luck, the animal would lose interest and swim off for a meal that took less effort. I leaned over the side, but the paddle stayed inches from my reach.

Instinct is just another word for smarts and I never had much of those. I couldn't watch the guy get eaten. So, with no time to waste, I threw myself over the side hoping that the bull wouldn't decide that I was tastier than the crusty old cop. Its powerful jaws remained clamped on Johnson's leg as the water reddened from shredded muscle. For the time being, the beast seemed content to hold on to its prize instead of gnawing the limb off. Meanwhile, Johnson screamed bloody hell.

I got close enough to use the paddle to pound at the alligator's bony head. No easy achievement while in the water. It withdrew its eyes into its skull and acted like I was nothing more than an annoying fly interrupting lunch.

I thought of climbing on its back and riding it like a mechanical bull but decided I wasn't a superhero and scuttled that idea. I whacked it on the head again and it opened its jaws. Johnson was now free and the gator channeled its anger toward the paddle. It snapped down on it several times until the blade splintered. With open jaws, it lunged at me, when with more luck than I'd ever experienced in my life, I was able to ram the business end of the paddle into the creature's mouth.

The reptile's teeth scratched my arm as I shoved the paddle down its throat. If this didn't work my future kids were going to be calling me Lefty. Assuming that I lived.

The alligator coughed and sputtered.

Eventually, the beast decided neither one of us was tasty enough to drown for.

"Sorry about that," I said as it swam off. And I meant it.

It wasn't easy to hoist myself onto the side of the boat with my scraped arm stinging even worse than when the little fish had attacked me when I found Keller. Finally, I managed to get one leg, and then the other, over the side.

Johnson was sputtering by the side of the boat. I grabbed the back of his shirt with two hands. "Help yourself, man. I can't do this alone."

He managed to get his hands on the gunwale and I was able to haul Johnson over the side as if I were landing a big fish.

Chapter Fifty-Two

Max was yelling to me from the shore.

"I called 9-1-1!"

I flashed back to the day on the dock when she helped me haul Keller out of the water and she had said those same words.

I used his belt to make a tourniquet on Johnson's leg. He was writhing and yelling in pain.

"I need a drink!" he pointed toward a cooler by the console.

As I scrambled over to the cooler I could see the alligator entering the water from the shore and swimming toward the boat. Obviously, he didn't consider us finished business. I suppose someone sticking a piece of wood down your throat isn't something you let go of even if you're a reptile. Now the gator was out for revenge.

A thud shook the boat as the alligator whacked the hull with its tail.

I'd heard of alligators tipping small fishing boats over, but Johnson's vessel was built for the ocean and had a decent beam and a good amount of freeboard, so I wasn't too worried.

"I need a drink!" Johnson said again. I flipped up the cooler lid and found a bottle of 100 proof Belvedere Intense. Johnson may have been an asshole but he had good taste in vodka.

"Hold on," I said as I opened it.

I turned and what I saw made me drop the bottle. The precious spirits created a winding stream down the deck toward Johnson who had managed to get to his feet. He stood at port side with his arms outstretched, a mullet in each hand. The crazy bastard was taunting the alligator with the fish by holding them a little out of reach of its snapping jaws as it launched itself from the water.

"Sit down before you make us tip!" I didn't have as much confidence in the stability of the boat as I had before.

He laughed and pretended he didn't hear me.

"You're going to get both of us killed," I said.

Johnson got on top of the bait box and drew in a deep breath. How he managed to get up there with the muscle in his leg exposed and oozing blood was a testament to his determination and desperation.

"I'm not going to go to prison for something that happened all those years ago. I've put a lot of men in there over the years. They'd rip me apart like a gator on a house dog. I'd rather end it on my terms."

Then with arms still outstretched by his side, he pitched himself into the river.

* * *

I was already exhausted and bleeding. Johnson and I were both lucky to get away alive from the alligator once. Trying it again was pushing my luck beyond all reasonable limits. I wasn't even sure if the old cop was worth saving if I could. It tore at me that I was put in the position of judging this man who did so much to help my father when he was shot. Although Johnson admitted to killing Keller and Hicks, it didn't mean I should turn my back on him.

Johnson may have tried to scream but all that came out was a muffled sound as he took in water. I picked up the ice chest and flung it at the gator, who had the old cop's arm firmly in its mouth.

To me, most animals are more trustworthy than people and I am totally against animal cruelty. But I knew the plastic chest would do nothing more than bounce off the beast's bony head. On the other hand, it would be a different story if it hit Johnson. Even as hard-headed as he was, the cooler would knock him out and he'd be a goner.

Lucky for Johnson, my aim was good and the chest found its mark on the alligator's noggin. The alligator shook it off, released Johnson, and disappeared.

Johnson spit off a stream of water and coughed until he could speak.

"Come back, you bastard!" he called to the beast as he pounded at the water with his good arm. He had to be the bravest, or craziest, dude I have ever come across.

The Belvedere bottle rolled under my feet pitching me toward the side. I grabbed the gunwale to stop from going over. I noticed the bottle wasn't completely empty. I picked it up and drained the vodka down my throat. No sense in wasting good booze, especially when I could use a little extra courage.

I stood and no sooner had I gotten to my feet than there was rocking as the alligator came up from below the boat. I almost fell to the deck again.

"Dive, Johnson," I yelled. Either he didn't hear or he chose to ignore me as the gator torpedoed toward him.

"Watch yourself!" Max had reappeared and was yelling from the shore.

As I looked her way, the gator launched himself in the air inches from me. I hit it on the snout with the bottle hard enough to make it fall back into the water and swim away.

"Help me!"

Good God! Not only was Johnson still alive but he'd had a change of heart about dying. My training had instilled in me the duty to always do my best to preserve a human life. That included the life of a murderer. Against my better judgment, I dove into the water hoping I could bring Johnson back to the boat before the monster returned.

Bad move, Al. The alligator I had driven off returned. I found it circling me. I dove hoping the same evasive action I tried before worked again. I felt a tug and then a violent yank as I was dragged through the water. Curiously I felt no pain. Was my leg gone? No, I would have felt that for sure.

It seemed that the cord that ran through the cuff of my pants was caught on the alligator's tooth and he was dragging me through the water.

I was towed like a barge behind a tug, but underwater. I tried spinning around to get free but that only made the animal swim faster. I felt abandoned and frightened, but didn't I give up hope. I tried to rip the pants off; too tight around the waist. I tugged at the cord around the waistband but I had tied it too tight. I was holding my breath as best I could when I remembered the knife strapped on my other leg. I managed to get it out of the sheath and cut the waist cord. I slipped out of the pants and the alligator was swimming away with them still hooked in its teeth.

I heard a gurgling sound like water going down a bathtub drain. It reminded me of the underwater sound effect you hear in submarine movies. Did Johnson get away and back to his boat? I broke the surface.

"Hey, don't leave me," I shouted.

But the motor on Johnson's craft was not running. I didn't see Johnson or the alligator. If I didn't do something soon the gator would return and they were going to find whatever was left of my body floating downstream in my underwear.

"Watch out! Watch out!" It was Max's voice. She was speeding in a small outboard toward the center of the river between me and the angry alligator who still had my pants. The old bull took off and she cut back the engine. She gave me a hand as I almost swamped the small boat trying to haul myself over the side.

* * *

A half dozen emergency vehicles pulled into the boat launching area. She caught the puzzled look on my face as she revved up the engine.

"I told you I called 9-1-1 before I ran down to the park ranger's office."

"And this boat?"

"I spotted it tied up at their dock. I hot-wired it."

"A skill you just happened to have?"

"I have a lot of skills you don't know about."

I left the comment at that but I intended to explore the subject further at the first chance I got. At the moment, I was trying to spot what must have been left of Johnson.

"I don't see him." I tried to control my voice to disguise the sick feeling in my gut.

"That was so terrible," Max said. "What could have been going through his mind to make him do that?"

"He worked with Martin Granville to pull off a kidnapping hoax. Twenty-five years later he finds himself a respected police major. Maybe he didn't want to face the shame of people learning of his past mistake."

Max was a little more sympathetic. "Or maybe it was that guilt had been eating away at him for all of those years."

"Only Johnson knows the answer." Whatever it was, I couldn't fathom how desperate Johnson must have been to torment the gator like that and then fling himself into the water with it. I continued to try to spot him but I saw nothing, not even the alligator. I wondered if there would be anything to find.

I didn't have time to wonder about it any further. Our stolen boat was surrounded by three white skiffs and a rubber dinghy all lettered D.N.R.

"I take it that doesn't stand for *do not resuscitate*."

Max scoffed. "Do you take anything seriously? They're Georgia Department of Natural Resources officers."

Four divers went in to look for Johnson before she could even finish the sentence. That was a heck of a lot more response than when I found Keller and they only sent out one boat and a diver.

"Where's Major Johnson?" A uniform on one of the boats called out. I couldn't help but notice that he had his hand on his gun.

"I told them a cop was in trouble. I knew that would get their attention." Max said.

I pointed to the bloodied water. "I don't see him anymore," I said.

"My friend is injured," Max said to the officer. "I'm taking him to the shore."

"No. Cut your engine. I'm tossing you a line."

It was only then that I had a chance to look at my injuries. My right arm was bleeding as well as my left leg. I put pressure on the leg wound. Did they think we would run off? I wouldn't get far in my wet underwear with these injuries.

"Then give me the damn rope and let's get moving," Max yelled to him.

Someone from one of the boats tossed us a line and towed us in.

Chapter Fifty-Three

The wound on my leg was more of a puncture than a bite. I was shivering in spite of the heat and the blanket I was wrapped in. One of the EMTs speculated that when the alligator hooked onto my pants its tooth pierced my leg. He dressed that wound and the scrapes on my arm.

"The bleeding is stopped, but you're in for a round of some potent antibiotics. Their mouths are a breeding ground for filth," he said. "You're probably going to have a nasty scar on that leg."

"I may get a bullet hole tat to cover it."

Max rolled her eyes.

He wanted me to go to the hospital in the ambulance. I refused and Max said she would drive me.

A DNA officer came over. He looked out to the river where divers and deputies in boats searched the water.

"Is Major Johnson out there? What happened?" His tone was accusatorial.

"He jumped overboard," I said.

He looked skeptical. "Your name?"

"Al DeLucia."

"Where were you at the time?"

"On the boat with Johnson."

"You didn't try to stop him?"

"He jumped into the water twice to save the man," Max said. "What more would you expect him to do? Listen, he needs stitches and antibiotics."

The deputy didn't seem moved by my plight. "Your name?"

"Max Brophy."

"So, you were on the boat as well?"

"I was on the shore for most of it."

"This is your boat?"

"Listen, this man is injured. Are you going to let him get fixed up or are you going to keep up this nonsense?"

Good for you Max, avoid the question about the boat.

"I wish I had been able to save him," I said.

"You saved him once. That's more than any other dude would have done. Why the hell did you jump in again? He obviously wanted to die." Max's voice was a mixture of anger and relief.

"He called for help. You were yelling to me about the alligators and I wasn't thinking straight. Maybe I could have done something else."

"You are blaming me?"

"No. That came out wrong," I said. I was confused.

The officer grabbed my arm and started to march me along.

"Hey, watch the arm. It's bleeding." He didn't care about my protest.

I thought he was going to make me get into an ambulance, but instead, he opened the door to a white SUV with a map of Georgia on the door.

"Hey, what are you doing?" I knew better, but I protested anyway and tried to break loose of his grip.

"Get in the vehicle until I find out what's going on with the rescue."

Rescue? Was he kidding me? If they were lucky they would be doing a recovery and even that wasn't going to be possible without finding that alligator and opening its stomach.

"What about my injuries?"

"You'll live. The EMT stopped the bleeding and he cleaned it. I have a few questions. You can get further treatment after that."

You get a whole new perspective when you see a situation from the other side of the badge.

"I didn't do anything. You have this all wrong."

Man, if only I had a buck for every time someone I arrested said that to me. I got in the car without giving him any more trouble.

Then he turned to Max.

"Okay, you too. In here." He touched Max on the elbow to bring her to the door.

"Why?" Maxine pulled away.

"For your own safety. In!" By this time the deputy was in no mood to put up with any more backtalk.

"What do you mean for my safety?" Max asked.

"There is an angry alligator around here in case you didn't notice ma'am, and a man was attacked. Right now, I have to deal with a rescue. I'll question you later."

It must have been the first time that Max was referred to as ma'am. She seemed stunned when she looked into the vehicle. I gave her a huge grin and patted the back seat of the SUV. She didn't see the humor in the situation.

"Not with him. Put me in another car. You never put two prisoners in a car."

"You are not prisoners. This is for your safety. I don't have time to argue. Get in."

The officer guided Max into the car with his hand on her head.

"You never know who you'll meet in the back seat of a cop car," I said.

Max pawed at the door even though there were no door handles or window controls in the back seat of the SUV. Maybe she had never been in a police car before. She slouched against the door fuming in silence. All of a sudden, she slammed her fist against the window.

"Damn!"

"What?"

"Just being around you is bad luck. You're a jinx."

"If you feel better blaming me, go ahead." I didn't see why I should be blamed, but I would take the high road.

"So, what are we supposed to do now?"

"Wait."

"For how long?"

"As long as it takes. Why were you out here anyway?" I asked her.

It turned out that Max had more faith in me than she had admitted to.

"Even as bad as you are, I decided that you wouldn't have left Big Al to go fishing without a good reason. I dropped Greenleaf off at the hospital and made an excuse to leave so she wouldn't insist on coming along."

"She probably would have wrestled the alligator."

Max scoffed at my joke. "I knew the boat ramp was the only public access to the river around here, so I came out to see what you were up to."

"And what would you have done if I was only fishing?"

"I'd throw you in with the alligator. Oh wait, you were in there with the alligator, and I saved you. And then you tried to blame me for distracting you."

"I told you that I misspoke. I suppose you're waiting for me to say thanks."

"It would be nice," Max said.

"I'm not good with words. And I'm not nice."

"Tell me about it."

"I'm better with actions."

I pulled her toward me and kissed her. And then I kissed her again.

"What are you doing?" Max asked.

"I'll bet you always fantasized about having sex in the back seat of a police car."

"I have not." She thought a minute. "Have you?"

"Only since I've met you. Forgive me?"

"Apology accepted," she said.

* * *

There was banging on the window. It was the deputy. Max and I laughed like high school students.

"What's going on in there?" He opened the door as the radio began to crackle.

"Carry on," the dispatcher said.

Max's face turned bright red. I was embarrassed only because I should have known the radio was on.

"Get out. I have a few more questions," the deputy said.

"You knew the radio was on," Max told him.

"I guess I forgot." The deputy's face was dark and he was clearly nervous.

"Did you find him?" I asked.

The deputy took a deep breath. "An arm."

"And?"

The deputy just shook his head. He didn't have to say anymore. There was probably nothing left to find.

A park ranger headed our way. I prepared myself to defend Max's actions in taking the boat.

"I was upriver and saw the man taunting the alligators. Before I knew it, he was over the side," the ranger said.

"See. I told you he jumped."

The deputy was practically in my face. "Do you think he might have slipped?"

"No, he jumped," I said.

"Did I hear you say he was pushed?" The deputy was an inch from my face now.

"Who could have pushed him? There were only two of us on the boat and I certainly..."

"That's what I thought you said," the deputy said.

"No, he jumped in," my voice was emphatic.

"You were both in the water when I got here. Are you saying he jumped in to save you and lost his life in the process?"

I realized what he was saying. The explanation of how the Ava Island police major died would be so much cleaner if Johnson jumped off the boat to save me. No embarrassing questions. No long drawn-out investigation.

The officer turned to the ranger.

"From your vantage point, could the major have jumped off the boat to save this man?"

The ranger didn't hesitate. "It looked that way to me."

"And you, Ma'am. Is there any chance that the major could have jumped in to save this man? From your vantage point, I mean."

Max looked from the officer, to the ranger, to me. She gave a heavy sigh.

CHAPTER FIFTY-THREE

"I suppose. I was on the shore."

I guess she finally got the idea.

My impulse was to let the world know what a scumbag Johnson had been. But I knew that, for all practical purposes, it was probably better that he died a hero. The cops were happy with the explanation and they wouldn't hassle us with more questions.

Chapter Fifty-Four

When the cops were finished the ranger gave me a pair of uniform khaki to wear and then Max and I shot to the hospital. I needed to get some stitches and, more important, I wanted to see what was going on with Big Al. I was hoping that he was having one of his "good" days so I could tell him that I finally understood what he had been trying to tell me about Johnson. I wanted to let him know that I couldn't have solved the case without him.

We walked up to the reception desk at the hospital.

"I'd like to see Al DeLucia," I said.

Max butted in. "Actually, he has to get some stitches first."

The woman didn't even take her eyes off of the computer. "You'll have to go around to the emergency room. Which one of you needs stitches?"

"He does," Max said.

"I'm fine."

"Do you, or not?" the receptionist said.

"I do, but I want to see Al DeLucia first."

"Your name?"

"Al DeLucia."

I think she was about to call the psych ward.

"Do you have identification?"

Now what was this all about? They didn't even ask for identification from me when I brought him in. I showed her my license.

"Okay, Mr. DeLucia, Jr. Now I understand. I had to make sure before I told you. Your father rallied this morning. He got up and dressed. He

248

insisted on leaving."

"You let him walk out? He has dementia."

"Calm down. We couldn't hold him, but our Social Worker, Ms. Jenkins, talked him into returning to The Palms. She and another lady accompanied him there."

I wanted to leave and come back later.

"I'm not going to be happy if we don't get there in time."

"You're not going to be happy if that leg gets infected, either," Max said.

She gave a good argument that I could lose my leg. It took an hour for them to see me and get me stitched up.

When Max and I arrived at The Palms we found Big Al lying in bed; his head cocked to the side and mouth hanging open. Greenleaf and Estelle sat by the side of the bed like mourners at a wake.

Greenleaf got up and hugged me. But she couldn't resist putting in a jab.

"Catch any fish?"

At one time her remark would have pissed me off, but I think I was beginning to realize that Greenleaf has this overwhelming desire for everyone to live in a perfect world of harmony. But the only way she knows how to achieve this is to cause conflict.

"A huge one," I said. "What happened here?" I sounded like the deputy who questioned us about Johnson's death.

Greenleaf touched the bed. "He's sleeping, but he should be all right."

"Oh," I said.

"You thought I was dead, didn't you, asshat." Big Al opened one eye.

Max ran over and gave him a kiss on the cheek.

"I never thought that," I said.

Maybe I did, but I should have known even the devil wasn't ready to deal with my old man yet.

"The Chief quit," he said.

"Maryann quit?"

"Took her pension. Stress disability." Al said.

"She decided as soon as she heard he was coming back," Estelle said.

I stood next to Estelle. "I'm going to have to talk to you. It's important."

"I know, Jill is dead. The police filled me in. I've come to terms."

I put my arm around her shoulder briefly. "When you were married to Granville, did you know he had his daughter kidnapped to hide her from his first wife?"

"I didn't marry him until a year later, but I knew his wife had been trying to get Christmas away from him. He said he had been fighting it. But he never shared with me that the kidnapping was a hoax."

"Bastard," Big Al said.

Estelle took one of his hands and Greenleaf went around to the other side of the bed to take the other.

"Take it easy," Greenleaf said. Then she turned to me.

"Your father didn't know Johnson was in on it. At the time, he thought his friend was helping him. Then a few years ago Daryl and Avalou told him Gerber had been paid by Granville to bring the girl to their farm."

"Didn't they think that was odd at the time?"

Estelle answered. "Granville had a foundation to relocate refugee children from Cuba. The Givens women thought Gerber and his wife were taking care of a foster child until she could be placed."

"Him and Johnson set me up." Big Al tried to get out of the bed.

Estelle touched his shoulder to make him stay down. "When your father realized what happened all those years ago he hired Andy Keller to help him prove it. Big Al knew he was having… you know… problems. And he needed some help with the investigation."

"Maybe things would have been different if he had his son to help him out," Greenleaf said.

The woman was the queen of backhanded compliments but I only smiled.

"Have you met my friend here?" Al said to Estelle. "He's a detective too." A smile slid across his face.

So, he still considered me his friend. I'd take that. While I wouldn't get any answers that day as to why he took off when I was eight, I felt confident that I would someday when he was in the mood to talk to his "friend" about the past which he still had a pretty good grip on.

Max stood beside me and put her arm around my waist. Most of the cases I had inherited were wrapped up. We knew the truth about Estelle's daughter Jill, and about the Granville kidnapping too. There was nothing to keep me from moving on. Still, somehow, I didn't feel it was quite time to leave yet. When it's time for leaving, I will know. For now, I'd found a niche at Blue Palmetto. Plus, I wanted to see what was to become of me and Max. Maybe I also wanted to find out what would happen with the old man as he slid deeper and deeper into his alternate reality.

I'd learned the hard way that plans are just bridges. I'm not afraid of bridges. It will take time, but I'm building one over the hostile waters of my past.

About the Author

Ang Pompano is an Agatha Award-nominated author, as well as an editor and publisher. He writes the Blue Palmetto Detective Agency and Reluctant Food Columnist series for Level Best Books. His short stories have been featured in numerous anthologies, including one that won the Anthony Award. A recipient of the Mystery Writers of America's Helen McCloy Award, Ang co-founded Crime Spell Books and co-edits Best New England Crime Stories. He also serves on the New England Crime Bake committee and the Sisters in Crime Connecticut board. Ang lives in Connecticut with his artist wife, Annette, and their two rescue dogs.

AUTHOR WEBSITE:
  www.angpompano.com

SOCIAL MEDIA HANDLES:
  Facebook: https://www.facebook.com/AngPompanoMystery/
  X: @AngPompano
  Threads: angpompano

Instagram: angpompano

Also by Ang Pompano

Novels

The Blue Palmetto Detective Agency Series
When It's Time for Leaving
Blood Ties and Deadly Lies

The Reluctant Food Columnist Series
Diet of Death
Simmering Secrets

Short Stories

Quincy Lazzaro Short Mysteries
"The Copycat Didn't Have Nine Lives" in *Still Waters*
"Promises to Keep" in *Deadfall*
"School's Out Forever" in *Best New England Crime Stories*
"Diet of Death" in *Malice Domestic Mystery Most Edible*

Mike St. Martin Short Mysteries
"Sand Bar" in *Stone Cold*
"The Noir Before Christmas" *Audio Recording*

Nike DeNardo One Woman Detective Agency Story
"The Bucket List" in *Red Dawn*
"Stringer" in *Seascape*
"Directions to Justice" in *Bloodroot*
"Minnie the Air Raid Warden" in *Snakeberry*

Anthologies (edited by)
Bloodroot

Devil's Snare
Snakeberry